PRAISE FOR *THE RENT COLLECTOR*

"This is the sleeper of the year, wryly funny, always
plausible, deeply moving, unforgettable."
—W. P. Kinsella, BOOKS IN CANADA

"B. Glen Rotchin... [uses] an old-fashioned realist approach to tell an
insistently small story with utmost care. The result is a genuine
pleasure, a first novel of insight and tenderness."
—MONTREAL GAZETTE

"Rotchin has done a masterful job of putting himself
inside a fatalist religious Jew ... he also has drawn
a tender portrait of a marriage with its joys and tribulations."
—CANADIAN JEWISH NEWS

"Rotchin's setting is a colourful backdrop for a story
of one man's stumbling attempts to measure up to
the weight of his heritage."
—THE GLOBE AND MAIL

"This complex, sensitive and erudite story thrusts us into a series of
historical, spiritual and religious grey areas .... Rotchin's warm,
aphoristic voice ... skilfully crafts moments of humour, wisdom
and sensuality."
—HOUR MAGAZINE

Finalist, 2005 amazon.ca/*Books in Canada*
First Novel Award

D1479118

The Rent Collector

A NOVEL

B. Glen Rotchin

ESPLANADE
Books

THE FICTION SERIES AT VÉHICULE PRESS

Published with the generous assistance of The Canada Council for the Arts, the Book Publishing Industry Development Program of the Department of Canadian Heritage and the Société de développement des entreprises culturelles du Québec (SODEC).

Esplanade Books editor: Andrew Steinmetz
Cover design: David Drummond
Author photo (p. 227): Terence Byrnes
Set in Adobe Minion by Simon Garamond
Printed by Marquis Book Printing Inc.

09 08 07 06   5 4 3 2

LIBRARY AND ARCHIVES CANADA CATALOGUING IN PUBLICATION
Rotchin, B. Glen 1964-
The rent collector / B. Glen Rotchin.

Novel.

ISBN 1-55065-195-1

I. TITLE.

PS8585.084343R46 2005   C813'.6   C2005-904606-6

Published by Véhicule Press, Montréal, Québec, Canada
www.vehiculepress.com

Distribution in Canada by LitDistCo
orders@litdistco.ca

Distribution in U.S. by Independent Publishers Group
www.ipgbook.com

Printed and bound in Canada.

For Annetta, Sivan, Sidney, Tamar and Eden.

And for the Rotchins and the Solomons.

ACKNOWLEDGEMENTS

I'm grateful to the following people who acted as most skillful, insightful and gentle literary guides: Rachel Alkallay, Annetta Black, Elyse Gasco, Elaine Kalman Naves, Randy Rotchin, Arleen Solomon Rotchin and Joel Yanofsky. Elfie Bédard, Joshua Freund, Steve Barry, David Griffin, Seymour Mayne, Armand Pinto, Rabbi Ron Aigen and my friends at Congregation Dorshei Emet were all sources of inspiration and instruction. Thanks to Andrew Steinmetz, editor extraordinaire, who is as good-humoured as he is rigorous. And to the Véhicule team: Simon Dardick, Vicki Marcok, Stephanie MacLean and Bruce Henry for their care and attention.

I'm especially indebted to my landsman and friend Harold Heft who understood and encouraged this story right from the very start.

An early draft of chapter one was published in the journal *Parchment*—my thanks to editor Adam Fuerstenberg. The information about Noël Chabanel was taken from the essay "Noël Chabanel 1613-1649" by Peter Ambrosie.

Contents

Even maasu habonim
Hayita l'rosh pina

The stone the builders rejected
Has become the cornerstone.

–*Psalms* 118:22

There are four types of character among people. He who says:
What is mine is mine and what is yours is yours, is a medium type,
and some say that his type is of the wicked city of Sodom.

–*Pirkei Avot* 5:13

A Place

IT WAS PLAIN to see that a person inhabited a place, but to what extent did a place inhabit the person? This was a question Gershon Stein often pondered as he toured the hallways of his building. You couldn't really understand a person without knowing where they were from, which implied that a place inhabited them as much as they inhabited it. If you were a Jew you were inhabited by many places. The biblical Zion yearned for in daily prayers and the Jerusalem Temple were as real to Gershon as the streets of Montreal and the industrial corridors of 99 Chabanel where he earned his living. The destruction of the first and second Jerusalem Temples was on his mind these days. *Tisha B'Av*, the ninth day of the Hebrew month of *Av*, when the Jews mourned their greatest national calamities, had been just a week ago. The most difficult fast day of the year took place on *Tisha B'Av*. It was far worse than the Fast of Esther (preceding the joyous holiday of Purim), and even harder for Gershon to endure than the fast of atonement on Yom Kippur because *Tisha B'Av* occurs at the height of summer when the solemnity of mood and the long days of sunlight conspire to make the hours of hunger pains interminable.

Gershon knew that he was the product of exile, and yet he also had the sense that displacement was itself a singular, definable place. Perhaps it was more accurate to say that the Jew was a specialist in that one place. The geography he knew best existed between myth and reality, the sacred and profane, heaven and earth, a land between good and evil, peace and war, hope and despair—the stretch of wilderness between Egypt and the Promised Land.

The ancient Israelites had twelve tribes. When the biblical nation encamped for the night after a day of travel, each tribe settled down into its pre-assigned location. The tribes of Dan, Asher and Naphtali settled to the north, Judah, Issachar and Zebulun to the east, Reuben, Simeon and Gad were to the south, and the formation was completed with Ephraim, Menasseh and Benjamin to the west. Levi, the priestly clan, was enclosed in the middle together with the Holy Tabernacle.

Sometimes Gershon thought of himself as belonging to a thirteenth tribe, the Tribe of Gershon, which set up its tents in an unprotected area outside the configuration, where the howls of hungry wolves could be heard, the ground was hard and sleep was fitful. Gershon felt this way because he also knew that of all the places inhabiting a person, some were out of bounds, not fully known or even unknown.

One of the places inhabiting Gershon was an uncertain place he had never personally been, yet carried within him as a legacy, a brand-mark. That place was a concentration camp. Holocaust survivors had numbers tattooed on their arms, but their children had nothing so obvious to identify them. Gershon was certain that he and other children of survivors were members of a separate Israelite clan, a tribe of in-betweeners, not quite victims and not quite survivors, not rememberers nor forgetters, neither here nor there. They were a tribe as uncanny and unsettled as ghosts, forever wandering, left to speculate about what happened and what it meant, since their parents, the witnesses, the true survivors, were unwilling to say or incapable of it.

A name for the Almighty was *Hamakom*, Hebrew for "The Place." God was one of those places that inhabited a person which could not be completely known, though in Gershon's case it was not for lack of trying.

For Gershon, experience was layered. Each stratum could be cracked open and peeled away. Going deeper, a person would inevitably arrive at the seed core, the inner beginnings, which for Gershon was the small toughened shell of a concentration camp and inside that, the hard impenetrable nut that was God.

The outermost skin of Gershon's existence was this building that he inhabited on a daily basis. His considerations of place were frequently inspired by contact with ordinary things—encounters with a light switch, a padlock, or even an electrical bill—during his workday.

Fifty years ago Chabanel had been an unremarkable street, but for the government armoury built there during the war. The sprawling arrangement of red brick and wood stored light artillery for the European conflict. Later, the raised superstructure of the Metropolitan Autoroute linking Montreal east and west was constructed just south of Chabanel. Then the huge industrial buildings were erected. The district became ghettoized by the garment industry and the armoury was transformed into a dye-house and fabric-printing plant. A legacy of the war, however, lingered. It was said that the ground along Chabanel was poisoned with lead, heavy metals and untold toxins. City officials were wise enough to zone the area industrial, so no one much cared anymore about what dangers might lurk below the surface.

Chabanel became the fashion centre of Canada. It all started one wintry morning in February 1960 in the restaurant of the Belgo Building downtown, when Shimmy Solomon stared into a plate of poached eggs. There they were. Two white mounds resting on top of a single slice of partially burnt toast. At first, they looked to Shimmy like a pair of firm breasts. But then he noticed the wavy strip of bacon next to the toast and the picture of a river greeted his imagination, the St. Lawrence flowing alongside the two mounds that made up Mount Royal.

Because Shimmy was a creative genius, he dismissed these references offhand, and decided to turn the plate around so the bacon lay south of the eggs. Shimmy immediately grasped two large white buildings. His eyes moved along the bacon strip and the Metropolitan Autoroute came into focus. It was time to move the Jewish business north, close to the highway. Merchandise could be shipped more easily to Toronto, Quebec City and beyond. Shimmy ran his fork along the strip of bacon and sent a tine puncturing one of the poached eggs. Yellow oozed from the torn egg-white over his toast until the surface of his plate was completely covered. Shimmy imagined Montreal fashion spreading across the continent.

Relocating the *shmatte* business was not an entirely original idea. In fact, Shimmy had simply latched onto a trend that was already well underway. As the garment business flourished, the Jewish migration proceeded west. The two went hand in hand. It was hardly an exaggeration to say that the prosperity of the entire Montreal Jewish community was built from rags. By 1960 the Jews had departed the midtown Yiddish slums of St. Urbain and Fairmount. They had bought posh houses in preferred west-end neighbourhoods like Westmount and Hampstead. They erected bungalows, split-levels and townhouses in Côte St. Luc.

The Orthodox Jews, however, remained ensconced at the base of Mount Royal in Outremont near Avenue du Parc, and that was where Gershon Stein and his family resided.

99 Chabanel was the first building in the new garment district, and in 1964 Shimmy Solomon became the building's inaugural tenant. It was clad entirely in white brick, just as Shimmy had imagined. It was enormous, comprising five hundred thousand square feet of industrial space, with seven floors and ten elevators. The loading dock in the back could fit eighteen forty-foot trucks at one time.

As the needletrade expanded sister buildings appeared along Chabanel, almost seven million square feet in all.

In its heyday, the mid 1970s, two thousand people made their living working in 99. Gershon estimated that there were less than six hundred now. Sadly, the building represented an industry and a community in decline. The Jewish population of Montreal was ageing and shrinking. Jews had fled in droves after the 1980 referendum on Quebec's independence from Canada. Gershon thought of a recent government survey, quoted in the *Canadian Jewish News*, showing that Côte St. Luc was per capita the oldest municipality in all of Canada. 99 Chabanel appeared to be ageing too, like a grey, grumpy, Jewish businessman, embattled and bitter to the very end.

The Rent Collector

GERSHON EMERGED from his morning meeting with Estella Mora, a gentle grin draped across his face. She had entertained him for about twenty minutes—that's what he called it, *entertained*. Every month Estella came to the management office to plead for an extension on her rent. It was a regular tango between them. She dressed as if she were going to a nightclub, this time sporting a pair of long black slacks and a lavender silk blouse with the two top buttons undone. The dark bags under her eyes were masked by makeup, and her long frizzy hair was neatly pinned up with a butterfly barrette which seemed to make the statement: I'm harmless as an insect with nothing to hide. She was not attractive. At her best, Estella was exotic-looking. Experience had taught Gershon that she was unashamed to exploit whatever sexual assets she possessed, in that entrepreneurial way young women who were trying to start a business sometimes did. There was no telling how far she might go to save her skin.

"I know that you helped me in the past. I appreciate everything." Estella opened her pitch. "It's just, the cheque of one customer came back. What can I do?"

"It's difficult, yes, but I need to get the rent on time. One month slips into the next so easily and before you blink you owe four thousand. You don't want to be two months behind, do you?" Gershon was not always this gentlemanly when he squeezed people for money.

"That won't happen." Estella moved closer. "I promise. I'm going to the bank this afternoon to cash in my retirement savings. You'll be paid every cent."

This was more than Gershon wanted to know. Not only did she look physically drained, the tank at home was empty too. If he had to sue her personally it would not be worth the cost.

"Last month you sold your car, this month it's your retirement. What's left?" he said.

As Estella was buzzed out of the office, Gershon shook his head.

"Again with her," Alfreda Bernstein said from her desk across the room. "Why don't we just get rid of her already? She's going to skip out one night owing a fortune. Why do you keep giving her chances? What pleasure do you get from it?"

The office secretary was tough-minded and fiercely loyal to Gershon—really, to his father. She had been working for them for almost twenty years. Not only did she dislike tenants who were delinquent on their rents, but she was particularly annoyed by women who flirted to get ahead. She would never stoop so low, she often said, as if it was a matter of choice. In reality Alfreda was a large, homely creature. Her competence was unquestionable, but it didn't hurt that there was not so much as a minuscule possibility of titillation.

Gershon thought about Alfreda's questions. Why did he keep giving Estella chances? What pleasure did he get from the exercise? She was right. Estella would eventually close down, or run away and almost certainly owe three or four months' rent.

It could be sympathy. He felt bad for her and wanted to help her get the business off the ground. Everyone needed a favour now and then, and it made Gershon feel good to know he could help someone out. On the other hand, his father had always told him that letting tenants get away with unpaid rent was not doing anybody any favours. On the contrary, it was doing everyone involved a disservice. The landlord was losing money, but so was the tenant. The landlord had an obligation to enlighten the tenant that if their business couldn't make enough money to pay the rent then they had no viable business to begin with. In fact, the landlord was doing the tenant a big favour by coming down hard on them. It gave both parties the chance to cut their losses. It was obvious that Estella Mora was a perfect example of someone who needed this kind of tough love approach. She was losing money by the day and seemed incapable or unwilling to face the fact that she would never recover. Not only did she have no business, she had no life. If he acted swiftly, mercifully, maybe she could keep her retirement savings.

Gershon didn't relish the role of executioner. He didn't want to be the one to pull the switch, which, if true, would make him a coward. Well, he could live with being a coward under the circumstances. But what about the way he kept Estella hanging in mid-air like a broken puppet? Maybe, he reflected, he derived enjoyment out of watching her hang on for dear life. And maybe, even more, he liked it when she flirted with him.

These thoughts disturbed him. He put them out of his mind by saying to Alfreda, "Estella's just trying to survive. You've got to give her that much credit. Everyone has a right to survive."

Gershon preferred to wait for people to die. He had to admit it to himself. It wasn't something to be proud of, but being proud was never one of Gershon's central preoccupations. It was not as if he fantasized about murder, God forbid. He was content to wait. That was his game. Waiting. Death was the one undeniable truth; it would come, proof that ultimately nothing was in a person's control. This was important because he came from a family of controllers. He felt that as long as his parents were alive, his life was rented. Maybe that was why he became a rent collector. There was always someone to whom he owed something.

The Stein family owned a great deal of property. Their principal holding was 99 Chabanel, but they also possessed several single-storey industrial buildings in Montreal's fashion district, as well as others along the highway toward Toronto. Gershon considered it ironic that his religious family earned its living in an industry that revelled in flesh. On his way down the street to make bank deposits, he would turn away from the large posters of barely-clad models with staring belly buttons and the store windows displaying rows of stiff plastic breasts saluting as he passed. Why did they put such things out in the open? Were people supposed to stand there looking? Inspect them like an honour guard? Gershon joked bitterly to himself that the Steins were the landlords of Sodom and Gomorrah.

When Sholem Stein walked down the hall, tenants would rush out from their offices to greet him as if he were bearing gifts, or like they believed he could magically make their wishes come true. Gershon's father was treated with reverence even though every tenant felt Sholem had cheated them during lease renewals.

Sholem was a legend in the industry. He had arrived as a refugee from Europe with a handful of ashes. A short, unthreatening man with sky-blue eyes and neatly cropped grey beard, he spoke slowly, thoughtfully, in warm tones with a thick but endearing Yiddish accent. There was something angelic about his comportment. His folksy charm put people at ease. Time and again Gershon witnessed hard-nosed businessmen turning tame at his father's utterances. Female tenants practically swooned in his presence. It was nearly mystical.

Gershon was envious of his father's easygoing manner and subtle cleverness. These were not qualities that could be learned. Sholem had survived death camps. Gershon decided that the furnaces of Europe were the kiln which forged his father's winning character. Or maybe it was the other way around, and his father had eluded the Nazi killers through guile, charisma and luck. Either way, Gershon knew he could never fully measure up.

"Listen. Don't speak. If you show them your cards you've lost the game!" Sholem would command.

Reserve was not in Gershon's nature. He was expressive. His chattiness annoyed his father to no end. Gershon wanted to please, to show what he knew. Under Sholem's tutelage Gershon had learned to keep his impulses somewhat in check. It was a difficult lesson. Sitting across the table from a prospective tenant, Gershon always felt uncomfortable. During the lease negotiations, he was fidgety. His hand would crawl up his beard and come to rest against his lower lip like a fat spider hiding under a ledge, ready to attack. When he secretly added ten percent to the measurement of a space, he adjusted his *kippa* back and forth, incessantly, like a gambler's tick. When he succeeded in negotiating a new lease, Gershon would triumphantly present the contract to his father, who inevitably responded that he could have gotten a quarter or fifty cents more per square foot. The disappointment was so painful that Gershon preferred to let his father handle the deal-making.

Gershon's cellphone beeped. Ruhama, again. It didn't matter that the office had five telephone lines, his wife insisted he carry a cell. He cursed it. "Don't forget to pick up a bread and a carton of milk! And be home soon," she ordered.

"Okay. Soon as I can. Bye." Gershon hung up.

The device hanging from Gershon's waist had taken on religious significance. Like his *tzizes*, the fringes that perpetually reminded Gershon of God's Commandments, the cellphone had to be worn at all times to demonstrate his allegiance. Ruhama's calls were to the point. Gershon appreciated this. But she was persistent. She knew her husband was a dreamer and needed to be monitored. In her mind, the cellphone had been bestowed by God as an earthbound leash for Jewish wives to offset the spiritual tether which tied their husbands to heaven. Ruhama thought of Gershon as being like a tent pole, steadfast and erect. His head brushed the clouds but his body was lashed down at the sides with taut wires nailed to the ground, pulling at him in opposite directions.

Flopping back in his chair, Gershon sighed. He surveyed his agenda to see if there were any appointments scheduled for the afternoon. His eyes stepped across columns, from box to box, until they locked on two words. Gershon was swept by a sudden chill. *Joey Putkin.*

When Gershon realized he was not cut out for haggling over leases he had set his mind on perfecting the art of rent collection. He had worked hard and done well. In the first twelve months after coming to work for his father in 1994, six years ago, he had reduced the company's receivables by half. There was only one persistent blemish on his record, Joey Putkin, an Israeli leather coat merchant who occupied sixteen thousand square feet in the basement at 99. Putkin was always three months behind.

It was bad enough he didn't pay, but Putkin's arrogance was insufferable. A flamboyant, chain-smoking braggart, his business had grown from a single tiny storefront to a multimillion-dollar chain in only five years. Putkin took satisfaction in proving his toughness by declaring his superior origins. "Business in Israel is like swimming with sharks. Here, in Canada, making money is taking candy from babies," he would tell Gershon.

Each time he had to meet Joey, Gershon became anxious. He despised Putkin and yet, in a strange way, he was indebted to him for an important lesson. Putkin's monthly rent was so high he could afford to be intransigent. When pressed for money, he threw up his hands and dared, "So sue me!" Putkin knew that Gershon, having already lost so much money, was unlikely to spend more on lawyers. This was how Gershon learned that indebtedness gave a person leverage. The more you owed, the more leverage you had and the more powerful you became. It was always better to owe someone ten thousand dollars than just ten. Here was the nature of the war Gershon waged on a daily basis and Joey Putkin was his most formidable adversary.

When Gershon called to collect, Putkin was usually unavailable. Gershon suspected he was being fed lies. Putkin was out of the office a bit too often; there were too many out-of-town trade shows. Gershon would traipse down to the parking garage and find Putkin's freshly washed silver BMW resting in its spot as usual.

If he accosted Putkin in the hallway, Gershon quickly found himself on the defensive. Putkin's mouth was like a loaded Uzi. He sprayed complaints like bullets, rapid-fire, and was gone before Gershon had time to react. "Have you fixed that problem we were having with the warehouse bathroom? When are you going to do something about these elevators, my customers are complaining. The shipping area is a mess and our trucking company is refusing to deliver. I'm holding you personally responsible for damages."

Every time he confronted Putkin, Gershon left the scene feeling outclassed.

"How 'bout if *you* go see Putkin this afternoon?" Gershon muttered to Alfreda.

"For heaven's sake, stand up and be a man," Alfreda replied, throwing him a baleful glance. "Face your problem. It'll only get worse."

It always did, thought Gershon. "I'm tired of talking. Anyway, the guy's got no respect for words. He pays when he feels like it, not from any sense of obligation. How can you deal with a person who has no sense of obligation? You can't make peace with someone like that."

Beyond the normal antagonisms between tenant and landlord, Gershon felt a deep personal animosity toward Putkin. His father liked Putkin. They were more than cordial when they met in the lobby, and Sholem frequently talked admiringly of Putkin's achievements, his shrewdness, his ambition and business acumen. Every word of praise pierced Gershon's heart like a well-aimed dart.

Gershon found Joey Putkin in his basement office, reclining in a leather-backed armchair. His feet were propped up on a glass desk. Putkin's fingers were locked together, palms down, across the top of his head. A heretic's *kippa*, thought Gershon, looking through the doorway. All in all, Putkin seemed pleased with himself, relaxed. Putkin leaned forward, then dropped his fists on the desk and faced Gershon squarely.

"So, you've come to collect," Putkin said.

Gershon might have chosen to reschedule his afternoon meeting had he known that Putkin was in rare form.

That morning Putkin had stormed into his basement office, late.

"The buyer from The Leather Barn has been waiting since nine o'clock," the receptionist had announced. Putkin scooped the small squares of multi-coloured message paper out of her hands and paused in front of her to flip through them.

"Fucking overpaid private school teachers are so lazy," Putkin had growled. "They'll do anything to work less. My kid's teacher says he's a trouble-maker. She wants us to put him on Ritalin. Shit. I had a meeting at school, that's why I'm late."

Putkin had shed his jacket, snatched an order pad from the desk and sped off down the corridor.

"Your father's keeping the client occupied in the showroom."

"Page him over the intercom. Send him on an errand to get more toilet paper or something. Tell him we're out of styrofoam cups!" he had barked back.

Joey's father Avi had come to work here after his wife died three years earlier. It was his way of filling a dark hole in his daily life, and Joey's opportunity to act the role of a dutiful son. Avi was a large jovial man who enjoyed telling off-colour jokes, especially to pretty young customers. Joey considered his father a nuisance around the office. He preferred working solo. His father's outgoing, friendly disposition nagged at him. But Avi was proud of his son, which made things difficult. He took ownership of Joey's accomplishments, reminding him, when Joey least wanted to hear it, that the apple doesn't fall far from the tree.

Joey had emerged from his meeting with The Leather Barn buyer wasted, and victorious. He was tabulating the profits in his head as he bid her farewell at the front door of Putkin Leather Designs Inc. For the tenth time he told her how gorgeous she looked, touched her hand, and then let the fingers drop gently, like a bouquet of flowers on a grave. It was a romantic departure worthy of film. Two lovers seeing each other off, perhaps for the very last time. The door closed behind the buyer leaving an atmosphere thick with the residue of longing.

Gershon, of course, knew nothing of Putkin's morning. His eyes ricocheted off the office walls and across the framed photos. He saw girls wearing tanned leather mini-skirts and zipped-up knee-high boots. His sightline grazed bare female arms gratefully clutching the jackets of chesty, heroic-looking men. On Putkin's side of the bureau there was a photograph of a woman holding her baby. Next to this was one of a little boy wearing a blue and white soccer shirt with "67" on the front. Gershon's eyes finally settled on the giant green bug behind Putkin. It was an army beret, the regulation IDF shirt and matching ripped khaki pants, pinned spread-eagle to the wall. He'd seen them on his other visits. But now the clothes made a unique impression on Gershon. They seemed to be displayed with the purpose to intimidate.

"You fought for Israel?" Gershon was looking for an amicable way to broach the subject of unpaid rent.

"Lebanon '83." Putkin sat back in his chair, turned his head toward his computer screen and began typing. His face glowed in pale blue light.

"I'm a bit surprised. You never mentioned you were in the war."

"There's nothing more to say." Putkin didn't budge from the screen. "Arab terrorist bastards. Now they want a country. What do they know about running a country?"

Putkin's fingers tapped staccato on the keyboard like he was sending an urgent message over the internet. "You think they won't send *katyusha* rockets into our cities every day if they can? Arabs hate Jews. It's inbred. They won't be happy till we're all dead," he said.

Gershon felt as if he had casually strolled into a restricted zone, booby-trapped with landmines. "God willing, one day there'll be a settlement," he said.

Putkin scratched his temple and glared at Gershon. "God willing? You say *God willing*? God has nothing to do with it. You religious guys think you understand, but you don't. I didn't see guys with *payas* fighting in my unit, I can tell you that. While you people were parading around synagogues carrying Torah scrolls on your shoulders, we were in the field with bazookas fighting for our lives!"

"I only meant that nothing is solved with violence."

"You know, the problem with you guys is that you live in the past. You never fought for your future. If we learned anything in the last fifty years it's that if you don't fight for your future, you don't deserve one!"

Gershon was losing his appetite for rent. The conversation was speeding past the point of no return. He would be lucky to get away unscathed. He sought some means of making an exit without appearing disrespectful. He stepped backward, trying to think of a neutral, harmless way to sign off.

"I guess we can both appreciate living in Canada," he said.

Putkin calmed down. "Yes, this great peaceful country, Canada. A wonderful place where almost nothing happens." He smirked. "Except maybe an old-time Jew like you and a modern one like me doing battle."

"I must go now. Another appointment. Excuse me." Gershon reached for the door knob. He hurried past the receptionist and exited the office.

He walked unsteadily as he approached the elevator, sucking in deep breaths of basement air. Gershon replayed the exchange with Putkin over and over in his mind while he waited for the elevator.

Had he lost? The money was not in his hands, it was true, but he didn't feel like a complete failure. Something was learned, something more valuable. Perhaps he was wrong about Putkin. As an Israeli soldier Putkin had put his life in jeopardy. He possessed a sense of obligation after all. This must be what Sholem saw in Putkin. They shared the mutual respect of brothers-in-arms.

Now Gershon was feeling presumptuous, even foolish. What had he ever done to struggle? He accepted his father's hard-earned hand-outs like a beggar. People shouldn't make silly assumptions. Gershon had to admit there was much he had to learn. He looked up and down the dimly lit hallway. Behind every wooden door strategies were being planned, decisions were being made, and destiny itself was taking shape. There was only One who knew the whole story, how it all ended, even before it began.

"You should've been there, Alfreda," Gershon declared as he yanked open the management office door. "It was ugly. A slaughter."

"I take it you didn't get the rent," Alfreda said. "Big surprise."

"Not even close. But I did get an earful. Now I represent everything that's wrong with the Jewish people. A weakling with *payas*." Gershon marched to his desk. "I realize it's not about paying rent with him. It's something more. The sight of me sends him into a rage."

"Gershon, don't take everything so personally," Alfreda reassured him. Pointing at him with her ballpoint pen, she said, "Everyone needs an easy target. Someone else they can harass so they don't take out their hostility on themselves. You're his favourite target. I think he feels threatened by you."

"Threatened by me? Why would he feel threatened by me?"

"We always attack the thing, or person, who threatens us most. It's the survival instinct."

"Why should I threaten him?"

"'Cause you're a Jew. And you really look like one. And he doesn't. He hates the fact that you look like a real Jew and he doesn't."

"I don't know," Gershon said. "Putkin's not the type who can be so easily threatened. He fought for Israel in Lebanon. Did you know that?"

"Really?" Alfreda stopped working and looked up. "It's hard to believe. Vulgar, money-grubbing, insulting Joey Putkin, Defender of the Holy Land. God help us!"

That night Gershon spoke to Ruhama about what had happened. They only talked about business in exceptional circumstances, like when Gershon was feeling guilty about a tenant collapsing in a heap of tears in his office. Ruhama knew all about Putkin, though. His story had been retold many times. Gershon turned to Ruhama for strength, and she considered it a solemn duty to encourage her husband, and, if need be, to harden his heart. She was clear-minded and purposeful. This time her response to Gershon was swift.

"Putkin didn't fight for the Jews," she said. "In the army he was fighting for his country. Any Canadian or American citizen would have done the same. The Jewish people can't depend on the likes of Putkin to defend them. On the contrary, his kind ensures that the Jews will die out, one way or another, either through war or assimilation, greed or intermarriage. Israelis are Americanized. They don't love God. They love only themselves and their country."

Gershon listened quietly. Ruhama was right. The survival of Judaism was at stake. Putkin wasn't a soldier for Judaism. Not at all. But could you fight for the survival of Jews and at the same time let Judaism die? On the other hand, Putkin had fought. And that, Gershon concluded, was something no one could take away from him.

～

The next day Gershon slipped back into his routine. The long hallways sprawled before him like a bed of oysters. Which black door would he pry open to find the pearl of rent today? The world was equally divided between those who were desperate to pay and those who were desperate to avoid it. On the first of the month, some rents would wash up on Alfreda's desk like bottled messages from people whose consciences refused to let them sleep at night. The remittance of rent was their SOS. The others were a forlorn shipwrecked lot who were battered by the elements and fortified themselves against uncertainty. Gershon did not consider it a question of whether people were inherently good or evil; God had created everyone with both a *yetzer hatov* and a *yetzer hara*, good and evil inclinations which they each struggled with daily. Whether or not a tenant paid the rent was simply a question of survival. The tenants did what they had to for one more day, one more week, one more month. Gershon's task was to make sure that when his tenants floated, he floated along with them, and when the boat sank, he wasn't on board.

On his way back from the bank, Gershon bumped into Avi Putkin coming out of the restaurant in the lobby, a brown paper bag in his hand.

"So my son's giving you headaches again, eh, Gershon," Avi said kindly.

"I'll manage," Gershon smiled. "If everyone paid their rent on time I'd be out of a job, right?"

It was easy to kibbitz around with Avi. Father and son were entirely different. Gershon wondered about the convoluted knot of genetics and history that had wrapped itself around the two, tying them together and yet leaving enough room for each to travel along a divergent path.

"He's not a bad kid, you know. It's just that he feels he's got something to prove," Avi explained.

"He's quite the warrior, your son. I didn't know he saw action in southern Lebanon."

"Action in Lebanon?" Avi looked puzzled. "What do you mean?"

"The army. The campaign in '83."

"In Lebanon? Basic training after high school, yes. After that he was stationed in the northern Negev, not Lebanon." Avi shook his head. "Joey never served in Lebanon. Thank God. They wouldn't send him there."

"Is that his uniform? The one hanging in his office?" Gershon had to know.

"Oh that. No." Avi's tone softened. "It belonged to his older brother. Yoav was killed in Lebanon. That's why they didn't send Joey. When one brother is killed in combat the military spares the next one from getting equal treatment."

Gershon was deflated. "I'm sorry," he said, finding the only two words that seemed to have any meaning.

"Yes, well, it could not be avoided. I suppose we all have to play the roles handed to us."

"He told me it was his uniform," Gershon mumbled.

"In a way, I guess it's his now," Avi said.

Later, Gershon returned to his office to find a cheque sitting on his desk. There was a note attached. *We live to fight another day. See you next month, Joey.*

Gershon lifted up the note and held it delicately between his fingers, as if it were a fragment of brittle parchment. He scrutinized it for clues. Avi must have spoken to his son. Gershon was suspicious. This payment of rent felt more like a tactical maneuver than an unconditional surrender.

Elevators

GERSHON WAS FEELING a sharp thumping in his chest. He was worried for a moment, but then he began to feel grateful for the sudden, unexpected pounding of his body. He never thought of the palpitations as warning signs. In his experience, warnings were generally more discreet, hidden enough to escape his vigilance, missed entirely, which is why Gershon remained perpetually in a heightened state of alert.

He was at his desk, passing his fingers across monthly figures, studying them like religious texts. The receivables were up this month. Joey Putkin hadn't paid the rent; nothing new about that. But there were a few others who always paid on time but still owed money on this, the tenth of the month. What did it mean? And that's when the palpitations had started. The frantic drumbeats of himself. He took a deep breath. Another. And another. He felt a surging warmth climb from his belly up to his forehead. Before a single bead of sweat could condense on the place where every morning he set the *tefillin shel rosh*, the palpitations subsided.

"Good day, folks!" Sonny Lipsey materialized at the front desk, buzzed into the office by Alfreda while Gershon was obsessing about his heart.

"For me! How sweet," Alfreda chimed sarcastically. Sonny held a bright bunch of flowers under his chin. He spoke into them as if they were a bouquet of microphones at a press conference.

"Honey, no one in this building deserves them more than you. Next time it'll be your turn. These are for my wife. I owe thirty-five years of marriage to flowers. Every Friday she gets them. Never missed a week.

It's to the point now if I ever forgot, she'd think I was cheating on her."

Sonny Lipsey was a well-known fixture of the Montreal garment business. He was a round-faced, humunculous jobber with a childish grin who sold end goods and leftover textiles to small manufacturers at cut-rate prices. Gershon dubbed Sonny The Poet of Chabanel, for the French beret he always wore, and especially for the light-hearted nicknames he gave industry characters. That was his shtick. His monikers were always on the mark.

There were The Dolphins: Charlie, Hyman and Irving Roth, three inseparable brothers who'd been in the business for fifty-one years. They all had sea-blue eyes, long torsos and prominent noses. The Dolphins always swam together.

Sonny called Shimmy Solomon The Great White Father for his crown of silver hair and the stature he enjoyed throughout the industry. Shimmy was widely revered for pioneering fabrication techniques that became standard practice. Shimmy's company, Simple Dress, was once the largest ladies' apparel manufacturer in the country. It had blossomed with three divisions and hundreds of employees. Sonny had nicknames for Shimmy's associates; beady-eyed Chairman Mao was in charge of sales, and Stalin was his square-headed, thick-mustachioed head of production, who occasionally purged the staff and plotted clever strategies for getting his workers to work harder.

With Sonny around, the *shmatte* business was a collection of heroes and villains. Superman inhabited the third floor of 99 and his arch-rival, Lex Luther, was two floors up. Sonny called basement-dwelling Joey Putkin, The Morlock King. Sholem Stein was Yoda and Alfreda was Princess Leia. It was something of an honour to be christened by Sonny Lipsey. It meant you were important, worthy, or at least noticeable. People stopped Sonny in the hallway to ask for a nickname. "I can't force it," Sonny would respond. "It has to come to me, like a vision, a poem."

Gershon didn't have a name. That was just as well, for he considered it juvenile, and not having a name from Sonny meant he wasn't one of them. He remained outside the fray, and that suited him fine. He didn't want to be pinned down, reduced to a joke or an artifact. Apparently no one except Gershon saw how a name from Sonny did that. Nevertheless, he appreciated Sonny's sense of humour. There was something appropriate about giving Garmentos (Sonny's term) schoolyard-type nicknames since they acted like children most of the time.

"Gershon, do something about the garbage in front of my door, will ya?" Sonny whined. "They keep leaving trash at the end of the hall. I think it's the Pakis you moved in on the floor. Shameful. They think they're still back in India."

"Pakistan," Gershon muttered.

"What?"

"Pakistan, not India. They're from Pakistan," Gershon corrected.

"Yeh, whatever. Please, just do something about it. My girl's coming in this afternoon and she doesn't have to see the mess."

"My girl" was common industry parlance for the female bookkeepers who showed up at the end of each month to do financial housekeeping: pay bills, balance accounts and straighten out government forms and remittances. Typically, these girls were bespectacled, frumpily dressed ladies with varicose veins and thick ankles. Sonny's girl though, was something extraordinary.

The first time Gershon saw her had been in Sonny's office. Sonny was short, so Gershon was startled by her height. She towered over Sonny by a head at least. And she was perhaps in her early twenties, young enough to be Sonny's daughter. Her hair was long, straight and jet black, framing a thin, oval face with a smooth complexion. Her expression was shy, her eyes almost sad, lonely. Her face shone with an unmistakable radiance. Gershon couldn't turn away. He was immediately, inexplicably embarrassed. As if, at that very instant, he had been caught in the shadows doing something forbidden.

Sonny did not introduce them. She acknowledged Gershon's presence with a half-smile and sat down at a desk stacked high with papers. The direct contact between them deflected Gershon's eyes to the ground. Sonny said he'd cut a rent cheque if Gershon waited. The anticipation of money immobilized him, but in truth he wanted to flee.

Miriam, he guessed. It struck him in a flash as his eyes crawled along the carpet that her name must be Miriam. Gershon realized immediately why a name had insinuated itself upon him. He wanted, or needed, to leave the room knowing something about her. Even if it was the wrong name, he now possessed a token he could carry away with him when they parted. But this added to his discomfort. He repeated the name in his head. *Miriam.* His muscles slackened. He was deflated, shapeless. He lifted his hand in front of his face. To verify his stubby fingers, count the lines of his palm. Nonsense. To sever the sightline connecting him to Miriam. He spoke to fill the silence and blot out the sound of her name in his mind. *Miriam.* What he said was thoughtless, mechanical. He did not hear himself speak. *Miriam.* Sonny was talking now. Gershon didn't listen. He felt a tug of reins in his direction. He shifted on the balls of his feet to feel weight, faced Sonny. His hand opened automatically. The cheque arrived in an envelope like parole.

In the weeks that followed he thought of Miriam frequently on his rounds. 99 was a different place for Gershon. It offered something unexpected and pleasant. His gait was a tad lighter. The rare times they crossed paths there would be the same half-smile of acknowledgement, but words were never exchanged. Gershon wanted to say something, but he knew even an insignificant hello was enough to breach a trust.

This wordless relationship—Gershon admitted to himself that he had begun to think of it as a relationship—troubled him deeply. He was a man of words. His business was a business of words. The world was a world of words. That's what he knew, what he'd been taught in school. It's what was confirmed every night at the *kollel* from nine to eleven o'clock in the ancient Talmudic arguments he cracked his brain on, and at synagogue with prayers uttered by heart, and in the blessings he recited before and after eating, many times a day. Words infused the world with clarity. They were all we had to illuminate the darkness of existence, define the soul. Or were they? Miriam's face shone that first day. It was undeniable. And it shone during every subsequent encounter between them. He was continually surprised by it. Her face was the *ner tamid* of 99, the synagogal eternal flame.

But what about the words for which he cared so much? All day long words were thrown back and forth in every corner of the globe. Between landlords and tenants, salesmen and clients, bosses and employees, husbands and wives, teachers and students. And what did they all mean?

On the other hand, Gershon was anguished by the possibility that the wordlessness he shared with Miriam meant too much. He had the sense she could see right inside him, to the faulty beating of his heart. Throw up a word and he might be protected. He never questioned words before in this way. The question for him was always a choice between words, unpacking their subtle distinctions, finding the precise ones, the ones that mattered, the ones that made the world matter. Wordless Miriam had sent him completely off the rails. He couldn't say where he was headed, and not knowing the destination was unsettling.

Gershon began seeing his marriage, his love for Ruhama, in a fresh light. There were bonds between people in words, and others that happened without them. His bond with Ruhama was built on a careful layering of meanings and understandings, through a process that took place over time like the gradual and steady erection of a grand and beautiful edifice, brick by brick, word by word. The foundation was Torah. From the time they stood under the marriage canopy and vowed to cherish one another according to the Laws of Moses and the People of Israel, their contract was signed in stone and confirmed forever.

Wordless Miriam had shown him more. Would Ruhama understand? Not every place was occupied by a building. The heart was a place too. Fragile, unpredictable, resilient, open-spaced, it could not always be imposed upon by commandment and obligation. Gershon thought of the Jewish declaration of the One and Only God, the *Shema*: "Set these words on your hearts and on your souls. Bind them as letters to your arms and signs between your eyes. Remember all My commandments and do them that you shall not follow your heart astray."

The heart was a safe-deposit box. A repository of loyalties, commitments, duties, purposes, faith, memories, even love. But it was also a sprawling warehouse of secrets, haphazard, untidy and dangerous. To harm Ruhama was the last thing he wanted to do. What he learned could be lost, forgotten. It could be buried. But Gershon was not good at forgetting. Knowledge shouldn't be held back, especially not from a wife. Especially not something like this—the revelation that slight alterations of the heart could also happen without effort or desire.

"The industry is dying," Gershon's older brother Chaim was explaining over a bowl of red borscht at the Chabad kosher restaurant. Chaim frequently returned to Chabanel to meet Gershon for lunch.

"They've been saying that for years, Chaim. The building's still ninety percent occupied. Everyone complains. The market's always had its ups and downs. The money they make is never enough. That's the oldest story there is."

"I'm not saying it's dead, not yet. But the prognosis isn't good. Look at what's happening. The government has contempt for the needletrade. They see it as third-world and black-market. So they're signing free-trade deals with African countries and the import quotas on Asian merchandise will be dropping in a few years. Canada will be flooded with cheap product. No Canadian manufacturer can compete with labour at twenty bucks a month. It'll be a pogrom. You're gonna wait for the pogrom?"

Chaim had worked in the family business. He had left four years earlier, leveraging his real estate connections and experience to start his own enterprise developing software applications for property management.

"Don't you think you're being a bit alarmist, Chaim? I mean, a pogrom?"

"You know what I mean, Gershon." Chaim slurped down another spoonful of bloody borscht. "You don't want to stick around till it's too late."

"So we'll change. I've been thinking about how the building might be converted into something other than industrial, something more than just *shmatte*."

"Conversion is costly. Pa would never agree to re-mortgage the building to finance it. The money's too good right now. You know the way he is. He waits too long. It nearly cost him his life once, now he thinks he can survive anything. Anyway, convert the building to what? The whole district is *shmatte*. Been that way for almost forty years. Your problem is more than transforming steel and concrete. You've got to change people's minds, their preconceptions."

Their prejudices, thought Gershon. Gershon folded his paper napkin in half, then in quarters and in eighths. He opened it again, flattening the tissue out on the tablecloth with fingers spread. He then traced with his eyes the checkerboard lines that appeared. Grabbing a salt shaker from the middle of the table, he ran it along the lines pressing hard to see if they could be erased.

"Gershon, sometimes the only solution is to get out before you're trapped."

Selling the building and starting over with the proceeds was an option Gershon had considered once or twice before but not seriously.

"The building still has value," Chaim reasoned as he dabbed at the corners of his mouth, spotting his white napkin with scarlet. "The current value can be turned into future value. Sell it now and with the proceeds you could buy an upscale apartment building, or an office complex for professionals and technology firms."

The notion was unpalatable to Gershon. He didn't see himself as upscale. And he had the sense that selling 99 was a form of abandonment.

"If you wait too long you'll find yourself at a disadvantage, trying to unload something nobody wants."

As they exited the restaurant, Gershon reached out and placed his hand on Chaim's right shoulder. They may have only been two years apart in age, but Gershon had always viewed Chaim as distant and aloof. His learning was far more advanced. While Gershon spent all his time reading *Berachot*, the rudimentary Talmudic explication of blessings, Chaim was already well into *Bava Metzia*, parsing complicated laws that concerned money matters. He was a faster reader and possessed a greater facility to grasp and explain Talmudic arguments. When Gershon needed help with his learning, Chaim couldn't be bothered, fearing that his younger brother would hold him back. Chaim had always been untouchable. Gershon appreciated Chaim's advice and wanted to feel, with a squeeze of the palm, or a hand on the shoulder, that he could depend on his brother to support him.

It was around 11:00 a.m. Ruhama knew this without verification on her wristwatch. The Filipina nannies had begun to colonize the park with their charges. They entered from all sides, via the maze of paths leading to the playground in the middle, their modest frames laden with lunchboxes and backpacks, pushing strollers and holding small, trustful hands.

Once inside the play area, the children scampered off, bouncing their bodies against plastic and wood. In the dizziness of their freedom some quickly ascended to the highest point of the playground and cheered, arms raised triumphantly like Kings of Castles. But just as many misplaced their footing, fell and flopped down in anguish, bruised and crying. When this happened their Filipinas ran to them, and hovered like guardian angels, smiling and soothing. They always smiled. When the children appeared safe from danger, the Filipinas retreated and spoke among themselves in sweet, hushed tones. Their voices were barely audible above the tranquil rustling of the maple leaves, strummed by a breeze. Ruhama tried to imagine what a mad Filipina sounded like, and couldn't. Do angels scream?

"Shoshana's Tushy On Potty," yelled Bayly, Ruhama's eldest daughter. At five-and-a-half Bayly could turn any word into an acronym that made sense.

"Good one," Ruhama congratulated. Shoshana, the three-year-old, threw her older sister and mother a disapproving frown. She had been potty-training hard these past two weeks and didn't appreciate it being mentioned publicly.

"My turn," said Ruhama. "Study. Study Torah On Purpose. Now every time you see one of those big red signs you'll think of learning Torah. A reminder on every street corner of the city."

"Silly Time Out Playing," responded Bayly proudly.

The acronym game had begun in the park one day. Bayly had noticed graffiti for the first time. She asked her mother what it was. Ruhama explained that some people wanted attention, so they wrote their initials on things to make others notice them. Like they're being famous.

The scribble that originally caught Bayly's attention was TVC, spray-painted in squiggly blue lines all over the playground, on the face of the slide, on a wooden fence and twice more on the jungle gym. Bayly was intrigued. The letters hadn't been there the week before. She liked the change. It reminded her of the way bulbs had come up in spring, the sudden push of yellow daffodils and red tulips like gifts from God. Not there one day, and then surprise! She liked the mystery of graffiti. The familiar playground near home now held secret messages that appeared out of thin air.

"What's it say?" Bayly demanded, turning her head and pointing. She could read the letters, but wanted her mother to say it aloud.

"It looks like the letters T V C," answered Ruhama.

Bayly noted silently that some letters were grouped together into words and others were pronounced separately.

"What's T V C?" Bayly inquired.

"Not what, but who?" Ruhama said. "They're initials."

"Initials?"

"Letters that stand for a name."

"Whose name?" Bayly asked.

"I don't know."

"So then the person's not famous. You said they were being famous,"

Bayly said, puzzled.

Ruhama smiled. "You're right, sweetheart. But it makes them feel famous to put their letters all over the place."

"But we don't know what they stand for?" Bayly was becoming frustrated.

"Okay," an idea sparked in Ruhama. "Then let's make something up. T V C...," she thought a bit. "Tuesday's Very Cold. It's a weather forecast."

Bayly giggled. She didn't know what a weather forecast was, but understood the object of the game right away.

"Television's Very Cool," Bayly announced, stunning her mother. Why did Bayly think television was very cool? They didn't own one at home. And where did she get "cool" from?

Ruhama resolved to get the game back on the right track. "Torah's Very Cool," she corrected.

Bayly was studying the markings, and slowly realized something about them. They looked like the writing in her Illustrated *Hagaddah*, the Passover story of the enslavement in Egypt and the miraculous Jewish flight to freedom. TVC was like the Egyptian hieroglyphs on the pillars of Pharaoh's palace. If you turned your head in a certain way it could be the picture of a man paddling a boat, or shooting a spear. And she immediately knew who the Egyptian master was shooting spears at. Bayly looked around. If the jungle gym was Pharaoh's palace, then the sandy playground became the desert and the tall triangle swings were pyramids built from Jewish oppression. Bayly got angry at the swings. Angry at TVC whoever he was.

"Terrible Very Cruel," she said.

Ruhama would remember how Bayly surprised her with that final acronym the first time they played the game and then abruptly demanded to leave the park. But Ruhama never asked Bayly why TVC meant Terrible Very Cruel.

Ruhama counted three, then four Filipinas entering the playground. She had become quite friendly with one of them, a caregiver named Olive whom she met regularly at the park. Olive served a non-observant Jewish family that lived up the street from the Steins. She worked twelve hours a day, six days a week. She prepared breakfast, lunch and supper for two children named Brittany and Jason. Sometimes, when they sat together on the bench, Olive complained to Ruhama. Never about her long hours or the workload, but that the parents she worked for were hardly ever at home, and the children missed them. These Filipina women *were* guardian angels. What would the children do without them? Brought from another continent, across oceans, they had been summoned to this place as if answering the silent prayers of children in need. Yes, these Filipina women were nothing less than angels provided by God.

Yet, Ruhama couldn't help resenting them a bit too. She was witnessing a whole generation of Jewish kids being brought up by Filipinas. She understood the predicament of immigrants and respected the way they worked hard to send money back home, or earn enough to bring their families over to Canada. But she also lamented the current state of the Jewish family. The Jews had fled the pogroms of Europe for North America to find a safe and stable environment in which to raise their families. Two or three generations later, both parents in the workforce, they delivered their children back into the hands of foreigners. What exactly had been gained? Eavesdropping on the children playing together, chatting to each other, Ruhama thought that she could detect a slight Filipino accent in some of the nanny-raised Jewish kids. If their speech was changing, what else inside them was being altered?

Ruhama looked down at her own child, Shoshana. She had ceased paying attention to the STOP game after hearing "Shoshana's Tushy On Potty." Now she was staring at an army of ants that coagulated on the cement next to the park bench around a hardened glob of pink bubble-gum, several shards of broken potato chips and a hunk of brown, dried-up apple.

"They have hearts too," Ruhama said pointing at the ants. "Hearts so small you couldn't see them if you wanted to. They may be tiny, but they have beating hearts just like you and me. They were created by *Hashem* too."

Shoshana seemed to understand. She dropped her head down toward the ants to get a closer look. The sudden brush of her brown hair against the ground sent the colony into a frenzy.

"Now you've frightened them," Ruhama said. "They're escaping to find safety and shelter. Can you imagine all their fragile little hearts racing now?"

∾

"You'd better go down to the third floor right away," Alfreda commanded as Gershon entered the office. "Someone's trapped in passenger Number Two between the second and third floors. I've called the elevator company. They said it'll take twenty minutes to get a serviceman here."

Gershon hadn't heard the alarm bell when he returned from lunch with Chaim. "How long have they been stuck?"

"I got the call from Emile about ten minutes ago."

Gershon was estimating how much time he could take hurrying down to the elevator based on how many minutes usually transpired before a person began to panic. An older person usually took about ten minutes. An older woman, five minutes, max. Younger people could typically endure the isolation longer. One of Gershon's greatest fears was an older person with a heart condition getting trapped. He was sure that one day someone would suffer a fatal attack in one of his elevators. The machinery was rusted and worn out. In the years Sholem had managed the property the elevators weren't properly maintained. It was one of the first things Gershon discovered when he started working for his father. The elevators broke down regularly and were a constant source of headaches. He begged Sholem to spend some money upgrading them, to no avail. Sholem was stubborn and preferred patch-jobs. He never considered the long run.

"Young or old? Man or woman? Alone or with someone?" Gershon blurted to Alfreda from the threshold.

Two people stuck in an enclosed space together with no escape were less likely to panic. They would fortify each other with conversation.

"Single, young, woman."

The way Alfreda said it, the description sounded like a personal ad in the newspaper. "Likes small dogs, windsurfing and bargain-hunting. Prefers walking stairs to riding up elevators," added Gershon with a chuckle on his way out.

When he arrived on the third floor, Emile, who owned a screen-printing shop down the hall, was talking to the sealed doors. He turned when Gershon came into view. "I think she's getting scared," he said.

Emile stepped aside and Gershon placed his lips close to the elevator doors. "Don't worry, the building manager's here," Gershon said, raising his voice to be heard through the sliding panels. "The elevator company has been contacted. A repairman is on the way."

No response.

"Are you there? Are you alright?" Gershon turned to Emile. "Did she speak to you?"

"Yes, a few seconds before you came."

"Miss, are you there?"

Silence.

Gershon was becoming anxious. What if this wasn't a routine entrapment? What if, even though she was reportedly young, the woman had a heart condition? Young people had those kinds of defects too.

"Mademoiselle, mademoiselle, êtes-vous là?"

"Yes, am here," came a muffled, heavily accented voice.

Thank God, just a language barrier. Gershon's effort at French opened one door.

"Don't worry. Restez calme, mademoiselle. Le technicien de l'ascenseur est en route," he stammered in his butchered French. He repeated the word *ascenseur* in his head. For the first time he realized the connection between the French word for elevator and the English verb "to ascend." But an elevator didn't just ascend, it also descended, so why not call it a *descendeur*?

He thought of the elevator. When a machine didn't work any longer it was called a "breakdown." But when two people ceased having a relationship it was called a "break-up." He continued to play with words, thinking of things he might say to keep the lady inside the broken elevator calm.

"Am okay," the quiet voice said. "Does he come soon?"

"Yes, he'll be here in a few minutes. Do you work in the building?" Gershon wanted to keep her talking so he could gauge her level of fear and, if possible, take her mind off her predicament.

Silence.

"La température est pas mal élevée. Is hot in here."

"I know. He's on his way. You'll be out soon," Gershon soothed.

In the years Gershon worked in the building he had never been trapped in an elevator. Since these malfunctions happened with regularity he considered himself blessed. He set his hands against the heavy doors and turned his ear sideways, listening for further signs of life.

Silence. Gershon wondered if this was the way priests took confession. What did they mutter to tweak the hearts of their anonymous clients, anyway, to start them talking, spilling truth. Is that what they were called, clients? Flock?

"Am sorry. J'suis desolée," came the small voice.

"Sorry? Why are you sorry?" Gershon raised his brow.

"C'est ma faute. So much trouble I make you."

"I'm the one who should be sorry. These elevators are old. We do our best, but you can't make a forty-year-old car run like new," Gershon joked mildly.

"No, I press that button."

"A button? You pressed a button? Which button?"

"Le rouge. Le Stop urgent."

The way she mixed French and English, together with her accent, Gershon thought he might have misunderstood.

"You say you pressed a button? Which button?" There were many buttons. Maybe she meant a floor button that had malfunctioned.

"Le Stop."

She had pressed the emergency stop between floors. Gershon understood perfectly now.

"Why? Why did you press the Stop button?"

Silence.

"You there? You okay?"

"I don't know. I see it there. I think what happen if…"

Gershon didn't need to hear any more. He stepped away from the steel doors, annoyed. All the empathy that had been building up inside him was leaking out, as if he were a cracked pipe. Why did people hit the emergency Stop for no reason? It was almost always a young person. They got their kicks from the disturbance they caused others. If they couldn't be sure the world revolved around them already, they would vandalize or sabotage something to get noticed.

The elevator serviceman strolled up. Without saying a word, he reached into his toolbox, producing a crooked wire-hanger-type object which he casually slid up the front of the cabin with the swift dexterity of a car thief. One twist, a yank and the heavy black doors began to separate slowly. A sharp beam of light from inside the cabin pierced the stark hallway like a passing solar eclipse.

The elevator enclosure was submerged partially below the floor. The repairman pushed the heavy doors out of his way, crouched down on his knees and stuck his arm deep into the cabin to his shoulder. Gershon imagined that this was how it looked when the police fished dead bodies from the river. He felt tremendous anticipation. The repairman rose slowly, pulling up what was below.

Thoughts turned to identifying the victim. First, Gershon saw a starfish of pale, delicate fingers. It was wrapped around the repairman's hairy, square hand. Leveraging his weight against the elevator doorframe, the repairman heaved the rest of her up, his bulk straining to hoist her weight onto the floor. The full figure of the victim began to emerge piecemeal from the depths. Gershon saw an arm. A shoulder. Then a foot came up. A bent knee. With one last heave, her body rose and plopped down onto the floor like a freshly netted fish on a ship's deck.

The girl's back was to Gershon. She paused for a moment to catch her breath, then rolled over on her side and faced him. It was wordless Miriam. And with her, the corpse of their first conversation.

Restaurant

Two Guys Delicatessen in the lobby of 99 was the oldest and most reliable of the Canadian-style eateries on Chabanel. At one time every building had its own restaurant. All of them served more or less the same menu, generically called Canadian cuisine: omelets, club sandwiches, hot dogs, hamburgers, french fries, salads, pasta and souvlaki. The Daily Specials were hardly ever special. They would typically feature a meat dish, beef stew or bourguignon, grilled salmon or trout, or fried chicken. But as the only gathering place in the building, the restaurant furnished the occupants with a sense of community.

It was one of the great tragedies of Chabanel that in recent years the restaurants had started closing their doors. 222 and 333 didn't have them anymore. 125 had a tiny Vietnamese joint. 433 had one that offered Middle Eastern fare. If the restaurants were any indication, and they were, the industry was getting smaller and subdividing into its constituent ethnic groups.

Two Guys was run by Greek brothers-in-law, Niko Costakos and Costa Dimitrakis. Niko tabulated bills and took take-out orders, while Costa was in charge of the kitchen. Their specialty was smoked meat. All the Jewish businessmen on Chabanel agreed it was the best this side of the Metropolitan.

If 99 was like NASA Mission Control, then Two Guys would be its Command Centre. At the peak of lunch hour, the vinyl-padded cubicles were loaded. Heads hunched over shiny place settings. Standing behind the cash Niko acted as Mission Chief. The restaurant was the one place where bosses and workers sat in proximity to one another. Workers sat in booths along the wall and bosses crowded into the dining-area tables near the front door. The static buzz of communication was heard between tables, and the waitresses carried critical data from each unit to the Central Station where Niko presided, behind the cash, parsing it all into digestible staff directives.

Reams of information about the state of tenant affairs could be gleaned at lunch by eavesdropping, an art perfected by Niko. Impromptu management conferences were often held in the restaurant. Sales underlings courted prospective clients. Shimmy Solomon could be seen pounding his fist on the table and jabbing his finger at Chairman Mao or Stalin. Joey Putkin rarely ate with his father, but Avi was a frequent customer, usually seated across the table from a pretty woman. Charlie, Hyman and Irving Roth had their special table reserved in the corner. When they weren't present it sat vacant, perpetually waiting for their imminent arrival—which is how The Dolphins liked it.

Among the entrepreneurs and sales personnel there was a short list of topics on which they exercised their limited vocabularies: money and sports. They bantered about stock fortunes made and lost, golf games squandered in missed putts, and they numerated admiringly the huge salaries paid to athletes. Labourers talked about recent parties they'd attended, how drunk they'd gotten by the end of the night, and the plans they were making for the coming weekend, which often involved getting drunk at some party.

Gershon didn't eat in the restaurant but he regularly partook of the gossip Niko amassed and peddled with great skill. He knew that if he wanted to find out about the comings and goings of the building he only had to consult Niko. When a tenant was planning to skip out in the middle of the night, Niko could be counted on to provide advance warning. When the rent was late, Niko offered Gershon a plausible explanation why. Niko knew everyone in the building on a first-name basis, and he knew lots of juicy personal tidbits. Gershon went into the restaurant the morning after the elevator incident.

"Niko, y'know that girl who works for Sonny Lipsey?" Gershon asked, softly scratching his beard.

"Gyerry, you like her?" Niko liked to call Gershon, "Gary" for short. But with his Greek accent, it came out "Gyerry." Niko showed teeth, a sign that he instantly recognized who Gershon was talking about.

"No, no, not that. I was just curious if you knew her name?"

While jotting down a take-out order, Niko said "Gyerry, you don't want to mix around with her." He stripped a sheet off the order pad, handed it to a waitress, and scribbled again like a psychiatrist taking notes.

"No, I just want to know her name." Gershon stepped back, sorry he'd raised the topic with Niko. All he needed now was word to get around that he had expressed interest in a girl.

There was a tattoo on Niko's left forearm, a faded blue anchor. When he learned something about a tenant it twitched, like a ship becoming unmoored by a heavy undertow. Gershon noticed how it bobbed up and down.

"Michelle. Michelle Labelle. Trust me, she's not your kind." When Niko said "trust me" he meant business.

"Of course not," Gershon said firmly. "She was stuck in the elevator yesterday. I just wanted to find out if she was okay, that's all."

If Gershon had simply wanted to know that Sonny's girl was okay, he could have inquired with Sonny Lipsey. But he wanted to know her real name. Michelle Labelle. It rhymed. How appropriate that Sonny Lipsey, The Poet of Chabanel, would have a bookkeeper whose name rhymed.

Michelle Labelle. Gershon let the syllables slide off his tongue, elle, elle, mich, elle, la, belle. It meant Michelle the beautiful. It sounded fake, made-up. Associations came to Gershon. There was a Beatles song with that name, wasn't there? Michelle Labelle. He'd remembered it. *Sont les mots qui vont très bien ensemble . . . I love you I love you I love you. . . .* And the last name, Labelle, sounded like . . . label. He couldn't let the name go. Michelle Labelle. It was like a mantra. Comprised of a certain combination of sounds which clung to the mind like burrs. Sounds so soft and rhythmic they might have been carefully selected by a squad of overpaid marketing professionals. It was a label, a brand name, ubiquitous, inoffensive and most important of all, unforgettable. Trapped alone in the elevator yesterday, stuck today in the cabin of Gershon's brain, crowded inside with all the prayers, blessings and Torah quotations Gershon knew by heart.

Now that he knew her name, what?

"She spoke French, but her accent was different," slipped out.

"She's not French, Gyerry." Niko was still listening. "She's from Hungary."

Hungary? That didn't make sense. "What about her name?" Gershon asked hesitantly.

"Probably short for something Hungarian. You know how the first thing immigrants do when they get to Canada is change their names."

Not my name, Gershon thought to himself. Mine is authentic. Goes back to the Torah.

"Gershon!" Irving Roth's voice boomed from the corner. Gershon hadn't noticed Irving sitting there eating his regular breakfast, a bowl of oatmeal with two lumps of butter and a teaspoon of salt. Gershon tried to avoid Irving whenever possible.

"What're you doing in the restaurant? I thought the food here wasn't good enough for you!"

The only time Irving ever spoke to Gershon directly was to mock him. No one in 99 upset Gershon like the youngest Dolphin Brother, except maybe Joey Putkin.

Gershon had once inadvertently interrupted a meeting between his father and Irving. He had entered Sholem's office and performed an about-face when he caught sight of the youngest Dolphin who, like Sholem, was in his early seventies. Gershon assumed they were discussing rental arrangements because Irving was only seen in the management office once every two years when it was time to renew the lease for his fifteen thousand square feet on the third floor. Gershon was on his way out when his ears picked up the mention of pork, and he stopped short.

They weren't talking about a lease. Nor were they commiserating about rising costs or cursing the municipality for escalating property and business taxes, subjects which Sholem typically used as a friendly prelude to negotiations. To Gershon's astonishment Sholem was explaining kashrut.

"It's better for you not to eat milk and meat together," Sholem was saying. "It's healthier." Talking about staying healthy was a way Irving might understand the Jewish dietary laws.

"The scientists agree about this now. It only took them two thousand years to figure out what we Jews have known all along." Sholem placed his hands against his lips in a pose suggesting wisdom.

Gershon became irritated. The way Sholem talked about health and

science you'd think these were the reasons behind the laws of *kashrut*.
"Tell him the truth," Gershon interrupted. "Go ahead. Tell him." He glared at Sholem. "Tell him that the laws of keeping kosher have nothing to do with health or doctors."

Momentarily taken aback by his son's intrusion, Sholem didn't respond.

"Those aren't the reasons." Gershon turned to Irving. "There isn't any *reason* for not mixing milk with meat. It's a *hok*, a Commandment which can't be understood. We follow the law because God tells us to, that's all!" Why should the Torah be diminished for the sake of Irving Roth?

Sholem spoke up now in a calmly dismissive manner. "It's good for you not to put milk with meat, Irving," he said, not looking at Gershon. "Better for the digestion."

"Why shouldn't he understand what a *hok* is? He's a big boy." Gershon challenged his father, waving a thumb in Irving's direction.

"Don't get so excited," Sholem said in Gershon's vicinity, smiling at Irving.

Gershon turned again to Irving. "We think about what we put in our mouths. We pause and take our time to say blessings, consider the meaning of what we're eating. There's no such thing as Jewish fast food. Food's not meant to be *fast*." He was burning now. "In fact, you want me to tell you precisely what it says in the Torah about not mixing milk and meat. I'll tell you. It doesn't say it's healthier. It says 'Don't boil a kid . . . a baby goat . . . in its mother's milk.'"

"Enough. Enough already. Leave us alone, Gershon," Sholem implored. "Please."

The moment Sholem said "please", it was as if Gershon snapped out of a spell. He felt ashamed of his outburst. Sholem was a master of such verbal wizardry, capable of saying exactly what was required to add weight, or shift perceptions.

Gershon left the office feeling sullen and regretting his behaviour. But why did Sholem take Irving's side? He said "leave *us* alone." Who was this *us*? Us was supposed to be the religious people, the people of faith, and *them* the miserable, cynical, godless, self-hating jerks like Irving Roth. Whose side was Sholem on?

Don't boil a kid in its mother's milk, Gershon repeated in his mind.

What did the words really mean and why did he feel compelled to instruct Irving? Slim chance that Irving Roth could grasp how some things simply do not bend to reason, and the job of a Jew was to accept this fact, swallow it, and bless the Almighty in gratitude. And maybe that was the difference between *us* and *them*. We sought meaning where there was no apparent reason. They sought reason where there was no apparent meaning. But whose side was Sholem on?

Quality Kosher Kitchen was pandemonium on Thursday afternoons. Friday morning was even busier, but not with strictly Orthodox Jews. The less experienced Jews, newly-committed adherents of the law, shopped on Friday. Thursday was the day old-hand practitioners did their Sabbath shopping. The Friday shoppers may not have known it, but Kosher Kitchen, as it was known in the community, prepared food fresh for the Thursday crowd. Friday shoppers were served leftovers.

Ruhama didn't like to cook. She considered it one of her major failings. She was aware that, traditionally, a Jewish wife was supposed to be an expert at preparing food. But cooking simply never appealed to her. And fortunately the trend seemed to be moving away from the traditional model.

Quality Kosher Kitchen had a delectable selection of pre-cooked dishes tastefully displayed in huge refrigerated glass cases. All the familiar Eastern European and Middle Eastern Jewish favourites were there, including a variety of salads and spreads like hummus, tahina, fatouche and babaganoush, as well as *cholent*, apple and raisin kugels, carrot *zimes*, and gefilte fish. Rows of glass jars with chicken soup glowed like lanterns next to plastic bags filled with freshly-made, baseball-size matzah balls. Nowadays a Jewish wife could still serve her family the traditional favourites without having to prepare them herself. Ruhama was grateful for the convenience. She never missed Thursday. Bayly and Shoshana joined Ruhama on her Thursday excursions, although she had misgivings about bringing the children along. She hoped they were not assimilating their mother's shortcomings.

The children enjoyed the mayhem of Kosher Kitchen. Ruhama would tell the girls that shopping there was like the kosher butcher where their Bubbie, of blessed memory, shopped for her chicken. She described for them how in the old days the *shoichet* clasped the feet of a live bird in his strong hands, wings flapping wildly. He then held the chicken still for Bubbie to inspect by blowing into its *tuches,* separating the tail feathers to verify plumpness. Once the test was passed, the bird was taken to be plucked, its throat slit and it was hung upside down. The blood drained into a bucket. Somehow this was not hard for the children to imagine in spite of what they witnessed at the store—the bright rows of plastic-wrapped drumsticks and breasts in open fridges, stamped with small blue expiry dates which Ruhama inspected meticulously.

Everywhere they looked Bayly and Shoshana saw Bubbies. The store was staffed by elderly ladies with thick accents who hollered and cooed from behind the counters and said "honey" and "dear" and *"shayna maydele"* when they served customers. On the counter automated machines spat out numbered tickets. Ruhama's girls noticed that having a number in your hand meant nothing. The Bubbies never bothered with them. They clearly had no appreciation for the wonders of technology. They called out "Who's next?" And since every Jew is born with the notion they're next, for both good and bad, shoving matches ensued, tempers flared, and the girls were delighted.

Bayly and Shoshana had their own plans. Squeezed in among the crowd of legs, they knew if they tapped hard on the glass near the danishes and pastries they would be rewarded for their cuteness with a chocolate macaroon or a handful of *rugelach.* Having the girls at her side gave Ruhama an advantage as well. When she asked for a container of potato salad or macaroni salad and it wasn't very fresh, the Bubbie serving her would "tsk, tsk," shake her head and look down at the innocent faces pressed against the glass, Bubbie-code for "I wouldn't serve it to my grandchildren."

Gershon was grateful for the box lunches Ruhama prepared for him, usually a cheese sandwich on an onion roll, a bag of sliced cucumber or carrots, some potato chips and a fruit. He ate lunch at his desk. Sholem also ate in the office. The lunch hour brought father and son together, as they paused, simultaneously, to eat in adjacent rooms.

Sholem brought his food in a paper bag, a sardine or whitefish sandwich, and an apple. Gershon had noticed that he always stank of fish in the afternoon.

When Sholem ate his apple, he peeled the skin off with the penknife he carried with him at all times. Gershon was always slightly startled when he spied Sholem slipping the knife out of his pocket. He found it indecent the way his father ran the blade along his apple's outer layer, unspooling a thread of skin. Sholem would then slice the apple into smiling half-moons and press each pale carved section against the knife's smooth metal, extracting them surgically, one at a time, and laying them daintily on the cushion of his outstretched tongue. Between mouthfuls he licked the blade clean and sucked the juice off his thumb. Sholem held the appleseeds in the pockets of his cheeks until the slice was completely swallowed, then spit them into his opened palm.

Their approaches could not be more different. Gershon bit into his apple with gusto. In ten bites the fruit was chomped and gone—core, seeds and all. Only the stem remained between the tips of his fingers, to be carelessly tossed into the garbage bin under his desk.

Gershon zipped through the required blessings before and after eating, but there was no artistry in it for him. It was simply a matter of necessity.

His mother had shown him how food could be a preoccupation. Sometimes, at six o'clock in the morning when Gershon was getting ready to go to shul for the morning minyan, the telephone would ring.

"But I brought you one yesterday, Ma," Ruhama would answer. "Okay, okay, I'll come later."

Ruhama would cry out to Gershon from the other room, "Do you think you could drop by your mother's house on the way to work?"

"Don't tell me, the bread you brought her yesterday wasn't fresh."

The bread was never fresh enough for Gershon's mother. She didn't leave the house without depositing a hunk in her pocket or a cellophane-wrapped end-piece in her purse. Sometimes Masha forgot her wallet, occasionally her house keys, but never the bread. Her wartime experience had left a mark, though the details were sketchy. She never spoke about those days. It was known that her entire family had perished in the Shoah, mother, father, four older brothers and two younger sisters. No one questioned her about it, out of respect. If Masha ever wanted to clear the air, it was understood that would be her prerogative.

Every couple of weeks Gershon drove to his mother's to clean out her freezers. He found four or five untouched loaves of bread frozen solid upstairs and another four or five bricks in the basement. Opening the sticky fridge door, a gust of cool vapour would escape, revealing little brown rectangles lined up like baby cadavers. Gershon saw them as everlasting remnants of a pain his mother was unable to let go. These breads were not memorials. Memorials stood for past events, yet they expressed the necessity to live in the present and build a future through the act of remembering. The loaves in the freezer represented potentiality, almosts, might-have-beens. They were like petrified lungs never having known a single breath of life, suspended in that no-man's-land between inhale and exhale, neither fully alive nor utterly dead.

Each loaf travelled a long circuitous route. Gershon would fetch one from the store, drop it off at his parents' house, pick it up from their freezer a few weeks later and return home with it, where it was defrosted and sweetened, made into french toast with maple syrup, or bread pudding with brown sugar and blueberries. By necessity, the one culinary proficiency Ruhama developed was recycling old bread.

Later that same day Gershon was speaking to Chaim from the phone in Sholem's back office, out of earshot of Alfreda. "Have you ever . . . um . . . um . . . noticed a girl?"

"What? A girl? Wait a second." Chaim muffled the receiver. He was talking to someone else in his office. "I'm sorry. What did you say, Gershon?"

Why was he making this harder? Gershon could barely get the words out. "There's this girl in the building. Did you ever notice something about a girl?"

"What are you talking about? Of course I notice girls. That's their job, to get noticed."

"No, I mean something different."

Chaim wasn't completely listening. "Gershon, you work in an industry where the whole objective is for women to get noticed. They all want to attract attention."

"It's not what I mean."

"Truth is, that's part of the reason I left the family business. I couldn't handle walking into those places to collect the rent and having to deal with all the secretaries flirting, their chests hanging out of their blouses, pants so tight. Couldn't take the smorgasbord of body parts. You know, you can't just ignore sin, you've got to run from it."

Yes, it was lust, pure and simple. That would make it easy for Gershon, provide him with an explanation that was both plausible and dismissible. He had felt the flush of desire for women in the building enough times before to know how to handle it. He scoffed at the exposed cleavage of attractive women, considering their flirtation low and pathetic. He would tag his feelings as sinfully indulgent and remove himself from the situation until his desire dissipated, which it always did in time. With Michelle Labelle he was gripped by another sensation altogether, an emptiness, a feeling of powerlessness that refused to let him go. It seemed to Gershon that those feelings remained because they had been with him all along. She had touched and amplified what was already a part of him. The lustfulness he was accustomed to feeling could be locked away, packed in a box and stored in the basement of his bones, where it was forgiven and forgotten. When the feelings stuck, as they had with Michelle, the desire was attached to something deeper and hidden, an anger or resentment, a lurking unhappiness, a dissatisfaction, or, worse, loneliness. He was not frightened by lust. Sexual desire was not dangerous. It was the other emotion which scared him, the deeper one he couldn't quite identify.

"There's this girl who works in the building. Her name's Michelle Labelle."

Chaim's voice came to attention. "You know her name? What else do you know about her?"

"Not much."

"Thank God. Keep it that way."

"I'm not talking about her body, Chaim. Her face was special. It shone."

A pause.

"What did you say? About her face?"

"It shone, Chaim. There was a light."

Pause.

"A light?"

"Yah."

Pause.

"It was *Hashem*, Gershon, not her."

Pause.

"What?"

50

"You might have seen her *neshama*. This could be major, Gershon. Just don't confuse God's light with physical attraction. We're always attracted to the light of *Hashem*. Look, you're a man. It might have been a physical attraction. Simply because you wear a beard and *payas* doesn't mean you're not tempted like everyone else. But if it was her *neshama* … Don't think that you can possess her *neshama*. That's a kind of idol worship. As much as lust."

The light was God's? Her *neshama*, her soul? The thought hadn't occurred to Gershon. What was it about her that allowed the light of her essence to shine through? And why to Gershon? Was it something between them alone? His mind raced.

"Be careful, Gershon. If it was lust, okay, that can be dealt with. But if it was, as you say, a light, be careful. You'll be drawn to it. Like a moth to a flame. It will grip you like nothing you've ever experienced before. You'll want to know more. There'll be questions and you'll want answers, desperately. The closer you are to the *neshama*, the more dangerous it is. You become exposed, vulnerable. Like I said, wanting to possess answers is a kind of idolatry, as much as wanting to possess riches."

It was true. Gershon could feel the questions welling up inside. The greed for answers.

"Chaim, what am I supposed to do? I can't ignore it, can I?"

Gershon replaced the receiver. He thought about the people who didn't bother with the soul, avoided it so skilfully, or denied its existence altogether. They walked around with obscured vision. It was easier that way. It enabled them to focus on the day-to-day. Strolling along Chabanel he silently counted the number of sunglasses. Nearly everyone wore them, shielding their eyes, or perched on their foreheads at the ready. It was more than just fashion. They hung on people's faces like constant fear.

Gershon was home from shul at nine o'clock, an hour after sunset. He entered the house quietly. Ruhama's great-grandmother's silver candlesticks stood apart on a shelf in the living room, draped in thick folds of wax. Shoshana was already fast asleep. The Sabbath meal was eaten without chit-chat. Bayly struggled to keep her head up during *Birkhat Hamazon*. She hated to miss singing the Grace After Meals, even if she was incapable of forcing out a melody. She would thank God in a mumbling drowsy fog.

Gershon and Ruhama dragged the twin beds which, in accordance with the laws of family purity had rested against opposite walls of the bedroom for two weeks, and set them back together again. It had been an exhausting evening already. To abide the Sabbath, certain lights were left on strategically overnight. One in the bathroom upstairs, in case someone had to urinate in the early morning hours, and another in the corner of the kitchen, streaming light through the main floor. The children's rooms were equipped with plastic nightlights that had automatic sensors to deter visits from unwelcome midnight creatures: a Ten Commandments for Bayly, and a glowing purple Barney the Dinosaur for Shoshana.

Ruhama had talked about having another baby for several weeks. The time was right and conceiving after ushering in the Sabbath would add sanctity to the act. Gershon sat down on the corner of their joined beds while Ruhama undressed in the bathroom with the door slightly ajar.

Ruhama entered the bedroom gently stroking her long, brown hair with spread fingers. Gershon was unmoved. In fact, he eyed his wife suspiciously.

Had this been a regular weeknight, she would have stretched for the bottle of skin moisturizer kept on the bookshelf next to Gershon's volumes of inspirational writings and Torah commentary. She would have squeezed some out and slapped her palms together to begin the ritual of spreading lotion to the preordained locations on her body. Gershon would have watched the series of familiar gestures contentedly, the sway of her body, her fingers moving from the crook of an elbow to the back of a knee, from the heel of a foot to the space between toes. He was always comforted by this dance, with its rhythmic predictability.

But it was Shabbat. Law did not permit rubbing moisturizer into skin. There would be no performance tonight.

Ruhama was petite. The only girl Gershon had ever known. The only body he'd ever touched beside his own. Her breasts were soft and full. The first time he felt them they were wrapped in cloth. It was their wedding night. She had not stood in front of him and unpackaged herself like a gift. Both he and Ruhama were already spent from rejoicing. Back in the hotel bedroom their heads continued to spin from hora after hora. Their nerves were jangled from being swung and tossed up and down on raised chairs. They undressed tentatively under cover of linen. The bedsheets offered a much desired level of modesty and more importantly, at that moment, the mattress absorbed the uncontrollable tremors of their naked bodies. They did not actually see the other's body at all. Instead, outlines were read by caress. Gershon's right hand was flattened under the small of Ruhama's back. The fingers of his left hand crept freely across the roundness of her belly and hips like a tangle of snakes rolling over a mound of rocks, occasionally coming to rest in the secure hidden corners of her flesh. She twitched with every pass. It was unpleasant. Eventually they both fell asleep, remaining, on the night of their nuptials, more or less pure.

Gershon drummed his fingers impatiently on the bed. He picked at the blankets. Ruhama wore a boxy cotton nightgown. The neckline was high, frills covered her collarbones. She moved around the bed to her side, untucking the blanket and topsheet in a neat triangle.

"Please don't sit on the edge of the bed. How many times do I have to ask you? You're breaking the mattress springs."

"It's my bed. I'll break it if I want to," Gershon muttered under his breath.

He stood up and, without turning to acknowledge Ruhama, left the room for the kitchen light downstairs. Gershon read for a long time. When he was sure his wife was asleep, he tiptoed back upstairs to bed.

Shabbat morning, Gershon strained to raise his body off his narrow side of the bed. He rubbed his lids open. *Modeh ani l'phanecha melech chai v'kayam,* he said. *I arise in gratitude before You, source of all life, who restores my soul with compassion. Great is Your faith.*

The rabbis taught that sleep was a kind of death. Overnight, the soul was lifted from a person's body and, if they were lucky, returned to them in the morning. From the first conscious breath to the very last before fading into unconsciousness at night, blessings were said by a Jew. The purpose of life was to utter God's praise. As the Prophet said, the dead do not praise God.

Thus the first blessing of the day was said in gratitude to the Almighty for the restoration of the soul. The soul was directly associated with wakening, consciousness, awareness of the world. Consciousness was the way the soul was nourished. God had ordained that it was every

Jew's job to expand and deepen his understanding of the world, thereby cultivating his soul. One who chose to turn away from the world, whether by remaining ignorant, alienated or disengaged, was stifling his soul.

Gershon reached for the pitcher of *negel vasser* on the bedside table. It was empty. Ruhama had neglected to fill the jug. She had never forgotten before. He put his feet onto the carpet and crossed the room.

Ruhama was gone, probably downstairs preparing breakfast for the kids. Out of the corner of his eye Gershon noticed that her bed looked like a pool of churning water, the sheets swirling angrily in the centre.

At the bathroom sink, he propped himself up against the corners of the porcelain basin and steadied his face in the mirror. He reached for the faucet handle and twisted, allowing the sink to fill with a stream of cold water.

Gershon dipped his hands in the water and dropped his face down into the centre of cupped palms. Lifting his head, his eyes slowly regained their focus. His facial features achieved sharpness inside the mirror's rectangular frame.

The night had not been kind. He felt robbed of rest rather than rejuvenated.

Behind soggy eyes, wet nose and dripping beard, questions began to reconstitute themselves in his mind. Matters he had pondered for hours in the kitchen after walking out on Ruhama. What if he'd actually seen Michelle Labelle's essence, a stranger's soul? How was it possible that he—who strived to know his own soul but hardly did—could perceive someone else's so readily? Maybe this irony was itself the message he needed to comprehend: it was easier to perceive the soul of another than one's own. Or maybe a person was *only* able to perceive the soul of another, and it was impossible for him to see his own. Perhaps this was why men and women were so strongly compelled to seek a connection to one another. Why they needed each other. Why God had created in humankind a limitless capacity for both love and loneliness.

Did seeing the Divine light in someone else change a person, like what happened to *Moshe Rabeinu*? In pursuit of a stray lamb, Moses chanced upon the light of God in the form of a burning bush at the foot of a desert mountain. Not only was the animal lost in the wilderness, but Moses was lost too. They called out to one another, the animal baaing and his master yelling. Precisely at that moment of greatest vulnerability, when shepherd and sheep were bonded together in their mutual failure, in their mutual yearning, God appeared to Moses in a continuous smouldering light. And when Moses brought down the Law from Mount Sinai the hair on his head and beard were bleached white, and his face glowed.

Gershon continued inspecting his face in the mirror. His eyes burrowed into the waves of dark brown hair covering his scalp. He thought he could detect the hairline receding above his forehead. He saw a few grey hairs here and there. He pulled at his *payas*, unrolling the lengths of sidecurls from his temples like tiny threadbare wings. A few more grey hairs. There were miniscule wisps of white tucked inside the reddish shadow of his beard. Probably, he just hadn't noticed them before. In spite of his persistent searching, the most Gershon could conclude from staring at himself in the bathroom mirror this Sabbath morning was that he was getting, if not wiser, then at least older.

Electricity

WALKING THE CORRIDORS of 99 you could hear the rhythmic stutter of sewing machines punching single and double threads through fabric, plainstitch and overlock, binding swatches together. Listening closely you could hear the whir of blades as the cutters slid their apparatuses through material stacked fifty or one hundred plies high, along tables sixty inches wide and longer than palace banquets. Listening even more carefully, you might discern the muffled whiz of computer plotters. They flailed to and fro, furiously mapping the flattened blueprints of garments on heavy rolls of white paper, making the markers used by the cutters who followed these patterns with their knives, then pulled the pieces apart, like giant jigsaw puzzles being disassembled.

The arms of sewers and cutters and plotters were all linked, through their machines, to 110-volt electrical outlets, thousands of them, pocking the walls of 99. These outlets were joined along wires and junction boxes to 60-KVA transformers installed in each of the premises. Branched off from an intricate network of kill-switches, the transformers received their power via a single, humming duct carrying massive currents through the spine of the building. A musty room at the bottom of the building housed the giant, hydra-headed basement transformer. This monster borrowed its strength from a 12.5 kilovolt electrical transformer perched precariously atop a utility pole, two metres from the south east corner of the building. If you were curious and inclined to journey farther afield, you could follow the wires, from pole to pole, then underground, traversing the city, beneath the St. Lawrence river, and through a series of switching stations in the Quebec countryside and onward, north, thousands of kilometres to the megawatt turbines, the mammoth beasts at Churchill Falls and James Bay.

Chabanel Street has always been charged with unseen energy. This energy articulated a two-fold law upon arrival: the longer the journey, the greater the power source, and, the more powerful the source, the greater the necessity for multiple stages of transformation along the way.

Gershon, who had been raised to view all of Creation through the prism of law, understood this implicitly. It was not difficult for him to imagine linked forces binding the universe into an oscillating whole deriving from a single awesome source. Everything came from one bang, one flash, one utterance, one distantly produced event of power and light. And from that one occurrence of force, transformations ensued, on and on, until today.

Gershon also understood that with every transformation, the voltage dissipated. As his yeshiva teacher used to say, with each generation the Jews became *shvach*, weaker in their commitment to Torah and learning. The 110-volt minds of today didn't hold a candle to the kilovolt intellects of the past. With each subsequent generation the light faded. First there were the Patriarchs—Abraham, Isaac and Jacob who spoke directly with God. Then came the mega-voltage of Sinai where God appeared to the Israelites in thunder and lightning and Moses brought down The Law. From then on the power had diminished precipitously, through flawed Kings David and Solomon, through the Rabbinic sages, Akiva and down, Rashi and down, Maimonides and down, the Vilna Gaon and down, the Baal Shem Tov and down, the Lubavitch Rebbe, and down and down, transformations, weaker and weaker. We are the weakest generation that has lived since Sinai, the teacher would say. But, he also offered some reassurance. Following us there will be weaker, he said, until we are in such an irretrievably hopeless state of decline that only the arrival of the Messiah can bring redemption.

Shimmy Solomon, The Great White Father, was fond of pointing out how the Montreal garment industry was transforming too. He thought about the industry a great deal and, like a nurturing parent, cared for it deeply. According to Shimmy, the industry had reached its apogee commensurate with the height of the Cold War, and started a rapid decline with the crumbling of the Berlin Wall. In fact, Simple Dress's best sales period coincided with the so-called Cuban Missile Crisis in

1962. His company sold three million units that year, when there were approximately nine million women living in Canada and so, as he said in his speech the following year at Harvard Business School, about one out of every three women in the nation wore a Simple creation.

After the Cuban Missile Crisis, there were two more peaks in company production. The first occurred during the Vietnam War and the second, early in the Reagan Administration. Shimmy could not say precisely why there was a correlation between nuclear tensions and dress sales, but it was plainly there.

Gershon hadn't seen Michelle Labelle for several weeks. His regular tours through the hallways turned up no sign of her. It could be that it was not the right time of the month. Her boss only called her in when the bills and remittances piled up. Yet surely a month had passed: the rent was due.

It was to the point that Gershon began doubting her existence altogether. Maybe she was a figment of his crazy imagination. An apparition. And what about the light? Maybe he'd imagined it. If she had quit her job with Sonny, there would be no way of confirming what he'd seen, or thought he'd seen. More questions for which he could only hope to find answers.

Alfreda stepped out from behind her desk and handed Gershon an envelope. "This came for you earlier."

An answer? Not likely. Gershon held it up against the window as he always did when mysterious envelopes arrived. Sunlight filtered through folded paper. There was no writing on the front of the envelope and nothing conclusive could be determined about the contents from the makeshift X-ray.

"How do you know it's for me?" Gershon asked, hoping Alfreda was mistaken.

"It was delivered by Avi Putkin. He said to give it to you."

He sized up the envelope. It was thicker and heavier than a cheque. Ignoring it wouldn't help.

"I signed for it. Avi wanted confirmation of receipt in writing, so you may as well open it," Alfreda said, watching Gershon fiddle. "If someone died you wouldn't be notified by letter."

Okay, no one died. So what could be so bad? Gershon slid his pinkie under an unglued corner flap. Alfreda was right. It was a letter.

To Whom It May Concern, it began. Gershon's eyes scanned down the page. *As a tenant of 99 Chabanel ... It has come to our attention ... the theft of electricity ... we are holding you responsible for any damages caused to us.*

Gershon's eyes doubled back. Theft of electricity?

We have been carefully monitoring our electrical consumption and noticed a substantial and unexplained increase in costs recently. Since we have not added machinery or increased production, we are holding you responsible ...

Is he serious? Gershon felt another confrontation with Joey Putkin looming. He turned to Alfreda.

"You're not going to believe this."

"You'd be surprised what I can believe."

"He's accusing us of stealing electricity from him."

"Stealing what?"

"Electricity."

"Stealing electricity? How's it possible?" Alfreda asked.

"I don't know. He claims he's paying for someone else's power. Like we hooked up another tenant to his meter." Gershon's eyes scanned down the letter again.

"That's a new one to me. That guy will try any excuse not to pay rent." Alfreda shook her head.

Gershon read on.

Commensurate with the additional cost in electricity we will be withholding rent until such time as the situation is rectified.

"Yup, he's withholding rental payments." Gershon had to smile at Putkin's chutzpah. "Does he really think he can get away with this?"

"Well, I suppose that's what makes him a good businessman. He gets away with things. Or, at least, he tries to," Alfreda replied.

If that's what it took, Gershon knew he would never be a good businessman. Business was not a matter of doing what was right, or fair, but rather how much you could get away with. Gershon always seemed to find himself on the receiving end of such tactics. He was a maintainer, concerned with keeping tenants relatively satisfied and paying their rents. He made sure the building machinery worked, the heating pumps pumped, the water pipes and electrical wires flowed. Unfortunately, all the pipes started from the basement and travelled up. Subterranean Joey Putkin was like a serious blockage right at the base.

Gershon hated himself for doing it, but he went to see Niko again, late in the afternoon just before closing time, when he was sure no customers would be there. Niko was standing behind the opened drawer of the cash register, counting money.

"I paid the rent, Gyerry," Niko said, as Gershon approached. "I brought it up to the office myself yesterday. Alfreda took cash. Here's the receipt." Niko reached inside the cash register and took out a pink slip of paper.

"I know. Thanks." Gershon planted himself in front of the cash register. "Listen, Niko. Remember you told me she wasn't my kind. I mean Michelle Labelle. You told me to stay away from her. What did you mean by it? That she's not Jewish?"

"No, Gyerry. Jewish shmewish. It's obvious she's not Jewish. Even you could figure that out."

"Then what?"

"She's not for you, because she's dangerous." Niko stared down at the twenties and continued counting in his head, flicking them from one hand to the other.

"Dangerous?"

"You don't want to fool around with her type. Don't be crazy. She has a boyfriend."

"Of course, I don't want to *fool around* with her," Gershon said. "But what do you mean, dangerous?"

Niko stopped counting and looked up. "He's a biker, her boyfriend. A bad guy."

"A biker?"

"On the weekend, sometimes, they come into the restaurant together. She goes shopping at Putkin's. He drives a Harley. One of those big noisy machines. They pull up and park right in front of my door. The racket disturbs my customers. She rides on the back with her arms holding tight around his waist. The guy's got tattoos up and down his arms. I think he's a Hells Angel."

"A Hells Angel? She's a Hells Angel?"

"Don't you see that she wears black all the time. A lot of leather.

Don't go near her Gyerry, unless you want to get killed. I heard he was involved in that boy's death."

"A boy's death? He killed a boy?"

"You know, Gyerry, the war. The biker war in the eastern part of the city. Over drugs. You don't want to mess with those guys. They're dangerous."

"What about the boy? What happened to the boy?"

"A beautiful little boy. Eleven years old, I think. What a shame. In the wrong place at the wrong time. Where have you been, Gyerry? You religious guys don't read the papers? It was big news. All over the television too. They showed his mother crying and crying. The Hells Angels and Rock Machine fighting over territory. A car bomb exploded. It killed a little boy playing in the street. The poor kid was caught in the middle. Tragedy. Wrong place at the wrong time."

"Michelle Labelle's boyfriend had something to do with it?"

"Well, he hasn't been arrested yet."

"Yet? They're going to arrest him?"

"The cops arrested a bunch, but not him. Rounded them up. I heard it was his gang. When they were killing each other it was one thing. Nobody cared much. Okay, let them all die. It's one way to get rid of them. But after the boy was killed, everything changed. They stepped over the line. Big public outcry. The cops cracked down hard on them."

Gershon remembered hearing about a boy being killed. Some tenants had talked about it, but he hadn't paid much attention. He considered the bikers and their drug war just another symptom of everything that was wrong with the outside world, the sickness of society, to be expected. It had nothing to do with him.

"That boy's death was the last straw," Niko said. "People all of a sudden realized that it could happen to them. To their own children."

"How could someone like her be with a guy like that?" Gershon asked.

"As they say, for every good one, you find a bad one standing right next to him."

"She's a Hells Angel," Gershon mumbled.

"I don't think *she* can be a Hells Angel, really," Niko said. "It's a men's club. But once you're connected with them, like being the girlfriend of a member, you don't get out too easily. You know too much. You see too much. They don't let you leave. You're trapped. What do they call it? Guilty by association."

"It doesn't mean what you're thinking," Gershon said.

"What?"

"Guilty by association. The phrase refers to people who are completely innocent of a crime, but who are condemned because they know the people involved. Knowing a criminal is not a crime. It's not the same as committing one."

"Like I was saying, she's trapped. Maybe she didn't do anything. But if she's a Hells' girlfriend, she must know something—probably, too much. She's stuck. Anyway, most of us are not much better. Let's not kid ourselves, Gyerry, we're all a bit guilty of something. Definitely more than a few sins. We like to fool ourselves into thinking we're much better than them, but let's face it, we're not. At least the bikers are honest about it. They don't let their members forget they're a bunch of criminals and sinners."

Niko made the motorcycle gangs sound almost like a conscience, a support group that made sure their members faced up to their guilt and didn't let them escape from it. Every person needed their own biker gang, Gershon thought to himself.

An observation suddenly struck him. There were similarities between the motorcycle gangs and the Orthodox Jews. The motorcycle gangs wore uniforms to identify themselves to each other and the outside world, and the religious Jews wore theirs. The bikers had black leather jackets labelled with insignias and helmets, and the Jews had black woollen overcoats, Stars of David, *tzizes* and *kippas*. The bikers were a men's club and the Jews were one too, in a way. The Hells members wore long beards and so did religious Jews. They had their clubhouses and bunkers, and the Jews congregated in synagogues and *kollels*. The biker gangs undoubtedly had their own rules, rites and rituals, though Gershon couldn't name any specifically, and the Jews lived by their unique rules, rites and rituals. The bikers liked sticking together as the Jews did. Maybe they even spoke their own secret language, or at least had a lingo, like the Jews. The bikers carved the city up into their turf, and, in a way, so had the Jews in every city they inhabited.

Of all the similarities, the one that struck Gershon most profoundly was what Niko had said. The Hells Angels didn't let a person forget their guilt, the gang kept its members in line. Gershon admitted that it didn't work much differently among the Orthodox Jews. His community kept him in line.

Apart from the one obvious difference that existed between the motorcycle gangs and the Jews, there was another one, thought Gershon, laughing inside. In a Montreal turf war, the Hells Angels would kick the Orthodox Jews' butt.

Ruhama was ironing. This was her thinking time. Bayly and Shoshana played with dolls in the living room, telling imaginative stories.

A basket was carried up from the laundry room filled with Papa's work shirts, the girls' Shabbat dresses, and Mama's blouses. It looked to Bayly and Shoshana like a huge, cushiony nest. The flat board flew out of hiding like a large fearsome bird and grew legs instantly with a frightening clack for landing. And when the appliance that looked like a toy boat came out, Mama would send it sailing back and forth over the wavy surface of fabric. They knew that when their mother brought the long padded table out from the hall closet and set it up next to the electrical outlet in the dining room it was a sign not to disturb her. Ruhama said code words like "hot" and "dangerous," but what she really meant was "privacy."

Gershon was agitated and uncharacteristically distant. The easygoing smile which normally creased his face was gone. *He knows it's time to try for another baby. What explanation is there for all the nights coming to bed so late?* Lifting the garments one by one Ruhama thought about how she supported her family and displayed them to the world, neat and clean. Right now, Gershon's collared shirt was wide and lifeless, a scarecrow between her outstretched arms. How different from her first impression of him.

He was a bear of a man with a bookish hairy face. He wore round glasses and his cheeks were soft and pinkish. When at eighteen Ruhama heard her parents in the kitchen talking about a boy from Montreal who came from a good, solid family, she became as curious as she was anxious. They would be coming to New York in a week. Why all the way from Montreal? As if the community in New York wasn't big enough to provide a suitable candidate. They told her, half in jest, that she was so special only a Canadian would suffice. But wasn't it freezing cold in Canada?

Didn't they speak French in Montreal? The community was smaller and stronger there, she was informed. The boy's family was prominent, respectable. They had real estate. They were acquaintances from the old country. Grandparents were landsmen who lived in the same *shtetl* in Poland before the war, deepening the foundation.

At first sight, Ruhama took in Gershon's slightly hunched shoulders and sympathetic eyes. He was tall, yet he was not imposing. He filled the room with a modest presence. His expression immediately put her at ease, in spite of the discomfiting pretext. In the past when suitors came to the house, they addressed the parents, announcing themselves formally, declaring honourable intentions, showing off their advanced learning. Gershon was unusual. He gently inserted himself, speaking to Ruhama directly, letting her parents circulate around them like bees at a picnic. He asked her personal questions but didn't pry.

Gershon was not shy. He unpacked himself, bit by bit, with humble admissions about family, the admiration he felt for his older brother and his own lack of confidence with his level of learning. He disarmed Ruhama with honesty. Every phrase felt to her like the genuine revelation of a person. She watched his hands curve gracefully through the air as he spoke. They seemed to float. He paused often. Words arrived with difficulty, thoughtfully, as if he was afraid the next one might be an intrusion, a puncture in the seamless transparency of their growing bond.

Ruhama shook out Gershon's shirt. The cuffs flapped up and down angrily. She spread it out flat along the ironing board, arms hanging loosely off the sides. Before pressing the searing metal on the shirt's spinal pleat, she touched it, ran a fingernail underneath. Physically he was a strong man. In many ways, though, he was vulnerable. It was part of his appeal. Ruhama had never been impressed by religious brutes who pontificated on spiritual rights and wrongs. She had rejected many of that type. On the other hand, she worried that if Gershon lacked fortitude he would be susceptible to unexpected shifts in wind. She manoeuvred the iron in and out between the buttons all the way up to the neckline. Holding the iron more firmly, she nudged the point against the tip of the collar, making it nod up and down.

If she wore his shirt it would conceal her head to toe. Free of creases, she folded it carefully and returned it to the basket.

Ruhama called out, "How're you doing, girls?" signalling she was now available for other activities.

"Wait. My story's not finished," replied Bayly.

There were five Mister Singhs at 99 Chabanel. Three occupied spaces on the fourth floor. Sonny Lipsey had fingered one of the Singhs as the culprit responsible for putting garbage in front of his door. Sonny had a name for Sikh Garmentos. He called them "Crooners." The Mister Singh from the sixth floor, Parvinder Singh, had a puffy face. He wore thick gold necklaces and diamond-studded rings. Sonny called him Elvis Singh. The oldest Mister Singh, who'd been a tenant at 99 for ten years, had blue eyes. Sonny called him Frank Sinatra Singh. Number three, who slurred his words when he spoke, Sonny called Dino Singh.

"They've got to be trained," Sonny said.

"They're not pets, Sonny," Gershon responded.

"Well, you've got to stop this new Crooner from putting garbage near my door."

The fourth floor had been divided and subdivided many times in recent years. In the industry's heyday it only had three occupants, now there were twenty-two. When Sholem saw that the market for large factory spaces had begun to dry up, he created new hallways, then built smaller, more affordable places to rent.

Sonny had the misfortune of being located next to the freight elevators. This was the darkest corner of the hallway on the east side of the fourth floor. His neighbours frequently put their refuse in the common area next to his door, because it was more or less out of sight. They wanted to maximize the utilization of their own limited space, and they looked for any corner to unload their trash. Gershon had to admit that this posed a serious problem. It was only a matter of time before there was an infestation of rodents, or worse, someone tossed a lit cigarette in the recurring mound of plastic bags, fabric cuttings and paper boxes.

"It's bad enough we have to live with the smell from their cooking. Hey, are they allowed to cook food in their places?" Sonny asked rhetorically. "Why don't you send a letter around, or put up a public notice? Better still, go and speak to them. Something has to be done. It's disgusting."

The fourth floor was overcrowded, there was no doubt about this.

It had developed a flea-market atmosphere. Merchants blocked the hallway outside their doors with mannequins and rolls of fabric that stood on end. Virtually all of them, whether small clothing manufacturers, importers or fabric wholesalers, sold to the general public. On Saturdays, the building bristled with cash sales. The merchants advertised liquidations and season-ending extravaganzas. Buses loaded with bargain hunters from outlying communities such as Hawkesbury and Trois-Rivières, frequented 99. Two of the tenants, Manny Minicucci the tailor, and Yossi Alfasi who made ladies sportswear, had big orange signs screaming BANKRUPTCY! EVERYTHING MUST GO! They had been going out of business as far back as Gershon could remember.

Posters and placards were everywhere. Most tenants defied the Quebec language laws which limited the use of English on business signs. All were either wild exaggerations or outright lies. DIRECT FROM THE MANUFACTURER. REDUCED 75%-90%. WE PAY THE TAXES. DRESSES FROM $9.99. There was a thought-provoking question, WHY PAY MORE? Even a declaration of unstable mental health, AT THESE PRICES YOU'LL THINK WE'RE CRAZY. There were other more clever efforts: HIGH FASHION AT LOW COST. And Gershon's personal favourite: BRAND NAMES YOU NEVER HEARD OF (BUT WISH YOU HAD).

Gershon enjoyed the fourth floor. Even on weekdays it bustled and howled with life. The elder Garmentos were less pleased. Sonny had his ongoing feud with his neighbours, and Shimmy Solomon disparaged the open-market huzzah; he considered the atmosphere symptomatic of the industry's sinking standards. Only third-world countries, he said, had such *souks*. These weren't businessmen—these merchants and so-called manufacturers were glorified beggars.

The market atmosphere of the fourth floor excited Avi Putkin. He was frequently seen strolling up and down the hallway, his mouth stretched into a wide grin. Avi said that the place reminded him of Tel Aviv back in the days when he owned a fruit and vegetable stall in the *Shuk HaCarmel*. On Friday mornings hordes would march up and down the lane buying fresh meat, fish, breads, spices, fruits and vegetables from the sellers. Dozens of kiosks offered exactly the same merchandise at identical prices. One's produce might have been a bit fresher, another's a shekel cheaper, but in general, it was not price or quality that determined

whether a seller was successful. It was showmanship. And this is where
Avi Putkin shone. He knew how to get attention. One of his best tricks
was making up rhymes on the spot.

"Miss, Miss, you look familiar. What is your name?" Avi would shout.
"Ruth? A dozen grapefruits for lovely Miss Ruth, spare a second and
shop at my booth, weren't we lovers once in our youth?"

"And you, sir, what is your name? Ron? A dozen lemons for Captain
Ron, buy them now before they're gone, a dozen more and I'll sing you
a song." And Avi would sing. His promenades along the fourth floor
brought him a kind of nostalgic ecstasy.

"Gershon, if I catch the Crooner putting his trash in front of my
door, I'll kill him," Sonny threatened. "And speaking of killing, how's my
cheque for *I VAIT* coming?"

I VAIT stood for Israeli Victims of Anti-Israel Terror. Sonny worked
hard for the charity, collecting more than ten thousand dollars annually.

"You mean you don't vant to vait?" Gershon joked in his best Yiddish
accent.

"Vhy to Vait?" Sonny returned, not to be outdone.

One day Sonny heard that Gershon wasn't in favour of the Jewish
State. He arrived in the office fuming. "What's this I hear about you not
supporting Israel?"

Gershon knew he had to be careful.

"I'm not against Israel. It's just that some of us think the *Moshiach*
should be here before the Jews have a country."

"You guys and your *Moshiach*," Sonny said. "Where was the Messiah
when we were being gassed and burned?"

"With all due respect, Sonny, please don't talk about being gassed
and burned. My family suffered too."

Gershon wanted to add that sometimes you needed to have faith.
But "faith" had become a dirty word. If you spoke about it, you were
either ignorant or naive. The modern brands of Judaism didn't rely on
faith. They were designed to empower. The politically Zionist Jews, the
ones who called themselves "cultural Jews" or "traditional Jews," had all
abandoned faith. And he hated to hear people talking about *losing* faith.
Faith was not something you lost or misplaced like a wallet or house
keys. Faith was something a person chose and worked for, or alternately
gave up on.

Speaking with Sonny, Gershon remembered he wanted to ask if Michelle Labelle still worked for him. Maybe that was the reason Sonny came to him again complaining about the garbage—maybe it upset his girl. And if so, there was a chance Gershon would see her in the building again. Ever since he had found out from Niko that Michelle was a biker's girl, that she was *dangerous*, he was even more intrigued by her. She had appeared to be fragile. Obviously, she was trapped. Gershon didn't need to know that she was a biker's girl to see it. But now he could imagine, more succinctly, the violence that kept her in place. The brutal means employed by her thug boyfriend and his cohorts to ply her into submission. Michelle wanted to escape the Hells Angels, but couldn't find the way to do it. Nonetheless, the light of her *neshama* had reached Gershon like a cosmic signal, a dying star. There was meaning in this.

But Gershon said nothing about Michelle to Sonny. It was bad enough he'd spilled the beans to Niko, he didn't want Sonny knowing anything about his personal interest in his girl. If he said anything now, Gershon would be in the position of having to explain the attraction of the soul. Sonny, clearly had no capacity to understand such matters. Gershon returned to the mutually comfortable, straightforward issue of money.

"Ve promised you a donation for *I VAIT*, and ve vill deliver," he said.

In August 1942 Sholem alighted on the main platform of the Warsaw train station looking for a sign. It wasn't long before he realized he would probably never see his family again. In one hand he held a heavy leather bag filled with religious texts and papers. The other hand scratched the bottom of a pocket which held the stash of *mandelbrot* cookies he munched on during the two-hour journey from yeshiva. He licked his fingertips to taste the granules of sugar caught under his nails.

When the train pulled into the station he remarked to his schoolfriend and travelling companion, Shmulik, how eerily vacant it seemed. Where was the bustle of people dashing for their trains? The stern, purposeful march of businessmen in fedoras and trenchcoats? The waves of well-dressed women with glossy red lipstick and boxy hats, who trailed tired porters pushing trolleys stacked with luggage? In their place, he saw helmeted men in greyish-blue uniforms. Bunched together like fists filled with marbles, they came into view gradually, as the train relinquished momentum. One group was huddled next to the ticket booth, another stood under the sign for toilets. From inside the cabin Sholem couldn't yet see the welcoming party, a gang of ten standing right next to the door of their train, guns poised.

Jude! Sholem was surrounded. He felt a sharp jab against his ribs, under the arm raised to his mouth. The sweetness of cookies was still on his lips. His leather bag thudded to the ground. Sholem resolved to stand firm, looking his captors straight in the eye. It was clear they wanted him to bow down, to demean himself before them. He could see it in their gleeful expressions. They were waiting for him to grovel. He didn't budge.

For the first time, Sholem knew what it meant to be strong and unyielding. More accurately, he comprehended the difference between the prideful rebellion of youth—the steeliness he maintained when his teacher slapped his palm with a stick, as punishment for chattering in class—and this now, the necessity for dignified defiance.

The Jews sat in a *hes* at school, a semi-circle, so everyone could see everyone else's face. The teacher had said it made all the students equal, no one sat ahead or behind, no one closer or further away, no one superior or inferior. This closed circle with Sholem in the centre was very different. It occurred to him that this ring of militants was a classroom of sorts and he was the subject they studied. It was also a tightening noose. He surveyed the faces around him. Many had smooth round cheeks. His captors were not much older than he was. Two even had chins underscored by dark scraggly beards like his. The similarities stopped there. Their heads were hard and flat. Their ears were bare and severe.

Sholem was shoved from behind. It was Shmulik being herded into the enclosure with him. One of the young soldiers reached down between the press of striped trousers and scooped Sholem's bag off the ground. He marched away from the group, inspecting it, smelling the leather. The click of boots on the polished concrete floor echoed off the train station's vaulted ceiling. The soldier unhooked the front latch and, deciding the bag would be useful, emptied the contents into a nearby garbage can.

This was the Gestapo's latest sport. They didn't have to waste time and energy going house to house looking for Jews when they could be netted like fish at the train station and dumped directly into boxcars waiting on an outside track.

The soldiers were pleased with their catch. Sholem and Shmulik were fine specimens, genuine Jews with the proper markings, skullcaps, sidecurls, knee-socks and long, woollen overcoats. Humiliation was a prelude. If these Jews put up a fight and could be kicked or punched in retaliation, all the better. It added excitement to the tedium of their task. Sholem understood immediately how to deny them. When he saw the white flap of *Chumash* and *Siddur* pages dropping into the trash like broken dove-wings, he vowed to himself not to participate in their lesson.

Shmulik was not so wise. He screamed. Twice. The first, a deep guttural wail protesting the desecration of holy texts. The second, higher pitched and stifled, answered the butt-end of a rifle thrust full-force to his kidney. Sholem spun and wrapped arms around his slumped friend.

Gershon was sure this was exactly how it happened. One day Sholem was plucked from the Warsaw train station, or as Gershon imagined over and over in his mind, grabbed by the *payas* and yanked like a carrot out of the earth. Gershon knew that Sholem did not go without some form of resistance. And there was obviously a lesser, weaker school friend with him. Someone he could save. Someone whose dignity he restored, or tried to, and in the process bolstered his own. The memory of the father became the fantasy of the son, or the story of the father became the memory of the son, or the imagination of the son became the experience of the father. Something like that.

The train ride must have been a stew of thoughts and anxieties and therefore a blur. Any attempt to recount the journey would do an injustice. So the next scene Gershon saw in his mind's eye was a second arrival. Always, it was arrivals that were important.

They disembarked outside the camp and were led single-file along a narrow pebble-covered path to the main gate. Sholem bent down, scooped up a handful of rocks and stuffed them into the pocket that had kept cookies. They were entering a cemetery. This was clear, in spite of all the apparent measures meant to keep people in. The fence topped with coils of barbed-wire, the watchtowers, men with guns. The soldier at the head of the line hummed a sleepy Brahms tune. He was a Pied Piper leading innocent children to an unspecified demise. Sholem's fingers flicked at the tiny stones in his pocket in rhythm with their march. Passing through the camp gate he took the rocks out and let them drop one at a time like a trail of breadcrumbs, as if to say, there is a way out of this place.

He was tired. He wanted a nap. Sholem counted six bodies lying along the base of the fence. Weren't they sleeping, eyes closed, dark mouths open? Why should their mouths be the hollow caverns of death? If only we were closer we could hear them snore. Sholem knew that from this day forward he'd have to rely on denial and silly thoughts like this to stay alive. So then: they were sleeping. Yawning. And he *was* tired. What about the round charcoal spots on their clothes? He looked at his own hands and touched the callouses where his teacher had scored his palms so many times for insubordination. He wondered how long it would be until he was testing them against the camp's electrified fence.

Gershon's deliberations ended. The decision was reached. He would not ask Sholem to handle Joey Putkin's electricity problem. He had resolved to take care of it himself.

Plumbing

GERSHON HAD A RECURRING DREAM. He saw himself standing in front of the Wailing Wall, the *Kotel,* in *Yerushalayim.* He was in the position of prayer, solemn-faced, nose barely touching a smooth layer of skin-tone stones. A prayer book was open between his palms, but he was not thinking about prayer. The pages were spread chest-high like a bird's wings and the lines of lettering were a bird's shadowy footprints in the sand. His mind was flying.

Suddenly, he felt a droplet of water land on his brow between the eyes, hard as a pebble. It surprised him. The droplet slowly made its way down the bridge of his nose leaving a wet trail and fell off the end to the ground. A tiny suicide.

At first Gershon thought about rain. He raised his head and noted blue sky. Not a single cloud. He felt another drop on his cheek, another on his chin, and another skim his earlobe. Maybe the azure sky has turned to water, like the word "sky" in Hebrew, *shamayim,* which included the word for water, *mayim.* The world was obeying the laws of Hebrew. An omen for the coming of the Messiah. Then he imagined Arab boys pissing down on praying Jews from the top of the Wall where it met the Temple Mount. He's heard this happened. Before they threw rocks, they pissed.

When Gershon looked up he did not see the faces of vengeful Arab boys. Water was spurting from a crack in the middle reaches of the Wall. He was pelted by more drops. And he spied another crack squirting water, and another and more water. A downpour. He looked around him and the Jews were swaying back and forth, rocking on their toes, but it was not the *shokel* of prayer. They were madly searching for anything to plug the leaks. They rolled papers, stretched and stuffed them into the cracks as fast as they could, but they weren't able to keep up. As soon as one leak was plugged, a new one sprouted. They danced around frantically wailing and waving their arms, calling out to one another and pointing at every new leak.

They jammed papers into the cracks, ones typically scrawled with personal prayers, wishes for health and long life and wealth and good fortune and world peace. They used whatever they could find. Some took the *kippas* off their heads to fill the holes while others used pages torn from holy books. Some took hankies and snot-blotched tissues out of their pockets and shoved them into the Wall. Others ripped sections of tourist maps. They even used dollar bills, anything to fill the gaps, stem the flow, dam up the Wall before it burst and the Holy City was flooded.

99 had its share of leaks and floods too. Gershon imagined that if all the water pipes on Chabanel could be straightened out and laid end to end they could reach across the Atlantic Ocean. Enough water circulated through the building on a yearly basis to fill the Dead Sea. He regularly saw evidence that the ageing, rusty network of pipes in 99 was losing its ability to contain the flow.

Why had the Jews built the clothing business? Why not the Italians or the Greeks who'd also made mass migrations during the same century? What was the reason for the Jewish fascination and expertise with fabric? Shimmy Solomon had a theory, one of his many. It went back to the Bible, he said. The Jews have always been nomads. They learned many things from wandering in the desert. Foremost among their lessons was to travel light. In addition to the clothes on their backs, they learned to make everything they needed out of fabric. Their shelters were tents, their furniture was pillows, floors were carpets. All could be rolled up, flattened down, folded, wrapped and packed away at a moment's notice. Fabric facilitated two central Jewish pastimes: searching for greener pastures and making quick escapes. They carried their lives on their shoulders from place to place before entering The Promised Land, and again in exile. This lesson had been deeply ingrained and reinforced time and time again throughout history. Jews were not farmers because that required land-ownership, which had been an impossibility. Jews and fabric were both a natural fit and a well-worn tradition.

Ruhama felt the fabric of her life slowing unravelling. Gershon was coming to bed later and later. The evening routine had stayed the same. Gershon arrived home from work at about six o'clock as usual. Most days the children were already fed and Gershon sat alone at the head of the dinner table carelessly shovelling food into his mouth. To his right and left were empty chairs behind rows of plates strewn with evidence of consumption, the sad remnant of Bayly's regular meal, a half-eaten bagel smothered in cream cheese, and Shoshana's plate licked clean. Shoshana always ate every last morsel placed before her. She never seemed to get full. She'd still be sitting there eating when Gershon got home if Ruhama didn't restrict her intake. As it was, Ruhama knew Shoshana would be asking for a bedtime snack.

When the family did gather, Ruhama talked about taking the girls to the park, how Shoshana was progressing with her potty-training, whether there had been any accidents. Bayly complained about Shoshana ruining her Lego-blocks construction. Ever since the start of potty-training, Bayly complained more often about her younger sister, who was getting too much attention. Shoshana kept herself squarely in the limelight by frequently becoming constipated.

Days would pass when Shoshana didn't defecate at all, ensuring that she would become the principle topic of dinnertime conversation between the parents, to Bayly's chagrin. Ruhama fed Shoshana prunes and bran muffins and diluted her juice with mineral oil, but somehow she persisted, holding it in stubbornly, red-faced. It was by now ritual that after dinner, Gershon ran out to the pharmacy to pick up suppositories and enemas.

Ruhama had stopped dressing Shoshana in underwear to make the insertion of a suppository a less complicated operation. Shoshana called the suppository a "bullet," a word learned from Bayly when she saw the tiny capsule in her father's hand for the first time.

Bayly shouted, "A bullet! Tati's going to stick a bullet in Shoshi's *tuchas!*" Shoshana was mortified at the news, but the word "bullet" stuck. These nights when Gershon took the box of suppositories out from the bathroom vanity, Shoshana ran from him screaming through the house, "No bullet, no bullet!"

The sight of his daughter fleeing for her life made Gershon feel like a rampaging Cossack. If you were standing outside the house by an open window you'd think a violent madman was barricaded inside, holding the family hostage. "No bullet, no bullet!" Shoshana pleaded as Gershon grabbed hold of his little girl, pinned her to the ground, kicking and squirming, and slid the tiny capsule between the squeezed shut cheeks of her rear. Initially, the suppositories did the job. To the relief of the entire family, Shoshana was soon running to the potty.

The longer the situation continued, though, the more skilled Shoshana became at holding it in. Ruhama would look in the potty expecting satisfaction and be surprised to find that somehow her daughter had developed a technique for taking the suppositories in, and then a few minutes later, spitting them out like watermelon seeds, completely intact at the bottom of the bowl. The heavy artillery would have to come out.

The enema was a more involved procedure requiring two sets of hands. Ruhama braced the girl's scrawny shoulders, as Gershon's squished out the liquid wash. Throughout they tried explaining to Shoshana how dangerous it was to hold poop inside. The doctor had warned that if enemas were used too often it could compromise the rectum's ability to expel naturally. In worst-case scenarios the body would have to be cleaned surgically.

Shoshana wouldn't listen. Holding in poop paid huge dividends in parental concern. The temporary discomfort was worth it. Ruhama wondered if Shoshana's handling of potty-training foreshadowed future developments. Would she be the type to keep things to herself, bottled up inside? Was this why Gershon seemed so remote lately? Maybe Gershon had been a constipated child. Maybe it was in the genes.

After dinner, the kids were bathed, read a story and put to bed. Gershon rushed off to *kollel*, the community study hall. When he arrived home two hours later, he would remain downstairs reading. Ruhama came into the living room in her pyjamas. Gershon sat at the far corner of the couch, his feet kicked up on the green hassock, the floor lamp by his side. He wanted to review the weekly Torah portion, he mumbled at his wife. She understood his comment as a dismissal and didn't respond. Climbing back upstairs, Ruhama would grip the banister more tightly than usual.

She couldn't sleep. Her body tingled under the bedcovers. Ruhama touched herself, fingers circling her navel, orbiting, descending. Having children was more than a Commandment from God. A desire for babies flowed through her body with the force of chemistry. This was His gift. At a certain time of the month, Ruhama felt the onset of an overwhelming, irresistible power. The veins in her arms and arteries of her legs channelled energy. The whole of her flesh was a receptacle into which the Divine poured forth. Divinity circulated, coursed through her body and took shape to form His Image. A baby. As long as Gershon abstained Ruhama felt incomplete. She knew only potential Divinity, the hint of Divinity, a scent of Divinity. Divinity as a flavour tasted, then lost, on the tongue.

Poor Gershon, sitting there night after night, struggling with words. Ruhama felt pity for him. She knew God in a way he could never hope to. God was as real to her as the flesh she inhabited. Gershon wanted so desperately to find God by deciphering meanings. She knew that no effort at decoding was sufficient. In fact, his endeavour was entirely off base. Here was God's punishment to men. Their futility. God implanted in them a yearning. They hungered for God, prayed for God, fought for God, killed for God, died for God. All born out of one great frustration. No man would ever know what it meant to conceive and nurture life. No man would have it growing inside him as part of his very being. No man will ever know such closeness to God.

Why was Gershon holding back? What if he had decided to deny her a Divine right? That's what it amounted to. Ruhama was angry. She felt the crush of spiritual and physical repression. What Gershon did was tantamount to disavowing God.

Was it that time of the month already? Gershon asked himself seeing Estella Mora waiting in the rental office reception area.

"Can I talk with you? In private," Estella said quietly.

She followed Gershon to the back office. Not until he was comfortably seated in Sholem's executive armchair did he notice Estella's attire, a tight black skirt and a loose-fitting solid pink polyester blouse. Her perfume immediately filled his nostrils. It seemed more pungent than his nose remembered in previous meetings.

She did not sit across the desk as usual. She paced back and forth in front of him, hands against her lips, looking for words. It was apparent they would not be following the regular script this time. There was a palpable tension in the room, a coil tightening with every step. Gershon waited and watched.

"I can't give you a cheque this month," she admitted boldly.

Gershon placed a hand flat on the table and swivelled his chair a quarter turn. He decided not to speak. Not yet. He would let her go a step further, see where she was headed before responding. Estella crossed her arms in front, bracing herself. She did not look at Gershon. She ruminated, her eyes crawling along the carpet.

"This business ... we're almost there. It's just, the money comes too slowly."

"Look. I have eighty tenants. They manage to pay the rent. Either you have a business or you don't have one," Gershon said, tightening the coil a notch.

"We have work. A lot. I have eight thousand garments hanging in my place right now. I need more time."

Gershon ciphered in his head. Eight thousand pieces. A liquidator might give him five, at worst three dollars per garment. Of course, there were also the costs of seizure and lawyer's fees to consider.

"We're finishers, you know, the end of the line. Imported goods come in, we change tags, re-package and ship. They pay pennies per piece. My business is handling. I have so many workers who make nothing, minimum wage. I have to pay them first. They have families."

So that was her game. She was playing the guilt card. Gershon decided to toughen his approach, to show he couldn't be swayed so easily.

"This isn't a charity. If you want charity there are places for that."

"I just need a bit more time. I'll pay two months next month. I'm not running away."

"Come on, Estella. Why should I believe you? Every month it's the same story. It never gets better. You can barely cover one month. So now, all of a sudden, you'll be able to pay two?"

Sensing futility, Estella took a deep breath and dropped her hands.

"Maybe ... there's something else."

Gershon waited for her to finish. Estella inched closer to the corner of the desk, her eyes fixed on him.

"There may be something," she repeated, landing a hand on top of his on the desk.

Gershon stared up at her, paralyzed. Her hand was weightless, resting on the bumps of his knuckles. It would have required hardly any effort to shake off, the slightest gesture could topple it. But Gershon couldn't move. Her palm felt hard and cold, her nails were chewed down to nubs. Then an image came to Gershon. Estella's curved fingers on top of his looked like mating insects.

She leaned forward and touched an upper button on her blouse.

A jolt of perfume sent Gershon back in his chair, slipping his mating hand out. He curled the freed fingers against his chest, inside the palm of his other hand.

"Please! Please don't humiliate yourself!" He spoke loudly to stop her from going any further.

"I can't." She straightened up and backed away. "I'm sorry. So sorry. I didn't mean to…"

Turning her face from Gershon, she pulled her hands together against her chest. "I'm so ashamed. I didn't really think you would. I'm sorry. Don't know what I was thinking." She was falling apart like her sentences and began sobbing.

Gershon had to say something to help her regain composure.

"I know you're trying," he inhaled deeply. "Maybe you should rethink this thing. Why should you put yourself in a position to suffer indignity? No one should be in such a position."

It was not that Gershon cared so much about Estella's dignity. He didn't want his own to be compromised. They depended on each other. Moments earlier they were playing the money game. Now, as the mist of their business relationship cleared, Gershon saw how, below the surface, he and Estella shared a secondary bond of aspirations and vulnerabilities. He needed to build her up again, give her some hope, for his own sake.

"Why don't you think of something. Take a few days. Make a plan. We'll meet again next week to see what can be done."

"Thank you. I'll come next week," Estella said, as she rushed out, straightening her blouse.

Alfreda entered as Estella was leaving.

"Next week?" Alfreda said. "What happened? Did she cry or something?"

Feeling exhausted, Gershon flopped back into his chair and stared at Alfreda.

"Don't tell me you think it was an act?"

"Well, she got what she came for, more time. And you got nothing."

The speed of Alfreda's assessment stunned Gershon. It was possible Estella had staged the whole thing. First, acting helpless, appealing for mercy. When that didn't work—the hand and the sobbing, every move predetermined. Bit by bit she raised the stakes, betting that at a certain point Gershon would fold his hand.

But what if he had called Estella's bluff and let her go a step further? What if he'd simply given her the floor to perform right there, and then, folded his arms and stared as she played with the buttons of her blouse between her fingers like they were pink candies? Would she have unfastened them all, slipped the shirt from her shoulders, unhooked her brassiere, lifted her skirt and dropped her panties? Would she have come behind the desk and reached for his crotch, unzipped his trousers, whispered sweetly into his ear, and asked for more time to pay?

No. She must have known all along that he wouldn't permit her to take it that far. She had read him perfectly. Alfreda was right. Gershon felt defeated.

He looked around the office. It was a mess. Alfreda was already back at work and concentrated on typing a document. It didn't seem to disturb her that the walls were cracked, the paint was peeling off in places and the carpet was faded and shredding. The desks were scratched and chipped and the veneer was stripped off, exposing the pressboard underneath in jagged patches. Gershon was certain that many of these pieces of furniture had been bought second-hand by Sholem years and years ago, when he started the business.

On the floor in Gershon's corner, long tubes of architectural plans stuck out from a brown cardboard box that had previously held paper cups. The vinyl orange upholstery seat on which Gershon sat had lost most of its cushion. During the time he worked in the office, Gershon had developed a persistent backache from this hard chair with its metal backrest that was loose and springy. When he wasn't doing rounds in the halls, Gershon sat stiffly upright on the chair, aware that it offered no rear support. If he leaned too far behind, the backrest would give way and he'd end up flat on the floor with a concussion.

Alfreda's corner of the office was more orderly. The filing cabinets behind her desk, packed with invoices, leases, correspondence and accounts, were neatly aligned and clearly labelled with addresses of Stein-owned properties. Alfreda had made efforts to overcome the space she inhabited with elegant, feminine touches. On her desk she kept a lamp with a pleasant powder-blue shade. Next to this was a potted African violet, which she watered daily.

Gershon watched Alfreda working at her computer. He had always trusted her and depended on Alfreda to get things done in the building. She was efficient and could also be understanding when situations took a turn for the worse. Her presence at this moment, in the same room with him, brought Gershon an unexpected sense of calm.

Prayer refreshed Gershon. It never failed. When he stood for the *Amidah*, the Standing Prayer, he came to complete attention. Lowering his chin in a posture of humility, he took three tiny steps backward. One deep breath. Then three steps forward, bringing his feet together, all the weight firmly centred over flattened soles. He exhaled and dropped his shoulders as his eyes came to rest on the text. *Adonai sephatai tiftach u phi yagid tehilatecha, God open my lips that I may utter Your praise.*

He knew the *Shemoneh Esreh*, the Eighteen Benedictions, from memory. Normally, he ran through them like he was scooting over a bed of scorching hot coals. It was a feat he could feel satisfied at having accomplished. These days, when he concentrated on the ancient script, his mind caught on every jagged letter. The prayers extended like long narrow paths of broken glass. There was a kind of pain in it, words penetrated, drew blood. He repeated the same word over and over. Forward movement was difficult. Not saying all the Eighteen, which actually comprised nineteen blessings, was unthinkable before. Each blessing extolled an attribute of the Almighty. If the Eighteen were unsaid, or half-said, it was like God didn't fully exist.

But Gershon yielded to a profound sense of personal exposure. Repeating only one word, one syllable, one sound, gave his prayer new intensity. Inside, his body was like a film. The mechanics of his mind snapped open and shut like a camera. Too fast, and the words he read failed to leave an imprint. Too slow, and the result was an unfocussed mash of blackness. Gershon realized that prayer required proper timing to let in the perfect amount of light. When this happened, his emotions operated like shallow pans of precisely measured liquid chemicals that turned negatives to positives and revealed a coherent composition of meanings. Otherwise, his soul was not much more than a vacant darkroom.

Prayer was more difficult than ever because Gershon understood how darkness was an essential part of the process. And it was necessary, because darkness was not enough, there had to be light too. Most people engaged prayer in moments of despair. It gave them a sense of hope and optimism. Estella Mora might have prayed before asking Gershon for an extension on her rent. The trick, Gershon began to understand, was to engage prayer as a means of confirming darkness, not escaping it. Genuine prayer was not meant to stave off ruin. It helped people to acknowledge the troubles they experienced and to embrace life in the fullest possible sense. Said with proper devotion, prayer affirmed a world rife with anguish and uncertainty. Lately, Gershon had sensed a rhythm underneath the melodies he hummed and the words he sang. It sounded like "I am, I am, I am."

Michelle Labelle could have had something to do with Gershon's renewed sense of prayer. Although it had been more than a month since his last sighting, she was still on his mind. Maybe it was Estella and Joey Putkin who had brought him to this point. Maybe Niko, Sonny Lipsey, Sholem, Alfreda. Chaim, Ruhama, Bayly and Shoshana and the Hells Angels. Maybe it was all of them, a stew of light and dark that congealed in his soul and produced something vibrant. That was how he felt now after a session of prayer: alive and real. And it was how he knew, for the first time in a long time, that he was doing it right.

Free-fall. This was the word that came to Gershon as he watched the elevator light blink 7 to 6 to 5 to 4. Of course, it was a controlled descent, although going to see Joey Putkin always felt like a free-fall. The doors slapped open on the fourth floor. Two ladies entered. Metal whacked metal shut. Gershon slid against the wall to give them room. The women wore thick kerchiefs covering their heads and chattered in Arabic. Their voices dropped from hallway volume to hushed, secretive tones. They were careful not to lock eyes with Gershon.

The fourth-floor Crooners sold colourful, intricately-woven fabrics desired by Sikh, Hindu and Muslim women who sewed their own clothing. 99 had developed a reputation in those particular communities as one of the best locations in the city offering a fine array of such merchandise at reasonable prices. They came in droves.

Recently, European and North American fashion trends, as seen in magazines and on runways, favoured a less-is-more approach. Models were sickly thin and designers rediscovered bare shoulders, cleavage, midriffs and navels. It was a boon for manufacturers. Less garment, more profit.

Less fabric, however, meant the mills and wholesalers would suffer. As their sales slipped, their inventories grew unwieldy. Gershon understood that these pilgrimages of well-concealed Sikh, Muslim and Hindu women draped in rolls of cloth, some in the name of modesty, others in the name of tradition, were saving the local fabric business and ensuring that a great many South Asians would be entering the business as suppliers.

Gershon continued to watch numbers descend. 3, 2, Lobby. The ladies swept out, their robes waving good-bye behind them. He was going down to the basement. Doors banged together like a locking vault. Along with the elevator, his stomach sank.

"He's somewhere in the warehouse. Please have a seat." The receptionist pressed three numbers on her telephone. She spoke into the receiver, her small, pleasant voice suddenly booming forth, echoing through the hallways. "Joey, please come to reception! Joey to reception!"

Gershon was glad she didn't mention who was waiting. Putkin might actually show up. Gershon strolled around the office perusing the posters on the walls. The models were in two types of poses. Either they faced the world with exaggerated grins, or they were brooding, the weight of the world on their minds. Here was youth, either carefree or deeply pensive. Men threw leather jackets over muscular shoulders, rushing off to important meetings where they were needed to make critical decisions. The women wore leather pants and vests, but were in the process of shedding them, buttons half-fastened, zippers half-zipped, while somewhere beyond the frame of reference an unseen voyeur, a Peeping Tom, waited in the wings to see what came next. Gershon realized *he* was the Peeping Tom outside the photograph. He shuddered.

There were several group shots where the models leaned on each other, propping each other up, or pushing one another with paws in the air, like playful puppies or kittens learning to pounce. They were caught in the midst of some action, precariously balanced on motorcycles or in zooming sports cars. Leather was the garment of speed and recklessness. As he considered their vehicles, Gershon parted company with this young crew. He was a careful person, always looking side to side, double-checking and rechecking when he drove, like someone behind the wheel of a cherished, irreplaceable vintage automobile.

The message of the posters was clear: the world is a wild, dangerous place. Leather was worn as protection, additional layers of tanned, toughened skin like hunters' trophies, proof of animal prowess and successful kills. Men who wore leather and dressed their women in it were warrior-chiefs displaying stature and wealth. Tightly-fitted on breasts and hips, leather could cover women without covering, clothe without clothing, hide without hiding.

They celebrated. But what? A kind of victory, a kind of freedom. They revelled in the strength and fitness of their bodies, the conquest of themselves, each other and the world around them. Everything was to be mastered, manhandled. The women submitted to the men, and the men demanded obedience from their consorts. Both submitted to base instincts and desires. In animal skins, they celebrated their animal natures.

Gershon sat down facing the receptionist and watched her manage the phone lines, steering incoming calls to intended targets with the press of flashing red buttons. Another poster several feet behind the receptionist's desk suddenly caught his attention.

He saw the image of a tall, thin woman. She was dressed in a one-piece red leather suit and spike heels. Her body was hunched over the sprawling figure of a man lying flat on the floor between her legs. Her long black hair brushed the man's bare chest. He wore a tribal mask that looked to be African, in the shape of a rhinoceros, its curved horn thrust up toward the pelvis of the woman. She also wore a mask, hers made of leather. It fit snug over her face.

My God. Gershon suddenly realized he was looking at Michelle Labelle. He could hardly believe his eyes. He wasn't a hundred percent certain, but the possibility alone horrified him. Michelle Labelle modelled for Joey Putkin.

If so, had Putkin spotted her in the building? Had he become taken with her too? Only Putkin was a different sort of guy. When he wanted something he didn't hesitate, he grabbed it. Putkin probably approached her openly in the hallway, made suggestions and offered her money. Gershon thought about Joey standing behind the camera telling her what to do, which poses to strike and hold. She obeying. Gershon's skin crawled.

Putkin burst into the office, blowing straight through the reception area like a fighter jet, a trail of cigarette smoke behind him. He flew directly into his office without acknowledging Gershon's presence.

After a few minutes, the secretary told Gershon he would be seen. He raised himself off the chair and paused. Looking through the doorway of Putkin's office, he felt he was about to enter a forbidden inner sanctum.

Joey looked up and smiled.

"Please, Gershon, come in. Sit down." He spoke cordially, pointing to a seat across the desk. "Give me a moment. I'm outputting a file."

The laser printer hummed. White pages rolled out like sickly pale tongues. Joey collected and squared them with taps on the desk.

Gershon looked up at the Israeli army uniform on the wall behind Joey's head, the spent shell-casing of Yoav's life. Every article of clothing told a story, kept secrets, hidden meanings of past events. Gershon noticed things this time he'd missed before. Two holes. One on the left thigh of the pants and another just above the left breast pocket of the shirt. His eyes were drawn to the holes, absences with slightly frayed edges. They possessed gravity like distant, white stars. Were these where the bullets had entered, the ones that had snuffed out Yoav's existence? The bullets had penetrated the fabric perfectly; the circles were remarkably tidy.

"Here's the problem," Joey said, licking his forefinger and dealing a sheet of paper off the top to Gershon. Long columns of numbers were stacked along the east and west margins of the page. Across the top was an underlined heading in bold letters: ELECTRICAL CONSUMPTION.

"On the left side you can see our electrical history for the past twelve months. On the right is the number of days for each billing period. Notice how about halfway down, the consumption shoots up even though the billing periods remain more or less constant."

Gershon wasn't listening to Joey. His eyes started at the bottom and moved up the page. When he arrived at the top he squinted. He didn't see numbers representing the flow of electricity or the passing of days.

What he saw was beautiful architecture, symmetry. The columns rose and supported a roof. The space in the centre was a portal through which his mind entered a foggy white blankness. He was in the Temple, the Holy Temple in *Yerushalayim*. Yes, the Temple where the Ark of the Covenant was kept, the High Priest spread incense, made sacrifices on the Altar, and where it was said raw meat did not deteriorate, or become maggot-infested, so pure and charged with holiness was the air.

Gershon's silence irritated Joey. He became more emphatic.

"How do you explain the sudden jump in consumption? Our production didn't increase. We didn't add machinery. How do you explain it? I'm paying for someone else. I only want what's fair, Gershon. What's mine is mine and what's yours is yours. You have to do something about it."

Gershon's eyes remained pressed against the sheet of paper.

"Perhaps," was all he said.

"What do you mean, *perhaps*? What kind of answer is that?"

"I don't know," Gershon said calmly.

"What do you mean *you don't know*? You have to know. Don't sit here and tell me you don't know! You better know!"

"I have to think about it."

"You have to think about it? What do you have to think about? Stop thinking and do something! What is it with you guys? Thinking, always thinking. *Do* something!"

Gershon sat still. He felt protected, insulated.

"What about the rent?" Gershon said, looking up at Joey, his tone gentle and fluid. "You can't withhold rent because you have a problem with your electricity."

"When you stop thinking, that's when I'll pay the rent!" Joey shot back.

"Okay," Gershon said rolling the paper between his hands into a scroll.

"What do you mean, okay. It's not okay!" Joey was burning.

Gershon rose from the chair weightlessly, like vapour. I'm water, he said to himself, please God, let me be as water. He left Joey Putkin's office without another word, and feeling high, buoyant, untouchable as a cloud.

Suppliers

"SHE WAS HERE," Niko said out of the side of his mouth.

"I'm sorry?"

"The girl you asked about, Michelle. I saw her a few days ago."

"Oh," Gershon said, not wanting to seem excited, his heart drumming.

"She bought a Diet Coke. What she always drinks."

This last bit of information explained a great deal. If she was drinking what she always drank, it meant she was okay and probably still working for Sonny Lipsey. It also meant Michelle Labelle would be on Gershon's mind a lot more in the coming days.

He had sought hints of her presence, the remnant whiff of a certain odour on the fourth floor at Sonny's end of the hallway, or the tell-tale rhythmic tap of her shoes coming around the corner. But she wasn't around. Then came the sighting in Joey Putkin's office. It had made him feel a combination of fascination and revulsion. The residue of that experience had stayed with him, as if an impure liquid inside his chest had evaporated, leaving a gritty, distasteful sediment.

What was her connection with Joey? What had he seen in her? Was it the light that Gershon had seen?

Gershon began delving more deeply into scripture than he had for a long time, staying up till the early morning hours with his books. Ruhama didn't bother coming downstairs anymore to question him. Their beds were once again on opposite sides of the bedroom.

He wanted to know about the nature of this light he had perceived. He knew he needed to go to the source, to the first mention of light in

Torah. He opened his book to *Genesis*.

"And God said, 'Let there be light.' And there was light. And God saw the light, that it was good; and God divided the light from the darkness. And God called the light Day, and the darkness He called Night. And there was evening and there was morning, one day."

How could it be that the light was called Day and the darkness Night? Day came with the rising of the sun, night with its setting. The sun, the moon and the stars were only created on day four, as he read: "And God said 'Let there be lights in the firmament of the heavens to divide the day from the night; and let them be for signs, and for seasons, and for days and years. And let them be for lights in the firmament of the heavens to give light upon the earth.' And it was so."

If the first light of Creation was not sunlight, the light of nature, what was it? It was a special light, supernatural. Gershon read Rabbi Sforno's commentary. He wrote that this light functioned only during the six days of Creation. It was the light of God's work. This primordial light represented Divine inspiration. Inspiration was the basis of all creativity, the life force.

"And God saw the light was good; and God divided light from darkness." The rabbis seemed to understand this literally; the light was good, and therefore the darkness was evil. The commentary said God made the separation because the wicked did not merit the light, so He set it apart for the righteous to bask in during the afterlife.

The light represented Goodness. It was supernatural. But at the end of day one, there was evening and there was morning, implying natural occurrences. For greater elucidation Gershon read Ibn Ezra's comment, which elaborated on the Hebrew words *erev*, meaning evening, and *boker*, morning.

The sage explained that *erev* came from *arab* meaning "to mingle," and *boker* came from *bakker* which translated as "to seek or examine." Gershon understood that there was a moral component to Creation. The separation of evening and morning was actually a process of moral discernment and extrapolation. He imagined God's mind reaching out across the firmament like a spectral hand separating exact order from intermingled chaos, extracting precise light from the morass of darkness like strings of toffy pulled from a massive stainless-steel vat. Finishing the process, He proclaimed that it was *Good*, which meant that God cared deeply for the world. He suffused it with Goodness. And He made people in His image, furnishing them with the intellectual capacity to discover the inherent Goodness of the world, if they tried. A big *if*. People had to *want* to see the Goodness.

But what happened to the light after Creation? Gershon remembered one midrashic explication that the light of Creation still existed, but only with the foetus while in the mother's belly. There, the gradually forming baby absorbed Torah, the moral teaching, from a Divine angel. At the moment of birth, Torah was forgotten. Babies emerged into the world as slates wiped clean. The rabbis said that people were fated to spend the rest of their lives struggling to reacquaint themselves with this previous experience, hungering for the womb and the memory of Torah learned at the feet of an angel. Gershon thought about Bayly and Shoshana fast asleep upstairs, nightlights flickering in their doorways. For all his years of struggle with texts and learning, they were closer to the angel than he was.

It became apparent to Gershon why the rabbis had said that the pure light of Creation was still present in the womb. That was where babies incubated, where the process of creation actually took place. It was where the soul, the essence of the individual, fused with physical being. At birth, when babies entered the world, another, opposite process took place. One which separated the person from their soul.

Slates wiped clean. Is that what babies were when they entered the world, clean slates? No. Newborns were definitely not clean slates. You only had to lay eyes on one in the moments after birth to know it. His babies, Bayly and Shoshana, had emerged from their mother red-faced, exasperated and squeaking at the top of their immature lungs. They were perturbed, annoyed at the intrusion. Their reactions reminded Gershon of the way he became when he was immersed in learning Torah, struggling with a notion, on the verge of grasping it, and someone rudely interrupted him from his studies.

Babies carried an imprint, like a transparent beauty mark, linking them to the Creator. Gershon remembered seeing it on the faces of Bayly and Shoshana as he held each of them in his arms in the hospital nursery moments after birth. Their pristine afterglow was undeniable. He was dumbstruck, awed by what he witnessed. With Bayly, his firstborn, he was so overtaken by mixed feelings of sheer wonder, joy and fear, he could could hardly catch his breath. He carefully put his newborn back in her basinet and went into the adjoining room where new mothers breastfed. Finding the room empty, he collapsed on a couch, placed his head in his hands and wept uncontrollably. He felt touched by something powerful and ethereal: the sudden sense that, fundamentally, he was as vulnerable as his newborn was. He depended on her as much as she depended on him. To Gershon the force emitted by her tiny presence was clear evidence of Divinity. The magnificence of Creation was still upon her, but fading.

Gershon's thoughts now turned from his children to his wife. Where was Ruhama's light? Had he ever seen it? Yes, one time that he could immediately recall, during the period when they were first starting their courtship.

Gershon had travelled by car to New York to go on his third "official" date with Ruhama. It would be their first meeting alone. He arrived in the late afternoon, after a nine-hour drive. He parked down the street from Ruhama's house. They decided to take a walk in the neighbourhood so Gershon could stretch his legs, and then go for an early supper at a nearby kosher restaurant. After their meal, they lingered over glasses of water, content to be in each other's company. The bill arrived. Gershon reached into his pocket to extract the American dollars his father had given him for the trip. His pocket was empty. He looked on the floor under the table. He checked behind his chair. No wallet. Flustered, he reassured Ruhama that everything was fine and asked her to wait in the restaurant while he ran back to look in the car. Jogging down the street a sense of dread grew inside him.

Fragments of shattered glass from the driver's-side window of his car could be seen from a hundred feet away. The concrete sidewalk shimmered in the streetlight. Shards crackled under Gershon's feet as he approached the car. He stared at the jagged ridges of the door framing the missing pane and simultaneously reconstructed the events in his mind. The wallet had slipped out of his pocket while he was driving. He had locked the door without noticing it on the seat in plain sight. A passing thief had not been so careless. Gershon's lapse had left him in a foreign country with no money, not a single piece of identification and a broken car window. Now a girl was waiting for him in a restaurant holding an unpaid bill.

Ruhama smiled when she heard Gershon's explanation. Then she beamed at him and began laughing out loud. Gershon laughed too, at first nervously, then feeling more at ease. With both of them lost in the absurdity of the moment, Ruhama reached out and took Gershon's hand into her two warm palms. She squeezed his fingers tightly until she realized what she was doing, and dropped them. Feeling as giddy and embarrassed as a helpless boy, and with Ruhama beaming up at him, Gershon knew, that if she accepted, he would make her his wife.

The light he had seen beaming from Ruhama's face that day in New York was spontaneous. It was searing, like laser light, welding the two of them together. Thinking of this now, Gershon realized she had never lost it. It was probably still there although no longer obvious. Perhaps it had been transformed, as energy is, through the machine of their marriage to a sub-visual wavelength, like ultra violet. If so, Ruhama's light depended on his sensitivity. He had to look harder for it and become like a specialized filter bringing out Ruhama's light. Looking down at the clothes he wore, a black jacket and pants, the garb of mourning worn by Orthodox Jews to commemorate the tragic destruction of the Jerusalem Temple, Gershon realized that he absorbed light. He stood for the absence of light.

"We have to call an electrician," Gershon said to Alfreda. "Putkin's going to withhold his rent until he can be convinced by an independent source that his electricity isn't being stolen."

"Let him pay for an electrician. He's the one with the problem," Alfreda replied categorically.

"He refuses to do anything. He's counting on us to ignore the problem, that way he can go five months in arrears. I'm not playing his game," Gershon said. "So we'll swallow the cost of an electrician, this time."

"If we pay for his electrician I hope we're not setting a precedent," Alfreda warned.

Gershon had forgotten about the slippery slope of precedent. Generally, when you gave a tenant something once, they expected the same treatment forever. Relationships with tenants were all about regularity, fixing norms of behaviour and rigidly sticking to them.

Leases outlined expectations. The landlord fulfilled his obligations as stated, not a single thing more or less. Deviating slightly from the lease tended to get you into big trouble. If the landlord did anything more than was strictly required it gave the impression of flexibility, which could be fatal. Having received the grossly mistaken impression of flexibility, the tenant might further assume that rent, due on the first of the month according to the lease, could be remitted on the seventh or the tenth. And if the seventh or tenth was acceptable, why not the twentieth or the thirty-first? Such was the snowball effect which, set in motion, crushed a landlord's ability to control his rent collection. Putkin already took advantage regarding the timely remittance of rent, so this was hardly an issue. Gershon's task now was to stop the snowball from growing any bigger.

"Alfreda, please call Mr. Krantz. It'll be nice to see him again."

Krantz was a competent electrician. But this was not why Gershon wanted him to work on Putkin's electrical problem as opposed to the half dozen other electricians they used. He was actually even a bit more expensive than the others. Gershon wanted Krantz because he liked him.

Krantz was a Lubavitcher. He wore faded blue jeans, construction boots and his *tzizes* hung out and danced around his waist while he worked. The spectacle of Krantz standing on a ladder fixing a light, or running wires along the ceiling, his arms in the air, *tzizes* doing a hora around his belly as he hummed a traditional Jewish tune, never failed to stretch Gershon's pursed lips into a smile. When Krantz was asked how he was doing, he always answered cheerfully, "Super-duper! *Boruch Hashem!*"

Gershon once asked Krantz how he stayed so happy. What was his secret for being positive and upbeat all the time? He expected the typically joyful Lubavitcher response, "God and all His Creation are glorious," and then perhaps, a rhetorical question, "What have I got to be worried about?" What Gershon heard, however, surprised him.

"Kip Gleason," Krantz answered.

"Who?"

"Kip Gleason," Krantz repeated in a sing-song voice. "*Salesmanship and Staying Positive, Accessing the Source of Your Inner Power, Mind-Body Success*, I've got all his tapes. You mean you've never heard of Kip Gleason?"

"Nope."

"The king of motivational speakers. I listen to his cassettes religiously.

Always have one playing in the car. I drove to Poughkeepsie to attend one of his seminars. The guy does wonders with words. He's a master of the power of suggestion. If you like, I'd be happy to lend you a tape."

Gershon knew how difficult it was to be a tradesman. If motivational tapes worked for Krantz, it only proved that on some level, everyone needed to find their own personal way of getting on with life. The extra few dollars Krantz earned was worth having him around. His pleasant disposition brightened the place up.

One of Gershon's first lessons when he began working for his father was dealing with tradesmen and suppliers. Alfreda brought Sholem a stack of invoices and placed them on the desk in front of him like a plate of food. He devoured them, one by one, a red pen poised in his right hand. He flipped past plumbers, electricians, painters, roofers, bricklayers, and companies that repaired elevators, boilers, motors, pumps, generators, air-conditioners and compressors. Heating-gas and telephone bills were initialled for immediate payment without further scrutiny. The invoices from tradesmen, however, were put aside for further inspection. On these, Sholem paused to verify each amount carefully. He drew his red pen across the bottom figures, striking out prices and replacing them with amounts sometimes ten, other times twenty percent less than the payment demanded.

There was also a handful of invoices Sholem didn't approve at all. These he put aside, saying they would be completely renegotiated. To Gershon, the process looked arbitrary, except that smaller companies were less likely than larger ones to be paid the full amount right away.

When Gershon asked Sholem why he was reducing the payments. Sholem answered, "*Gonivs*, thieves, they all boost their prices."

Some suppliers didn't appreciate this treatment and after being undercut a few times refused to service 99 altogether. Even Krantz, at one point, stopped quoting on jobs for Sholem, knowing full well that his prices were being used to drive down estimates from other suppliers. When Krantz was hired it was without bargaining.

Gershon didn't argue with Sholem's techniques. He had no right to question a successful businessman. His father had built up a considerable enterprise from scratch. Nonetheless, when Gershon started dealing with suppliers himself, he decided to try a new approach. It didn't take long for him to learn that Sholem was right after all. There was, indeed, an extra ten or twenty percent added to each invoice—the amount they knew Sholem was going to subtract. It was a vicious circle, suppliers boosting their prices to hedge against Sholem's slashing. Everything balanced out in the end.

Sholem used the suppliers' approach of boosting prices during lease negotiations. If he wanted to get four dollars per square foot for a particular space, he demanded four-fifty. The tenant offered three-fifty, both parties realizing full well that they would eventually settle in the middle.

Gershon had learned that bargaining was a necessary part of the process, a way of making everyone involved feel satisfied with the final deal. But it puzzled him. Couldn't Sholem just demand his desired price and stick to it? Couldn't the tenant say what he expected to pay? Both sides had fixed prices in mind anyway. Instead they danced, showing one another goodwill, demonstrating they could be flexible, instilling confidence, when in reality none existed. The deal, if it was to be reached, was a foregone conclusion from the outset. There was merely the illusion of negotiation. A ritual took place in order for the two sides to develop a sense of trust, which itself was illusory. Neither side really trusted the other.

With suppliers, there wasn't even a pretense of negotiation. Everyone assumed they were being shafted. Once the service was rendered, the work completed, the supplier was at a tremendous disadvantage. Shrewd businessman that he was, Sholem recognized when he had the upper hand and acted on it decisively, with the stab of a red pen.

All the experience Gershon acquired navigating business relationships gave him cause for concern. He wondered if, in some subtle yet irrevocable way, he was becoming suspicious and cynical. How much of his business experience was poisoning his relationship with Ruhama? How much was affecting his manner with Bayly and Shoshana?

Gershon decided to take a walk outside. Tenants had been complaining about potholes in the parking lot on the west side of the building and in the loading dock area at the rear. He figured he'd see how bad the pavement damage was, and whether or not repairs were called for. The fresh, early September air might do him good.

The midday sun was potent. 99 appeared gowned in bright white. It radiated, majestic as a Sabbath bride. Rounding the corner of the building he paused to enjoy the view. On the spur of the moment he decided to inspect the brickwork more carefully. The compact rectangles were precisely laid one on top of the next, row on row, rising up thousands upon thousands, hundreds of thousands of bricks in all. He examined the corner itself, where the front of the building was married to the western wall. The joint was coming apart, separating from the structure. Long, wide cracks traveled down in jagged lines. The corners of the building were particularly vulnerable, unprotected from the natural forces of wind and snow which battered the structure from opposite sides.

The wall-facings were straight and solid. But examining the western wall more closely, Gershon saw that the bricks were not as perfectly aligned as they seemed at first glance. Some bricks stuck out fractions of an inch. Where the bricks were flat and even, the wall was strong. Where they jutted out, Gershon noticed thin, insidious cracks in the mortar. These spots caught extra rainfall, accumulated frost and were slightly more exposed to bluster. Once fissures began to appear, a process of erosion started which would not abate. The cracks would widen. The bricks here would eventually separate like the ones at the corners.

These structural irregularities were texts in which history could be read, line upon line. They documented minor lapses in concentration, where long ago the bricklayer had been preoccupied by personal thoughts, a disturbing memory, an argument with his wife, trouble with the kids, family illness, money difficulties. Or they marked momentary distractions, a suddenly spilled coffee, a mishandled cigarette, an upsetting comment overheard, an insult dispensed. These seemingly insignificant glitches of workmanship—hardly noticeable mistakes, preserved in stone—would ultimately be the cause of great damage. Ignored long enough, left unattended, Gershon was sure the entire wall would eventually completely collapse.

He walked along the western side of the building, past the parked cars, snug side by side, their headlights and hood ornaments pointed toward the wall. It was a tranquil scene. In a few hours, 99 would empty *en masse*. The cars would fill with people, doors swinging open and slamming shut, keys being inserted into ignitions, motors revving. One by one the cars would back away from the building and turn onto Chabanel, their drivers taking them home.

Gershon looked at his watch. He wondered how long it would take to walk from the front of the building to the shipping area in the back. He set out, periodically checking his watch, while stepping around the potholes and making mental notes. A paving company would indeed have to be called for an estimate on repairs.

Twenty seconds into his march Gershon felt a tap on his head and another on his right shoulder. He stopped walking. Before he could think "bird-droppings," his eyes caught sight of a trail of smoke hanging in the air beside him. He followed the thin, dissipating plume down to the smouldering butt of a half-smoked cigarette rolling along the ground. Turning his face upward, he surveyed the open windows of 99. Did someone see him coming and decide to drop their cigarette on his head like a tiny bomb? It was impossible to have such good aim. But what if he'd been wearing his fedora? The cigarette would have been trapped in the brim of his hat, instead of bouncing off his shoulder. His head might have caught on fire. He pressed the sole of his shoe down on the asphalt to extinguish the butt and carried onward.

Thirty-eight seconds was his finishing time. He turned the corner and stood facing the loading dock area at the back of 99, hands on his hips.

Gershon saw that more than half of the shipping bays were filled with large and small vehicles. There were long container trucks, sixteen-foot cubes and minivans. Some were being loaded and others unloaded. The minivans belonged to the Chinese sewing contractors. Gershon watched a particular pair of contractors at work. A man stood on the loading-dock platform with a rolling-rack. The other man, on the ground three feet below, handed up to his partner bunches of plastic-wrapped garments on hangers. The contractors moved in and out of the docks inconspicuously, not seeming to mind the loud noises and the stench of piss.

The forty-foot container trucks were filled with rolls of fabric on wooden skids. Whereas the sewing contractors laboured to move their goods by hand, the unionized truckers had the benefit of machinery. They slipped the wheels of their jiggers underneath pallets of goods, pumped hydraulics to lift them off the ground, and with a push steered the massive loads out onto the dock. The truck drivers yelled at each other across the docks, cursing and joking in a version of French Gershon could barely understand. The sounds of heavy loads being shifted in and out of metal containers echoed along the platform. Skids being placed inside the freight elevators thudded and cracked as they landed on the metal floors. The elevator security gates clacked down, doors slammed shut, and the elevators creaked as they rose, heaving their merchandise up into the building.

Gershon noted a man on the dock who carried a mammoth roll of polar fleece on his shoulders. Standing outside in the sunshine, Gershon perspired on the back of his neck, under his arms and on his forehead. He imagined how the fellow he was watching sweated under the weight of fluffy winter fabric. But this was unavoidable, he knew. In the summertime they made winter clothes for the next season. In the winter, when the temperature outside was minus twenty degrees and the streets were narrowed between piles of snow, they worked on the summer fashions. This place which Gershon managed was completely backward.

Leaving 99, Gershon turned his vehicle from Chabanel south onto St. Laurent Boulevard. At Cremazie, he passed under a raised portion of the Metropolitan Autoroute. This was the route he took every evening driving home from work. He glanced out through his windshield at the giant angular pillars that supported the elevated highway, the squat concrete legs that carried the tremendous weight of rush-hour traffic which was stalled above his head. He quickly surveyed the underside of the structure, noticing how it was corroded in places. Chunks of concrete had begun to separate from their moorings and hung down on rusty wires. He worried that one day a piece would fall and crush a car passing underneath, maybe even his car. That would be an example of supreme bad luck. What was the chance of such a freak accident actually happening? Perhaps it was incalculable. He decided that death by a falling block of concrete through the car windshield was probably the very definition of being at the wrong place at the wrong time.

These thoughts brought to mind a conversation with Alfreda earlier in the day. She had talked about the most recent suicide bomb attack at a Tel Aviv discotheque. Twenty-two had died, mostly teenagers. Maybe the chance of getting killed by falling concrete was similar to dying in a nightclub suicide bombing.

Alfreda wanted to know what Gershon thought about the motivation of the suicide bombers. Specifically, what he thought about the act being considered by the perpetrators as their ticket to heaven. She wanted to hear Gershon's point of view since he believed in heaven, and she didn't.

Gershon hadn't wanted to get involved in a discussion about religion and politics with Alfreda. But the news of the latest attack had made her distraught. Her feelings and opinions had to be expressed.

"It's the belief in heaven, Gershon. It has always been the cause of so much suffering," Alfreda said.

"It's politics," Gershon replied. "The Palestinians are fighting for land. For power, control. Their so-called leaders are doing what politicians have always done. Sending kids out to fight their battles. Exploiting the most vulnerable with brainwashing techniques."

"Interesting, Gershon. So you think religion is brainwashing?" Alfreda teased.

"That's not what I meant. A genuine belief in God never justifies the killing of innocents."

"But you agree that it's their belief in heaven. That's what is being exploited," Alfreda said. "If they didn't believe in heaven they wouldn't be susceptible to brainwashing. I say people should forget about heaven and focus on solving their day-to-day problems."

"*That* is the real problem. They see no solutions to their daily circumstance. The suicide bombers are the most despondent, hopeless people. Kids who should have something to look forward to in life, but don't. They live in slums, they have no jobs, no prospects, no future. If the politicians would sit down together and figure out a plan, generate some hope ..."

"Then they would have no need to believe in heaven," Alfreda interrupted.

Her conclusion made Gershon uncomfortable. He decided to broaden the discussion.

"Well, if we didn't believe in an afterlife what would be our ultimate purpose here? I mean a person lives about seventy-five or eighty years. Most of the time they struggle to earn a living. And for what? The odd, momentary thrill? And in this part of the developed world we're the lucky ones. We have the occasional pleasures we can enjoy. For most of the world's population life is just an unending chain of pain, misery, exploitation and suffering. Come on, Alfreda. Do you seriously believe that this is what life is about? There's got to be more to it than that."

"There's a job to do. We've got to fix things here and now," Alfreda answered pragmatically. "All I'm saying is that you don't have to believe in heaven to think that life is worth living."

"Then why bother doing anything more than improving your own private lot—unless you believe that there is a larger meaning in life? Something beyond serving your own personal pleasures and immediate needs. We Jews reject this. We follow the Torah because we believe that life has a deeper significance. A Divine purpose, not a selfish one."

"I thought you guys followed Torah because you thought it would get *you* to heaven," Alfreda said.

"No," Gershon said.

"The Torah is *your* roadmap to heaven," she added.

"At least I've got a roadmap," Gershon said. "Most people are guided by nothing more than their own whims and desires. The Torah must be followed because it is the Law from God. A person's intentions don't matter."

"Can't argue with that," Alfreda said. "You know what they say about *intentions*. The road to hell is paved with good ones. I still say that most religious Jews follow Torah because they see a payoff in the end. And if that's why they do it, then fine. They should at least be honest with themselves and admit it. Admitting something is the first step on the road to recovery. Hey, that's interesting. We have the road to hell, the road to heaven and the road to recovery. A whole lot of roads."

So which road was Gershon riding? Now, crossing under the Metropolitan, Gershon wondered whether the highway overhead was the road to heaven, hell or recovery. He could see that the superstructure was not properly maintained. Aside from the falling concrete, he knew that the asphalt surface above him was buckling too, and drivers occasionally had to swerve to avoid dropped debris. Almost every day there was an accident or two and the highway was lined with burning orange caution flares.

During the day, Ruhama occupied herself with the children, sustaining their minds and bodies with art projects, boardgames, jigsaw puzzles, books, and outings to the neighbourhood playground. She was conscious of their delicate metabolisms, how a slight deviation in diet might upset the fragile balance, and she planned their meals with care: cheese sandwiches and freshly washed vegetables, peeled carrots, or sliced cucumbers, and cups of sweet apple or orange juice diluted with water.

When Bayly was a baby, Ruhama had collected a substantial library of books on infant health and nutrition. There was a great deal of talk at the time about the dangers of pesticides, even chemicals long considered safe by government authorities. Not wanting to take any chances, she bought only organically grown fruits and vegetables from health food outlets. She puréed large quantities of carrots, potatoes and squash in a blender and froze the digestible mush in ice-cube trays. For lunch or dinner, she could instantly produce a nutritious meal by defrosting a cube or two in the microwave oven.

With childbirth, Ruhama had become acutely aware of her surroundings. Random or planned events, nature and its variants—anything, it seemed—might affect the newborn adversely or positively. Her job was making sure the bad was adequately filtered out and the good provided in fat doses. And, of course, not only did the world alter the child, the child changed the world. It became a place where every spoonful mattered, and every gesture and utterance had palpable significance. This was how the world renewed itself, thought Ruhama, beginning in her body, through Bayly and again, through Shoshana. God willing, she would have a hand in helping the world renew itself again with the birth of a third child.

At night, Ruhama experienced a pleasant exhaustion, pleasant because it was accompanied by a sense of accomplishment. True, the children tired her out with their constant demands, but they gave as much as they took. In contrast, Gershon's brooding silence merely drained her. She began to dread his arrival home. She became instantly agitated upon hearing the handle of the front door click open, as if these days Gershon himself was breaking into their home. When he entered the house Ruhama felt her lungs contract, her chest tighten. His presence created a void, a black hole. Bayly and Shoshana ran to him and flopped against his legs, wrapping arms around the anchors of his large thighs. At the first opportunity, before Gershon could remove his coat and hat, Ruhama pulled the children back and whisked them upstairs.

Ruhama bled her monthly bleeding. She lost hope. She removed blotched pads from her undergarments and tossed them in the wastebasket, blaming Gershon. God sustained him, but what sustained her?

Gershon withheld attention, thoughts, caring, all things that added up to love. One time, Bayly asked Gershon if he loved her more than God. He answered deftly. He said loving Bayly was the same as loving God. And loving God was the same as loving his daughter. The two were inseparable. He could no sooner make a choice of one over the other, than he could choose his left hand over his right. Bayly was still in that early developmental stage when children are ambidextrous. He didn't tell her that with the passage of time people became left-handed or right-handed. They took sides.

If the measure of love was how much you did for someone else, Gershon's love for God was unquestionable. He devoted swaths of time and effort to texts, ritual, prayer and *mitzvot*. He was good-hearted and compassionate in his treatment of others, which made it hard for him in business. Ruhama supported him when he lacked strength. But who supported her?

Autumn was almost here and her closet looked bare. Ruhama counted three sweaters, a grey, an olive green and a black. The green one was too tight, she remembered from last year. Probably the others didn't fit either. There were four long woollen skirts, all pleated and in dark shades. They hung heavily on skinny metal hangers. Next to them, the white blouses were lined up stiffly in a row, like people waiting to use a bank-machine. One by one they would be worn, ironed and replaced, worn, ironed and replaced. She needed a new wardrobe, and right now she was looking for something to wear for the upcoming High Holy Days. Ruhama couldn't be expected to wear the same threadbare wardrobe year after year.

But there was no money. Every time she wanted new clothes, she had to beg. Gershon hated spending money on clothes. He wore the same uniform day in and day out, the plain white shirt, dark jacket and woollen slacks. The fedora and black overcoat. He didn't understand a woman's needs. Ruhama would push him to demand more money from his father, a higher wage. Sholem was rich and Gershon was being paid the same salary he received when they first met. Now there was a family to support. A wife and two children. It was an insult that Sholem didn't pay him more, but Gershon was too respectful to question his father, demand his due, their due. It was just like Gershon not to realize when he was being taken advantage of.

~

"Mizter Shteyn iz here?"

Alfreda shook her head, knowing the man referred to Sholem.

"Gershon, for you!" she yelled, sliding open the top right drawer of her desk and extracting a leather-bound chequebook.

Gershon entered the front office and Alfreda silently handed him the chequebook along with a ballpoint pen. Nodding to the man, Gershon opened the book flat on the front counter.

"*Sholem Aleichem,*" Gershon said to the man.

"*Aleichem Sholem.* You can give a nice donation?"

Gershon turned pages of perforated cheque stubs. The book was filled with pre-signed cheques of one hundred and eighteen dollars each. The office was prepared for the charity-seekers that came every other day. Gershon only had to fill in the name of the recipient.

"The yeshiva needs your help," the grey-bearded man said, watching Gershon find an unused cheque. His hand moved inside his jacket and produced a paper, unfolding it to indicate his credentials. "Yeshiva Am Chai" was printed in bold letters across the top of the document. He watched intently as Gershon copied the name on a cheque.

"You think maybe I can have two? There are so many students and every year more, *Boruch Hashem,*" the man said, staring at the cheque-book.

"One per customer," Gershon replied, grinning. "We don't want to run out."

"From what I hear there is no danger Mr. Shteyn will run out." The man took the cheque and shoved it into his pocket without saying thank you.

No one who came for charity ever left the office empty-handed. On Purim, the traditional time for giving *tzedakah* in generous amounts, Sholem walked around with bulging pockets stuffed with cash. Dozens of charity-seekers came to the office that day. At night, they would line up outside his house. Thousands of dollars were distributed.

"*A shtickl Toyreh?*" the man asked.

"Sure, why not?" Gershon said, handing the chequebook back to Alfreda, his back to the man.

"I speak in *ainglish* for the nice lady to understand," the old man said, without looking at Alfreda.

"So we come to *Brayshis* soon again, *Genesis*."

Gershon thought about how funny that sounded, "again, *Genesis*." How many times can you begin? If you began over and over, as the Jews did reading Torah every year, as they did throughout history, was there ever really one beginning? One ending?

"The Almighty, blessed be The Name, brings the world into existence. He makes heaven and earth and from the ground He brings out Adam." The man opened his palms and scooped up imaginary dirt off the counter. "And from Adam, He takes a rib and makes Chava, Eve.

"And what is she called, Chava? *Aizer k'negdo*." The grey-bearded man glanced at Alfreda. "It means 'a helpmate', someone by his side, so he would not be alone, a person to share his experience with.

"The word *aizer* comes from *oz* which means 'force'. She's a power." The man squeezed his fingers into a fist and thrust it out toward Alfreda.

"*K'negdo* means 'at his side', yes, but also, 'against him'. She's a force against Adam. The woman goes against the man, that's her nature." He brought his two hands up and flattened the palms together pressing hard.

"The woman and man lean against one another, each must be strong. If one side is not strong, together they fall." The man's hands tilted and dropped to the side.

"We luuurn … " his voice trailing off as he sang, "that to be a true helpuuurr … to do *Hashem's* wuuurk … of repairing the wuuurld … we must go against one anothuuur … and be strong enough to correct each othuuuur. Now you know why opposites attract." He looked at Alfreda who responded with a smirk. "It's all part of God's plan."

"Was it God's plan too that she would give him the forbidden fruit?" Gershon said abruptly, feeling a pang of irritation. "Was that how she corrected him?"

The man grinned at Gershon. "You don't think Adam needed correcting? Even Adam was created with a *yetzer hara*, the evil inclination. You think he was blameless?"

"Well, no."

"So, let me ask you, what was his sin?" the man inquired, eyes widening at Gershon.

"He didn't listen to *Hashem* when he was told not to eat the fruit."

"No," the man replied. "He was *kofer tov*. He failed to acknowledge

Hashem's goodness. When *Hashem* asked him why he ate the fruit, what did Adam respond?"

"It was because of the woman," Gershon replied.

"Precisely." The man stuck a finger out at Alfreda. "Adam pointed fingers. He blamed her. As *Hashem* created the world in Goodness, Adam did not appreciate that Chava was also given in goodness, so he would not be lonely. It was not Chava who sinned against Adam, the opposite is true. By blaming her, it was Adam who sinned against her, and in doing so against the Almighty. And soooo ... whaaaat was his punishmainnnt?" the man asked, in melody.

"Immortality was taken away and they were exiled from Eden," Gershon said flatly.

"Yes. And we luuurn, my young friend ... that God's face was the canopy of *Gan Aiden*, it shone on the plants making them grow, bloom and bear fruit in quantity, they never wanted. But outside the Garden, just as we have to work the land to harvest food, it is our deeds that bring out God's goodness in the world. The sages tell us that more than prayer, ritual practice and learning *Toyreh*, the greatest *mitzvos* we can perform are good deeds done for others. We are partners in the continual work of Creation. The first partnership is between man and woman. This is what Adam refused to recognize."

Gershon was attentive now. "So, because Adam didn't appreciate all the goodness he was given by *Hashem* in *Gan Aiden*—an inexhaustible supply of food and the companionship of the woman—he had to learn it, by working for it."

Gershon's lesson learned, the old man smiled. "Why else do you think marriage is no picnic? The goodness is there, we must work to bring it out. The Almighty punishes in exact portions. His Justice always brings the two sides to balance. That which is lacking must be replaced, *midah k'neged midah*."

The man took the cheque out of his pocket and waved it between his fingers like a tiny flag. "Maybe, just one more? For the yeshiva?"

Gershon asked Alfreda for the chequebook again. He scrawled "Yeshiva Am Chai" on another cheque. He felt he'd gotten his money's worth.

Footage

"THE LONGER THE ZIPPER the better the stripper."

Arnie Free made Gershon laugh. Alfreda glared at him in disgust.

Arnie was a Lifer. That's what Sonny Lipsey called the tenants who had been at 99 for twenty-five years or more. A one-man operation, Arnie manufactured leather shoes and boots on the fifth floor. He had come to pay his rent and was describing a business outing the night before. He loved to talk, rambling on and on excitedly.

"There's big money in making boots for strippers. Okay, it's a niche market but not as small as you may think. Do you have any idea how many strippers there are in Quebec? The perks aren't bad either. Last night…"

"Spare us the details," Alfreda interrupted, but there was no stopping Arnie.

"Last night I went backstage to meet the ladies. They tried on samples, modeled the new designs. And best of all, my visits to the strip clubs are tax-deductible research and development."

Arnie depended on such niche markets. Strippers adored the cherry-red and lipstick-pink boots he fabricated with transparent five-and-a-half-inch stiletto heels. The leather boot climbed up the thigh to the crotch and flared out from the hips. Gershon was saying that it didn't seem to make much sense for women who took their clothes off to buy such expensive boots.

Arnie repeated, "The longer the zipper the better the stripper. They love my hipboots. All those little metal teeth coming apart across the skin, down the slope of the thigh, running over the bump of the knee and peeling open along the shin. The horny guys go nuts. They slobber, tongues hang out." His tone became serious, business-like. "The exotic dance profession is all about packaging, Gershon, not what's inside. Once the clothes are off, the fun's over."

Besides strippers, Arnie's other major client-base were Hasidim. He sold specialty black loafers to ultra-Orthodox Jews who didn't tie laces on Shabbat. He also made knee-high, thick-soled, *shtetl* boots for the Hasidim who mimicked the fashion of their Eastern European predecessors. These styles were favourites in Borough Park, Brooklyn and the reclusive community of black-hatters that lived near the airport thirty minutes drive north of Montreal.

Arnie lived and worked in two distinct worlds. He could serve the religious Jews because he was a born Jew, raised in a traditional home and educated in parochial school. He understood their mindset, how to talk and behave around them. As for servicing the strippers, well, he was also a charming man.

Gershon was curious how Arnie managed to keep the two polar ends of his business apart. It was not hard to imagine a very uncomfortable situation arising, one that would harm his business. What if, for example, he was measuring the foot of a stripper in his shop and an Orthodox Jew appeared unexpectedly for a repair? Apparently, there was never a problem. The strippers were fitted at their work-site or on house calls. The Orthodox Jews were sized by mail, from foot-tracings. Every few weeks he would receive from New York or Mirabel, a legal-size manila envelope stuffed with giant peanut-shaped outlines. Arnie cut shoe soles from these.

"They have very bad, beat-up feet, the dancers. Callouses and corns," Arnie explained. "I treat them with extra care. I fit them in private."

Hasids and strippers were joined in their preference for footwear that had a polished, glossy appearance, but for different reasons. The dancers liked the way shiny boots caught stagelight, accentuating their leg-lifts and high scissor-kicks, reflecting sharp beams of blue light in a spray of directions. The Hasidim considered spotless footwear a means of honouring God. It was their manner of declaring publicly that they abided the biblical instruction to "walk in the way of the Lord."

"They both have unique needs, heavy on material content and craftmanship," Arnie said about his two types of customers. "So they pay top dollar. And they pay well. I never have to wait for a cheque. Never had one bounce on me either."

Gershon wished he could say the same. "Maybe we should advertise space for rent in stripper trade magazines. Get some solid customers," Gershon said to Alfreda, half-jokingly. "They have trade-magazines, don't they?"

"Yah, and while we're at it, why don't we convert some industrial space into bedrooms? Turn the place into a full-fledged bordello. We can charge by the hour, take cash up-front," Alfreda scoffed.

It was not such a far-fetched notion. Alfreda was referring to the time Frank Sinatra Singh was unknowingly running an escort service from his premises. The first sign was the traffic in the building, which had suddenly increased after business hours. The night watchman reported seeing white limousines inexplicably pulling up at the front door during his shift.

Shortly before these bizarre occurrences started, Frank had hired two petite Chinese girls. Graduates of a design school, he set them to work making patterns. They turned heads, arriving to work strikingly dressed in tight, revealing clothes, which was nothing to sound alarm bells. Women who worked in the garment trade frequently dressed in immodest, appealing ways. It was a sign of commitment and ambition.

The girls were hard-working and Frank Sinatra Singh extolled their impressive output. The Orientals would take over the entire industry, Frank said. They already controlled most of the sub-contracting business. Montreal was flooded with hundreds of underground Chinese sweatshops that paid wages long ago deemed unacceptable by union standards. With the industry now largely de-unionized, the average price for assembling a pant or blouse had plummeted to levels not seen in twenty years.

The Jewish entrepreneurs who still dominated the business called themselves manufacturers when in reality most had ceased manufacturing anything. They were salesmen and warehouse managers. Every aspect of local apparel fabrication was being farmed out to sub-contractors. The Jews acted as brokers. They maintained their advantage by controlling the all-important relationships with buyers.

Shimmy Solomon, The Great White Father of the Montreal industry, had observed that Jews were in a unique position. Historically trained to operate in multiple milieus and polyglot, Jews were situated favourably to bridge the gap between the university-educated retail marketers and the immigrant-based sub-class of producers. Success in the needletrade increasingly depended on the ability to straddle a cultural gap, and speak two different languages: the sales-speak understood by sophisticated merchandisers who discussed computerized inventory management, just-in-time delivery systems, market-share and customer satisfaction, and a street jargon used when haggling with Chinese contractors over pennies.

Standing at the bottom of the economic ladder, it was perhaps predictable that some members of the Chinese community would try to get a leg up by branching into other areas of the fashion industry. The buildings along Chabanel, where thousands worked and buyers from out of town regularly visited showrooms, offered a potential clientele. Arnie Free was expanding from Hasids to strippers, and Frank Sinatra Singh's young protégées had themselves discovered a niche market, one which could be exploited without even leaving the building.

Generally, the girls were quiet sorts. When they chatted in Mandarin, Frank assumed it was nothing more than task-related. He had become suspicious when they began receiving an inordinate number of phone calls during the day. They stayed at work later and later. Then unfamiliar men began arriving, tapping on the office door window. Together with their guests, the young ladies would steal away to the privacy of back rooms.

One morning there was a commotion in the hallway. Frank Sinatra Singh's door was locked shut. The two Chinese girls paced outside nervously. A leather-clad tattoo artist yelled and slammed his fists against the door. Frank emerged from his premises brandishing a baseball bat and threatening to call the police. After the trio had finally fled, Gershon went to question Frank. He said he had fired the girls a few days earlier and now they had returned with their pimp to claim back-wages.

"They're hard-working. They have the immigrant hunger for success. This business just doesn't give them opportunity. Not the same way it did when I came to Canada," Frank said, his voiced tinged with regret.

True, the industry as a whole was in a state of disarray. Government bureaucrats congregated in the dining section of Two Guys Restaurant where the bosses previously sat, their leather briefcases and portable computers on the floor next to their chairs. The bosses had started to order meals up to their offices ever since teams of auditors had been dispatched to Chabanel to track down unpaid sales taxes. Niko wasn't unhappy with these new customers. The lunch business had improved a bit. He found that tax assessors had hearty appetites. They consumed Daily Specials and stretched the lunch hour as long as possible, lingering over coffee and double portions of dessert.

The auditors came to 99 in waves, sniffing around in offices, looking for unremitted sales taxes. The contractors made it a regular practice to keep the money for themselves, discreetly closing their businesses and reopening under different corporate names in a commercial shell-game they played with the authorities. Since the Jewish manufacturers were traditionally at the centre of the industry, the government held them responsible for millions in unpaid taxes, plus interest and penalties. The Roths and Shimmy Solomon were audited regularly. Shimmy announced he would close his doors and put hundreds out of work before paying the government a single penny more. Sonny Lipsey called the situation the Roman Siege of Jerusalem.

Gershon thought that if anyone in the building would understand his interest in Michelle Labelle, about the light he saw, it was Rosie K. Rosie was a kind, bubbly-cheeked black man with a dense beard. He was giant and generous, in equal parts. Born in St. Lucia, he spoke an island patois to the Haitian ladies who visited his fourth-floor wholesale textile outlet. He greeted Gershon enthusiastically whenever they met in the hallway. Rosie insisted on shaking Gershon's hand each time. It felt like a mitt, which, considering Gershon's own large hand-size, always left a strong impression on him. Gershon rarely met anyone who made him feel small. On the basis of physical size alone, Gershon felt a certain kinship with Rosie. Large people like them experienced the world differently. They endured problems with shoes, clothes and cars which smaller people didn't, not to mention the preconceptions and jealousies the less endowed held against men of physical stature.

Like Rosie, Gershon also had thick, sumptuous lips. As a child, Gershon had been teased more than once by classmates about his "nigger-lips." It didn't hurt their relationship that Rosie was also Jewish, or at least he thought of himself as Jewish. He was married to a Montreal Jew,

Côte St. Luc-born and bred, making their two children officially Jewish according to *halachah*.

Rosie and Ellen had met shortly after his arrival in Canada. He began working in the textile business, learning the trade as a salesman for a wholesaler that sold fabric to Ellen's father, who manufactured dresses. Ellen worked for the family company as a secretary. She said that with Rosie it was love at first sight, a claim which made her father apoplectic. He cursed the day he allowed his daughter to work in his business.

Initially convinced that their "spoiled, immature daughter" was going through a phase, Ellen's parents treated Rosie with indifference, serving only to spur their daughter on. When Ellen announced that she and Rosie were moving in together, her parents tried every known tactic to dissuade her from ruining her life. Finally, after they were married in a small ceremony at a Reform Temple which her parents reluctantly attended, did they begin to acknowledge Rosie's presence at family dinners. "Don't you dare call me 'Dad'," Ellen's father told him. Rosie obliged, grateful that his in-laws hadn't chosen to sit *shiva*, the seven-day period of mourning, the traditional method of demonstrating disapproval at inter-marriage in Jewish families. "If she had to marry a *goy*," Ellen's father told her mother, "why not a black, immigrant one? Our daughter has never settled for half-measures. So, we'll dance a hora to her stubbornness."

Rosie and Ellen agreed that they would raise their children as Jews. He learned about the Holy Days, taking courses with the Reform rabbi who had married them. Rosie even became actively involved in the community. He joined committees at Temple. When Holy Days approached, he always used the appropriate salutation with Gershon and wished him "Shabbat Shalom" every Friday afternoon. Rosie enjoyed talking with Gershon about Judaism, particularly Kabbalah. Although Gershon didn't normally care to discuss Jewish mysticism with anybody, preferring discourse on less complex core texts, he listened to Rosie contentedly so as not to dampen his curiosity and enthusiasm.

Rosie would understand about Michelle Labelle. Maybe Rosie would even consent to helping Gershon whisk her away. They could find a safe-haven for her in the building. Somewhere she could stay, apart from the Hells Angel. There was a vacant room upstairs on the seventh floor, suite 709, the old Stein management office. It was the perfect sanctuary. Two air-conditioned rooms and a clean bathroom. Rosie could help take

Michelle there. But would she come willingly? Or would they need to ambush her? He didn't like the sound of that word, ambush. Abduct. Kidnap. None was right. The appropriate term was something in between abduct and save. Was there a word between abduct and save?

This was the most unsettling season of the year. It was not quite a season, rather a time between official seasons. A time of year which wasn't accorded the dignity of a name, neither here nor there. Summer was over but autumn hadn't yet made full entry. Nonetheless, the signs were unmistakable. Change was afoot. Ruhama noticed the sun beginning to take a short-cut across the sky. The lofty sun, which had looked down at the earth haughtily all summer long, was now making a rapprochement. The squirrels were out scavenging, greedily stuffing their cheeks with morsels of food dropped by carefree children. They seemed to know the summer abundance of scraps would soon dry up once schools were back in session.

The park lacked splendour. The oaks, maples and poplars were still awash in emerald green, but they were losing their lustre. And the dappled gilt of gold had not yet taken hold. Pacing along the path, Ruhama kicked a green leaf on the ground, sending it briefly back up into flight. She considered how some leaves dropped prematurely. These were not leaves from Jewish trees, she said to herself. Leaves from Jewish trees were programmed to hold on stubbornly right to the very end.

One maple leaf floated face down in the stone pond next to the playground. It was a curious place to have set a basin of water. While their children played nearby, vigilant mothers circled the pool anxiously, round and round, like hands on a speeding clock. When children approached the edge of the water, as they always did, because they couldn't resist the clarity and shimmer of water, mothers would stop in their tracks and throw out arms like grappling hooks.

Ruhama listened to the yips and yelps of children on the slides, monkey-bars and swings, chasing after one another, the sharpness of their taunts and teases. And she thought about the coming winter. They will soon be sliding on toboggans or building ice-forts in the park and their sounds will be muted, muffled by snow.

This is my world, thought Ruhama. So different from Gershon's. The park had become a refuge of sorts, a home away from home, where tensions were stifling. She could easily reconcile herself to the slow inevitable shifts of nature. The situation with Gershon was something else. It provoked frustration. Gershon had a building he could rush off to in the morning. She had the park. Here was the space between them, the distance from a building to a park. Gershon had the safety of walls, floors and ceilings. His life was a series of erected boundaries, delineated frontiers, compartments. Hers was comprised of breaking down barriers, crossing borders, cultivating and nurturing the expanse of available soil. She worked with nature; he worked against it.

Ruhama recalled the time Shoshana was brought home from the hospital. Her newborn's room was freshly painted and furnished with the changing table, cushiony nursing-chair, dresser and cradle which had been used for Bayly three years earlier. On the floor was a stack of baby gifts. Bayly hollered and whined at the appearance of her new sister. Ruhama tried to make her feel more comfortable by letting her open all the new toys and play with them. Bayly threw each one in turn to the ground. Flustered, Ruhama scolded her daughter and left the room for an instant with the baby swaddled in her arms. When she returned, Bayly was gone. Ruhama panicked. She scanned the corners of the room, looking behind the furniture and calling out. She found Bayly, quietly curled up inside one of the large overturned empty toy boxes.

Gershon's office must be just like that. A shelter. A place that was his own. He didn't have to share it with anyone. If not the entire office, than at least a desk, his small corner, his paper box.

Ruhama's life was completely shared. There was not a single room in the house she could call her own. Not even the bed, which was really half a bed, pulled apart and put back together. That was precisely how she felt—pulled apart and put back together. The children did it. She hung on their emotions, their every need and whim. When they were in pain or upset for any reason, Ruhama felt incomplete. When they were happy and content, she felt reconstituted. In her marriage it was the same.

Still, the discussion with Gershon about money had gone quite well. He understood Ruhama's desire for new clothes for the High Holy Days. He was not patronizing. Ruhama believed him when he said he would take care of it. When Gershon said he would take care of something he always followed through. He was dependable in that way. The timetable, however, had to be his own. Gershon would determine when their chances of success with Sholem were greatest. Ruhama had to trust him.

Sitting on the park bench, Ruhama thought about Montreal, her adopted city. She could never have imagined, in her wildest dreams, that this was where she would end up marrying and making a family. During the time of the 1995 referendum on separation, she hated the place. She begged Gershon to take her back to her family, to New York where the road signs were readable and she could approach sales clerks without fear of being treated with condescension for speaking in English. Gershon cursed the Separatists for destroying property values. But he refused to leave. He was rooted to the city, arguing that the Jewish community was strong here, and that Montreal was a wonderful place to raise children. The political difficulties would blow over, he assured her. She trusted him. And by the slimmest of possible margins, he was right.

The enormous blazing crucifix that branded the city's skyline at night from the top of Mount Royal was Ruhama's constant reminder that she could never feel completely comfortable here. She tried to understand how Gershon's family managed to feel at home living at the foot of a cross. This patchwork city was blatantly pieced together, domain stitched to domain. The rich lived up on the mountain, the poor in settlements down by the river. The English-speaking upper-classes resided in the west, working-class French neighbourhoods blanketed the east, right up to where the smokestacks of oil refineries spit black smoke into the air. Perhaps this was what comforted the Jews here. There was no effort to conceal divisions. Each group knew its place and kept to it.

Ruhama reflected that in New York, ethnic and economic boundaries also existed, but underlying it all, there was every American's faith in mobility, the American Dream. They believed in the very depths of their hearts that social barriers were permeable. Embracing this notion was a basic article of faith in America. Gershon was right when he pointed out how unsafe U.S. cities were. Ruhama knew that the violence of her native country resulted from the frustration and disappointment born of unfulfilled dreams, the unbridgeable gap experienced by most people between espoused ideals and reality.

Ruhama surmised that Canadians didn't hold to such fairytales. On the contrary, it was apparent to her that in a land so vast and sparsely-populated a person could get lost unless they kept to their place, language, heritage and kind. Remaining distinct meant remaining alive. This was the message she heard over and over again, particularly in Quebec. When the Jews were hated here it was quickly out in the open. The Québécois were not shy. They expressed themselves. And not just at street level with spray-painted graffiti and overturned tombstones. Within the powerful classes and the elite, anti-Semitic slurs were brazenly publicized. Nothing was kept secret for the sake of upward social mobility. The Jews of Quebec appreciated the advantage of having their enemies clearly identified, and knowing where they stood. In this way, Montreal was a comfortable place, indeed, for a Jew to make his home.

In spite of the barriers that separated communities, Ruhama also saw that some mysterious power held the city, the province, the country together. It had to be more than just common ground, or common interest, common values, common anything. The word "common" did not touch what was happening here. It was a kind of miracle. A bond of the spirit. And suddenly with her mind holding the word "spirit," Ruhama felt hopeful once again, even at home, at least for a moment.

"*Nu*, what happened with the girl?" Chaim asked.

"With the girl? Oh, nothing." Gershon replied.

"What do you mean, nothing? Well, nothing is good sometimes," Chaim said.

"I haven't seen her in the building, but she's here, somewhere."

"Are you still thinking about her?" Chaim prompted.

"Yah," said Gershon. "Well, not really. Less about her than what you said. About her *neshama*."

"What have you told Ruhama?"

"Nothing."

"Like I said, sometimes nothing's good."

"Chaim, what do you think the road to heaven is paved with?"

"What? The road to heaven?"

"Yah. You know that saying about the road to hell being paved with good intentions. Alfreda mentioned it to me the other day and it stuck in my mind. They don't say anything about the road to heaven. What do you think the road to heaven is paved with?"

"*Mitzvot*," Chaim said. "God's Commandments. They're the connection to heaven, Gershon. The *mitzvot* came from *Hashem* and it is through the *mitzvot* that *Hashem* comes down to us."

"Like a two-way street."

"Exactly."

"Do you think it matters why we do them? *Mitzvot*, I mean."

"No. We just have to do them."

"What if we're doing them for personal reasons?"

"We just have to do them," Chaim repeated. "There are so many *mitzvot*. How can we comprehend all 613? If we had to understand them before doing them, we probably wouldn't do them at all. Our reasons for doing them matter less than having a sense of obligation."

Gershon thought about Joey Putkin. Putkin had no sense of obligation, at least not with Gershon. That was the essence of his problem. Putkin despised religious Jews. He hated being obligated to one every month, to pay rent. And Gershon thought about other tenants, ones who paid and others who didn't. In some cases, like Estella Mora's, it was a matter of their ability to pay. But in Putkin's case, where money was not the issue, reluctance to pay was about attitude.

Chaim said, "That's the problem nowadays. A person's decency to others comes from his desire to feel good about himself. One morning he wakes up in a good mood and says, I think I'll treat people well today, and he feels all proud. The next day he wakes up in a bad mood and doesn't feel like being charitable. The *mitzvot* stand in complete opposition to this. It doesn't matter whether a person feels good about doing them. They're Commandments, as immutable as the laws of nature. Here's how I think about the *mitzvot*. God made the world. Torah is like an owner's manual and the *mitzvot* are like His operating instructions, direct from the manufacturer. Say you have some new gadget, a complex technology. You can't use it properly unless you read the operating instructions, right? The world is infinitely more complex than a computer, or a cellphone, and yet no one bothers to read the operating manual."

Gershon reached down to his waist and touched the cellphone attached to his belt next to his *tzizes*. His phone was the latest model, according to the manufacturer, "developed by top researchers in microchip technology." The owner's manual also instructed Gershon that the phone had many advanced easy-to-use features including, "full graphic display of 5 text input lines and 1 icon line with variable font."

The device was "easy to dial through the VR feature and enter letters through the T9 text input mode." The instructions revealed that the phone possessed "enhanced web browsing & data services, as well as downloadable ringtones and images for personalization." Presumably, these phrases were meant to excite the gadget's new owner. They filled Gershon with dread.

The list of instructions was vast and impenetrable. The booklet was over a hundred pages long and translated into seven languages, including English, French, Spanish, Greek and Japanese. Had he been reading the Japanese version instead of the English one it would have made little difference: RING MODE, press [4] [1] select the parameter; LOCKING THE PHONE, press [*] [enter password][1] select the parameter; RESETTING PHONE, press [*] [enter password] [4] select the parameter, "yes"; CLEARING STORED PHONE NO., press [*] [enter password] [5] [1] select the parameter; LOCK CODE CHANGE, press [*] [enter password] [2] select parameter [enter new password] [enter again]. Gershon gleaned that a password was crucially important, but he didn't have one. Without a password, he had the sense that one could not gain access to a world of untold thrills and wonders. He settled for comprehending and mastering four magical words. ON. OFF. SEND. RECEIVE.

CLEAR was the most important button of all. A button he could rely on. In frustation, he always ended up pressing the CLEAR button, not once, but twice and three times, because nothing was CLEAR to him and he desperately wanted the button to make it so. Gershon watched in awe those people who were capable of handling their cellphones expertly, making the devices retrieve information from the netherworld of some unseen digital universe. They had command over their technologies. They knew their gadgets intimately and touched them delicately in special places. In gratitude, the devices surrendered to them whatever they desired at the time. These cellphone wizards, who had absorbed their owner's manuals cover to cover and could conjure voices and information out of thin air, were the same people who called Torah esoteric.

"The first thing you learn when you open up the operating manual of a new gadget is that the manufacturer's warranty does not cover misuse," Chaim said. "It's stated clearly at the very top. There you have it, Gershon. God does not warranty His Creation if we misuse it. The *mitzvot* are Commandments, His operating instructions. If we want the world to work properly we are obligated to use it properly by following the *mitzvot*."

"So you're saying that ignoring the *mitzvot*, denying the obligation to heed them, is tantamount to abusing the world?"

"Like using your cellphone to hammer nails. Having a sense of obligation is key. Think of how it affects our personal relationships."

Chaim paused in thought. "You know, in hindsight, I think I stopped working for Pa not so much because I wanted to build something on my own, as I was ashamed of myself for not being able to face my obligation to him. Look at what our parents went through in Europe and after. What they had to overcome. How they struggled to survive, and succeeded. We should always be grateful."

"But, the obligation you're talking about now, to our parents, with everything they went through—it's like a debt that can never be repaid."

"You do the best you can. Nothing more can be expected. Just don't deny the obligation exists. They have an obligation too, our parents. Their survival was part of it. You and I are part of it. And their parents had an obligation to their parents who had one to their parents…"

"All the way back to the Patriarchs, Yaacov who had an obligation to Yitzhok who had an obligation to Avraham, each trying their best to repay a debt. So we come from a long line of debtors, is that it? All the way back to the first debt, to the Almighty Himself. Chaim, the obligation, the debt, is unrepayable. The interest alone would kill us," Gershon chuckled.

"Why do you think the Torah says one Jew can not charge another Jew interest on a loan?" Chaim laughed.

"Look at your own list of creditors, the people you owe so much. You and I talk about being obligated to our parents, but you also have to consider your obligation to Ruhama. Look at what she's given you: Bayly and Shoshana. In the final analysis, moving forward, accepting obligations is what living is all about. For whatever reason, the obligation I felt to our parents chained me to them. I was incapable of taking the next step. I failed, got divorced. I didn't have children. I ran away from Pa and the business. The weight of obligation was too much for me to bear. But you took on more and more. You married and have two beautiful children. I envy your courage Gershon. You have accomplished great things. You've become fully engaged and implicated in the world. By taking on obligations to your wife and children, you've honoured our parents and *Hashem* in the proper way."

Gershon was stunned by Chaim's admission. He had always thought of himself as the weaker of the two. He wanted to hug his brother, but resisted. Instead, Gershon shared words he thought might comfort Chaim.

"Chaim, why does it feel sometimes like doing the best you can isn't good enough?"

"'Cause, Gershon, somewhere deep in your heart you know the truth is, you're not doing the best you can."

There is no force on earth that jogs the memory like physical illness. The smoker who develops lung cancer or emphysema after many years of smoking will immediately think back to the first cigarette he ever lit up. He remembers how old he was, the name of the school chum who offered it to him, locates in his mind's eye the precise place where it happened in the corner of the schoolyard on a certain street, in a certain neighbourhood in a certain city. He senses, once again, the thrill of engaging in defiant behaviour for the first time, and reconsiders the wisdom of taking his life in his own hands.

The woman who discovers a lump in her breast while lathering in the shower, senses a tingling at the tip of the toes or feels the uncontrollable twitching of a pinky that signals the onset of a terrible process. She thinks back to how it may have started. She searches her memory for exposure to toxicity, rapidly assembles an inventory of the unhealthy foods she has eaten, regrets not continuing her exercise regime, and thinks of the times she lived too close to power lines or sewage outlets. She enumerates the stressful relationships she should have abandoned, but didn't.

This is memory as utility. This is wanting to find a source, an origin, the key to unlock a secret. A cause must be exposed, a sin disclosed so restitution can be made, a poison pinpointed so an antidote can be found, the error revealed so amends can be initiated. The course of illness generally entails rifling back through the catalogue of personal events and experiences.

Holocaust survivors are a totally different breed, particularly religious ones. As fatalists, they participate in no such mental activities. Sholem had vocalized neither regret nor humiliation in the two weeks after he entered the office, lost his footing and collapsed in a heap. Resting in his hospital bed, he showed no sign of anguish at having suffered the indignity of being carted through 99 on an ambulance stretcher by two burly uniformed men, his tenants lining the hallway, gawking. Alfreda had run to him, knelt by his side and hesitated before touching him. She rolled her sweater into a ball, lifted his head off the floor gently and placed the improvised pillow underneath, before returning to her desk to dial 9-1-1. Next, she called Gershon on his cellphone. The paramedics showed up first. By the time Gershon entered 99 his father was already being wheeled into the hospital emergency and Chaim was at his side.

The doctors said the prognosis was positive. The patient was making good progress. A stroke of the same magnitude suffered by a lesser man might well have killed him. Some paralysis remained in the left hand and leg. If the will was there, they reassured, the strength of his extremities could be regained, at least partly, with extensive physiotherapy. In the hours immediately following the trauma, Sholem could talk in a slurred speech, but understandably. He simply chose not to.

Every morning Sholem did ask one question. He wanted to know what day it was. He didn't want *Shabbat* to arrive and pass without his knowledge.

Gershon and Chaim stood dutifully by his bed. They went to synagogue together and prayed, adding the *Mi-sheberach* for those who had fallen ill to their long lists of prayers. They also had their mother to tend to. She was frantic, and refused to leave the house. She paced from room to room like a caged mouse. Ruhama went to stay with her every day. She brought Bayly and Shoshana in the hope that their presence would offer some solace and distraction.

Gershon was sickened by the sight of his father lying in the hospital bed. The pale covers, metal bars and bags of fluid hanging above his head were disheartening enough. But it also occurred to Gershon that he didn't ever remember seeing his father sick in bed. Not even at home as a child growing up. It seemed as though his father was never ill. When he was suffering with a cold or the flu it was ignored; he went to the office regardless. Sholem worked like a machine. And he had expected the same from Gershon and Chaim, driving them hard, refusing to accept aches, sneezes and sniffles as reasons for missing school.

Their mother had exactly the opposite orientation. In her estimation, a simple headache was sufficient grounds for keeping her boys in bed. It was also reason enough to call the doctor several times, to make trips to the nearest pharmacy to stock up on every available medicine, to take the patient's temperature, both orally and rectally every two hours, to cook gallons of chicken soup and to worry. Whether a runny nose, a cough or a stubbed toe, the response from their mother was equally manic. Given her agony and their father's disapproval, Gershon and Chaim usually chose to downplay whatever ailments they might have felt. They maintained impeccable records of school attendance.

As soon as Sholem arrived at the hospital, they stripped him of his clothes and took away his wallet and identity cards. Men and women in lab coats surrounded him, smiled fake smiles, prodded him with instruments, inserted needles, strapped him to machines and spoke an unfamiliar medical lingo. To Gershon the scene seemed like some kind of death camp nightmare which took his father backward in time, to a place where his future rested in the hands of technical fanatics, experts in chemistry.

Gershon had a more disturbing realization—perhaps the unease he felt looking at his father lying in the hospital bed, in this incapacitated condition, was somehow his own sense of incapacity reflected back. He imagined that the clear tubes attached to his father's flesh were actually sucking the life-juices out of him, not the other way around. The hospital was a terrible place. People died here. The only hope was escape. Escape was a feat Gershon knew his father was capable of. He'd proven it before. He expected his father to be back at 99 soon. He hoped and prayed for it. One morning Sholem would wake up, raise his chest and shoulders off the bed, swing his legs around and plant his two feet squarely on the ground. Testing his weight, he would rise up on his thighs and placing one shaky foot in front of the next, walk out of the hospital just as he had many years ago through the front gate, under the black wrought-iron words *Arbeit Macht Frei*.

Walls

KRANTZ HAD COMPLETED his inspection of Joey Putkin's premises and submitted a written assessment. He confirmed that Putkin had good reason to suspect something was amiss. He had traced one electrical line through Putkin's factory, up through a hole in the floor. It led into an air-conditioning unit installed inside the office of a new tenant's six-thousand-square-foot space on the second floor.

Gershon wasn't completely shocked, but the result was unexpected and prompted questions. Had it been done intentionally or as an innocent mistake? It would not be the first time that one tenant had drawn power from his neighbour in error. Years of dividing and sub-dividing spaces had created a tangle of electrical lines passing through different locales all over the building.

The second question concerned who would pay for the mistake. And there was a third, related question. Should Joey Putkin be told?

There was no doubt about one thing. If Putkin was aware of the facts he would reduce his rental payments to recoup his costs from Gershon. Gershon would be left the task of collecting the money from the guilty party, who would almost certainly resist paying. On the other hand, as long as Putkin was kept in the dark he would withhold rent. Gershon knew he was in a lose-lose situation. The only thing he had on his side at the moment was knowledge, and knowledge was power. If the truth were concealed or twisted there was a chance that Gershon could avoid losing out. Perhaps he could have the line transferred to the proper meter secretly and then, once the evidence was covered up, tell Putkin he was mistaken. Gershon could pay Krantz a few extra dollars to fudge his report, write up a new one. It would ultimately save the management a lot of money.

The fact remained—Gershon's disappointment derived less from the prospect of having to make a decision, than the reality that Joey Putkin had been right.

His second disappointment of the week, a much greater one, came in the days immediately following the onset of Sholem's sudden illness. Sholem's accountant Jerome Levy had summoned Gershon and Chaim to a meeting in his office downtown.

Jerome was a thin, salt-and-pepper haired man with a nervous manner who wore rectangular reading glasses at the end of his nose. When he presented the year-end financial report of Sholem's consolidated holdings, Jerome looked grandmotherly, speaking in a high pitched voice, his eyes sliding down to draw figures from the document in his hands and back up over the rims of his spectacles to keep the attention of his impatient audience. His approach to explaining the itemized revenues and expenses on a balance sheet was akin to describing a recipe: a pinch of this ingredient, a dash of that one, mixed together in a bowl, baked for a predetermined period of time and the result was a savoury net loss. In spite of Sholem's obvious wealth, Jerome always found a way of declaring a net loss at the end of the fiscal year so his client could avoid paying income tax.

Sholem was appreciative and considered Jerome a dear friend. He and his wife were invited to all the family *simchahs*, bar mitzvahs, weddings and *brisses*. Jerome had worked for Sholem right from the very beginning. He had been the midwife for every real estate transaction Sholem had ever delivered. It would not be an exaggeration to call him Sholem's trusted confidante. No one knew the intimate details of Sholem's business dealings like Jerome.

Seated at a mahogany conference table, solemn-faced Jerome began the meeting with papers propped up firmly on his fingertips. He explained that given Sholem's current debilitated state, it was advisable that his sons be made aware of their father's assets and the details of his arrangements. In the event, God forbid, that their father was incapable of managing his own affairs, the boys would have to take over. The first document he presented was a Power of Attorney, not yet signed by Sholem, naming Chaim, Gershon and Jerome as jointly possessing authority over bank accounts and matters of corporate decision-making.

Giving them equal power under the circumstances didn't surprise Gershon. As the architect of Sholem's financial edifice, Jerome would be heavily relied upon for his knowledge and advice. For their part, the two sons could ensure that the interest of the family remained paramount. Not that there was any question of Jerome's honesty and integrity. But he was not, strictly-speaking, family.

It was the next document presented by Jerome that upset Gershon— Sholem's Last Will and Testament. After some formal introductory remarks written in an impersonal legalese which made Gershon feel uncomfortable because it didn't sound remotely like his father, Jerome read aloud: "The shares of 99 Chabanel Inc., a duly incorporated holding company which exclusively owns and operates the property situated at 99 Chabanel Street West, the whole being located in the city of Montreal, province of Quebec, I do hereby leave to my eldest son Chaim Stein."

Gershon waited, expecting to hear more. He looked at Chaim and then at Jerome who stared back over his reading-glasses, adding nothing.

"What did you say? I mean, what did *he* say?" Gershon asked Jerome, referring to his absent father. Chaim got up from his seat and moved around the table to look over Jerome's shoulder at the document.

"Pa left the shares in 99 to me," Chaim answered as his eyes scanned down the page, his voice shaky.

"No. No! There must be a mistake! I can't believe it!" Gershon said. Jerome handed the document to Gershon.

"How could he do this?" Gershon shot out at no one in particular, confirming with his own eyes what Jerome had read aloud, the paper bending between his palms like a tightened elastic. "Jerome, you knew about this? When was the Will last revised?"

"About nine months ago," Jerome answered.

"And you let him do this?" Gershon accused. "I was involved in the building at that time and Chaim had nothing to do with it? How could you allow him to do this?"

"Maybe he planned to change things eventually, but this is how the situation stands at the moment," Jerome said stoically.

"I had no idea," Chaim reassured his younger brother, as they made their way together out of the office.

"Honestly, Pa never mentioned anything to me about this." They waited side by side for the elevator. "I'm sure he was just waiting until you had taken full reins of the business, showed that you had it under control."

"You're not even married. You don't have kids. We're the ones who need the money. You have no idea what private school costs."

Being unmarried was a sore spot for Chaim and Gershon knew it.

"Marriage probably had nothing to do with his decision," Chaim retorted. "I have more business experience than you. Pa probably just wanted to be sure that everything was in solid hands after he was gone." The brothers entered the elevator. Gershon hit the lobby button. The doors slid together quietly.

"Are you saying I'm incapable of running the business? You think I'd piss it all away? As it is, I manage the building totally on my own."

"Look, we don't know what Pa was thinking. And right now he's in no position to tell us. The fact is I worked with him. I know the business. And now I run my own successful company. So maybe he thought I was better suited to take over."

"And leave me a salaried employee for the rest of my life? The rest of *your* life?"

"Gershon, I wouldn't keep it. I'd split the shares with you. It's only fair."

"Split the shares?" Gershon was outraged. "What do you mean, split the shares? Like you said, you've got your own business. The shares in 99 should be mine. That's fair. You have no right to them."

"I've got my own business because I worked hard and risked a lot to start one." Gershon comprehended that this remark was Chaim's retaliation for his shot about not being married.

"Why should I work for your benefit?" Gershon hit back.

"Pa started the business to support the whole family, not just yours. It belongs to all of us," Chaim said.

"Not anymore." Gershon stomped away, crossing the office building's cold, marble lobby. Revolving glass doors spit him out onto the cloudy street.

"It's not just the *eruv*. They've also started ticketing parked cars, knowing full well we can't move them from one side of the street to the other on *Shabbos*. This is part of an organized campaign."

"They hate to see our children playing in the streets. They think we're taking over. How can they resent our children? What kind of people resent children? Can we help it if they choose not to have them?"

"We should be their worst problem. No, instead let them have dead-beat alcoholic neighbours, welfare cases who peddle drugs, vandalize property and commit crimes."

"We need to run candidates in the next municipal election. Vote them in. It's the only way to stop the harassment."

"What's next? I'll tell you. Kristallnacht. Quebec-style."

Gershon had no desire to participate in the debate. He sat back and listened sceptically. Grynzpan always had something meaty on his plate to complain about. For Heller, griping was a favourite pastime, second only to learning *Taharot*, the impenetrably complicated Talmudic laws associated with ritual purification. And Rosenberg, a senior member of the study-hall, took advantage of his stature by exaggerating. No one responded to his doomsaying and morbid predictions. They were silently respectful. Everyone acknowledged that Rosenberg had seen too much in his lifetime to be challenged.

In *kollel*, it didn't matter what they argued about. Rather, everything mattered equally, whether current politics or Talmudic commentary. The thrill in their voices was palpable. Gershon listened to the joyful swirl of arguing for the sheer sake of argument. This was the music of the place. The lively banter of dissonant voices. A backdrop refreshingly antithetical to the sleepy piped-in Muzak heard throughout shopping malls, in office waiting rooms and on automated phone systems.

It wasn't as if decisions rendered in *kollel* had tangible consequences. Decrees were not being handed down, legislation was not enacted, punishments not imposed. In fact, the arguments were never-ending, which was part of the attraction. The rabbis of the Talmud admitted as much when they couldn't make heads or tails of Divine law. They wrote *TÉKU*, an acronym meaning the difficulties will be settled only with the arrival of Elijah The Prophet, whose presence heralds the onset of the Messianic era.

Nonetheless, in *kollel* pros and cons were volleyed back and forth with the fury of a championship tennis match. They fought over every point like it was their last. Gershon realized that this was the essence of the reason he came night after night. He basked in the aura of seriousness, the urgency of sudden-death overtime. Every man who came to the *kollel* did so out of a sense that the debate mattered, regardless of the outcome. Not that there was a great prize to be won or that lives actually depended on it. Even more. Souls depended on it.

In Outremont, where the Steins lived among approximately four thousand other observant Jews from various sects, the erection of a new *eruv* was the source of a major controversy.

An *eruv* is an unbroken boundary which encircles a Jewish community. Montreal had several of them in quarters where sizeable numbers of Jews resided, namely Hampstead, Côte St. Luc and St. Laurent. There was even an *eruv* in the west-island suburb of Dollard des Ormeaux where upwardly mobile Jews had settled in large numbers.

Eruvs were created using existing permanent physical structures like telephone poles, utility poles, fences and buildings. These were connected by strung-up fishing line or wire at least twelve to fifteen feet above the ground in order to avoid obstructing pedestrian and automotive traffic. So fragile were these connections they had to be checked regularly by religious authorities to ensure wind or rain had not dislodged sections from their moorings. An *eruv* was a continuation. Like electrical circuitry, it did not work if there were gaps.

Living within the imaginary walls of an *eruv* allowed observant Jews to carry objects in public on the Sabbath. Outside the *eruv* borders, Jews faced many difficulties. Mothers walking to synagogue were not permitted to push strollers, or even lift their crying toddlers to comfort them. Fathers wanting to take invalid family members to worship were unable to push wheelchairs. The front doors of houses had to be left unlocked because keys could not be pocketed. Prayer books were not to be carried from home and reading glasses had to be worn.

Typically, the only public indication that the territorial limit of an *eruv* had been crossed was a small sign placed on a residential lawn next to the sidewalk and written in Hebrew saying, *Soph Eruv,* "Eruv Ends." In this respect, one might think of an *eruv* as similar to the lines on maps dividing districts and provinces, unseen yet understood. Or the unguarded frontier separating Canada from its powerful neighbour to the south, which in many locations across the country was indicated solely by a sign announcing "You Are Now Entering the United States of America. Please Report to a Border Crossing." *Eruvs* were a frame of mind.

The new Outremont *eruv* was supposed to run along Côte Ste. Catherine Road, Ducharme, Pratt and Hutchison streets. But an application made by local religious officials to obtain the needed permits from the city council had been refused on the grounds that provincial law did not give municipalities the power to authorize the use of public space for religious purposes. The city's half-Jewish mayor stated publicly, "We cannot exceed the powers provided for by law. Our decision was based on a straightforward objective legal analysis." Most Jews understood and put great stock in a so-called "straightforward objective legal analysis."

Other Jewish representatives charged discrimination, claiming the mayor and city council were caving in to complaints made by non-Jewish residents annoyed at the growing presence of religious Jews in their midst. When the issue was debated at council, fifty opponents of the *eruv* were present. One councillor, spearheading the movement against the request, said it was objectionable on the grounds that the Jews were trying to impose religion on the rest of the community. "We live in a multicultural society," she argued. "No single group should be allowed to claim public space as its own. They make me feel like a stranger in my own home."

The entire Jewish community was buzzing about the *eruv* controversy. With the imminent arrival of the High Holy Days, Gershon's *kollel* was frantic with opinion, interpretation and analysis. So adamant and forceful were the participants, they might have been fighting over the thickness of fortress walls.

Gershon's study partner Joshua Gutman said, "It's fine when they want to put up a brightly lighted Christmas tree in front of City Hall, but God forbid we should have our practically invisible boundary. This is nothing but intolerance. You know, there's no separation of religion and state in Canada." Gutman made his living as a lawyer. He was a *Ba'al Teshuvah*, a Jew who had been raised in a non-observant family but had returned to religion.

"In fact," he added, twisting his elbows like he was popping a celebratory cork out of a wine bottle, "do you know what it says in the Canadian Charter of Rights and Freedoms? The very first line says that Canada is founded on principles that recognize the supremacy of God! Who says we don't live in a theocracy!"

Ruhama had mentioned the *eruv* controversy to Gershon. She said it was a shame. She thought about the logistics of Holy Day observance and the inconveniences confronting her in the absence of an *eruv*. Ruhama didn't talk about the political ramifications that preoccupied the men: the purported insult to the community, how it represented discrimination or was an expression of anti-Semitism. Ruhama had seen a map of the new *eruv* in a community newspaper and remarked that the proposed circuit would have made a nice, brisk walk for regular exercise.

Gershon knew from his experience in 99 all the different types of walls. There was wood, plaster, Gyproc. There was brick and steel-reinforced concrete. Each had its advantages and disadvantages. Some were protective firewalls required by municipal regulation. These were erected between neighbours. Others were flimsy, not extremely durable. Interior office walls, for example, were built in a flash and could be torn down just as fast.

Gershon decided that the *eruv* walls were like so many structures that defined a person's life, imposed and self-imposed limitations of sentiment and behaviour. Barriers of the mind and heart that blocked views, stopping hands on one side from reaching across to hands on the other. But such walls also bounded communities to their kin, families to their brethren and individuals to their sense of meaning and purpose. The principle task of every person was to build their own *eruv*.

Every battle, whether won or lost, resulted in the erection of walls. Sholem had known the unscalable walls of the death camp. Vast sections interrupted by guard-posts, peaked towers patrolled twenty-four hours a day by guards who surveyed the grounds and kept everything orderly. Maybe this was a legacy Sholem was trying to transcend with his zealous entrepreneurial ventures in property development after the war. He was building his own walls with dimensions of his own choosing.

Gershon could also understand that for some, personal boundaries were expansive. They included immediate family, extended family, the local community, and communities oceans away, even communities of the living and of the dead.

Gershon felt as if the boundaries of his life were shifting. There was the wall with Sholem; he measured it daily like a prisoner pacing the courtyard, obsessively searching for a soft place in the earth to tunnel under or an unguarded spot to leap over.

What if the wall between him and Michelle Labelle came down? What would he discover about her? The more dangerous question was what would he learn about himself? That he was capable of thoughts and feelings and perhaps even acts which were out of bounds, off limits? Maybe it was not her light that had drawn him to her. Perhaps it was a desire to test the boundaries of his own soul.

Gershon decided that the soul was expansive. Its nature was to grow. He imagined that the soul was part of God's vast spiritual ecosystem connecting all living things together, spreading shapelessly like water over the landscape to permeate and nourish the world. It revitalized by bringing life-giving energies to low points, finding every available opening and penetrating every vacancy of cracked, parched soil. Without the procreative energy of the soul, Gershon was certain that the world would wither and die as surely as the grape starved of sunlight and rain shrivelled on the vine.

When a man and woman desired each other, it was an expression of two souls, two forces wishing to join. Gershon surmised that they could just as easily and with equal force repel each other. The trick was to harness the power, control and contain it. The primordial, soulful yearning of two people could be moulded by obligation and devotion into something meaningful and enduring. They created an exquisite container of genuine love. This was what he had with Ruhama. The very thing that they had laboured together for years to shape and upkeep. Their marriage, the trust and expectation they established together, the hope and disappointment they had risked, the family they had created, was their exquisite chalice. It was something to celebrate, like the wine-filled goblet he raised in the air every Friday night with his family surrounding him as blessings to the Almighty were said in gratitude.

Gershon thought of Chaim. What Chaim had said about Ruhama and the kids temporarily displaced the resentment Gershon had been feeling since the meeting with Jerome. Gershon rarely felt sorry for Chaim. He realized that he was more comfortable feeling jealous of him. It was more normal. He had been envious of his older brother many times.

The first time, he remembered, concerned a beard. Gershon took after his mother. His hair was fair and thin. Chaim possessed their father's dark, mature features. His cheeks and chin effortlessly sprouted hair. At his bar mitzvah, Chaim had already begun to grow a respectable beard which he sported with pride. Gershon fixated on Chaim when his brother sat learning at his desk, rocking back and forth and stroking the sides of his face. He envied the way Chaim, lost in thought, could run his fingernails along the angle of his jowls and massage the strands that hugged the bulb of his chin. Gershon imagined that this hairiness gave Chaim increased powers of concentration, made him smarter and more studious.

Acknowledging his younger brother's predicament, Chaim counselled Gershon to start shaving. It would toughen the follicles. It would get the hair to push up faster, with more vigour. So Gershon scraped up some money and ran out to buy an electric razor, the Norelco rotary model permitted by Jewish law because it did not pull the hair out when it cut, but sliced it off at the surface.

For weeks he shaved every day except on *Shabbat*, sometimes twice and three times a day. His skin became blotchy and raw. His face exploded with acne. He shaved until the blades became clogged with dry bloody puss, the electric motor sputtered and it was too painful for him to continue. The razor had done its ruthless groundwork, tilling his skin like soil. Left to heal, and with a little extra patience, a sparse, scraggly crop eventually appeared. Every morning, after thanking God for making him a man, Gershon added an extra blessing, a prayer of gratitude for His gift of hair.

Sitting in *kollel*, listening to the *eruv* debate and soaking in the camaraderie of men, Gershon was at peace with himself. *Kollel* was the only place Gershon felt completely at ease these days. He had choices in *kollel*. He could choose to join in with the general buzz of discussion, or learn texts with a study partner. If he wanted, Gershon could sit alone with a book opened up on the wooden desk in front of him and let his mind wander outside the boundaries of Torah texts.

It hit Gershon that a mind did not always need to parse concepts. Sometimes, though in his case he realized it didn't happen often, a mind could free itself from the rigours of reasoning and simply meander along an indeterminate path. A mind could break from its gates like a horse. With the comforting buzz of debate in the background, Gershon's daydreaming, or perhaps it was the unhindered wandering of his soul, sounded like this: *There was the light of God and from Him came the light of Creation and the light of God was the pure light of holiness and the light*

of Creation which came from the light of holiness was a white light com-
prising all colours and all souls and the light of souls was white light which
was separated through the prism of the world into different colours and
every colour had a unique quality and there was the colour of anguish and
the colour of disappointment and the colour of love and the colour of pain
and the colour of hatred and the colour of joy and the colour of suffering
and the colour of hope and the colour of despair and the colour of triumph
and the colour of survival which by itself was three or four colours mixed
together including the colour of memory and the colour of forgetting and
the colour of living and the colour of dying all of the colours mixed together
were the white light of God and all of them separated through the prism of
the world were the flickering coloured lights of humankind as it struggled
which could be separated and rejoined together two at a time making new
colours as primary colours were layered on top to make secondary colours
and tertiary colours just as Sholem was the colour of survival Masha was
the colour of anguish and they mixed together to make Chaim who was the
colour of determination and Gershon who was the colour of uncertainty
who mixed together with Ruhama who was the colour of faith who joined
with Gershon's colour to make Bayly who was the radiant colour of curiosity
and Shoshana who was the shimmering colour of innocence.

On his way home from *kollel*, cutting a solitary wake through the black
night of the outside world, Gershon felt refreshed. His eyes skipped along
the sidewalk. He thought about the game Bayly and Shoshana always
played when, holding Gershon's two hands at opposite sides, they marched
to synagogue on *Shabbat*. The girls chanted, "Step on a crack and break
your mother's back! Step on a line and break your father's spine!"

He remembered seeing Michelle Labelle's soul as a pale yellow glow,
the colour of loneliness. The object of souls was to join together, all the
colours, all the souls, crying out to one another seeking completion, a
unity of pure Divine white. He thought about the impossibility of
complete unity. What was possible was partial unity, if such a thing made
sense, but making sense did not seem to matter at the moment. With
the soles of his leather shoes scraping along the sidewalk, under the partial
light of streetlamps, it came to him that his main job, the one he had
temporarily lost sight of, was to guard and nourish the souls of his wife
and children. Their souls needed completion. And like the missing piece

of a jigsaw puzzle, only he could fill the gap. Obligation, as Chaim had said, was the glue that bonded the spirit.

Gershon's anger toward Chaim and Sholem for not leaving him the shares in 99, which were rightfully his, together with the cool night air, had brought him to his senses. He had to protect and fight for his own family, the one that did not include Chaim.

But could he confide in Ruhama? Should he? Gershon took strength from knowing how much Ruhama and the children relied on him. The certainty of it was one of the few things *he* could depend on. Yet, he wondered whether he would be capable of keeping the bad news about Sholem's Will to himself.

"Do you keep secrets from me, Ruhama?"

"Of course," Ruhama said, hoping to get a rise from Gershon.

"Good," Gershon said sharply.

"Why, good?"

"Secrets are needed," Gershon said. "They keep the world intact. There are certain things best kept hidden."

Ruhama was grateful that Gershon finally seemed to be opening up to her. She had observed that he generalized when he was trying to deal with personal pain.

"We have to learn to live with them," Gershon explained. "As difficult as it is to live in a world with secrets, living in a world without them would be intolerable."

"So, ignorance is bliss?" Ruhama tossed out, hoping he would tell her what was really bothering him.

"No, ignorance is the opposite. Ignorance is a form of wilful disengagement from the world, which is not blissful, it's hellish. I'm talking about respecting the secrets that exist at the core of everything and everybody, but at the same time not turning away. I'm talking about acceptance, bravely embracing those aspects of the world which can't be fathomed and shouldn't be tampered with. That's why the Almighty said to leave it alone, the tree in *Gan Aiden*. God wanted us to understand that the essence of life was faith, and faith was based on respect for the unknowable. Ignorance is a kind of arrogance, a way of turning away, dismissing outright the possibility that life is both meaningful and fundamentally unknowable."

"What about the secrets between a man and his wife?" Ruhama asked, trying to pull Gershon back down to earth.

Gershon resisted. "It wasn't shame that made Adam and Chava cover themselves. It was their way of putting their secrets back where they belonged."

"This afternoon Bayly asked me why they persecute K," Ruhama said.

"Persecute Kay? Who's Kay?"

"Not a person, the letter K, at the beginning of a word. They're learning to read words like knock and knee…"

"Know," Gershon interrupted.

"Yah. So she wanted to know why K isn't pronounced. She felt bad that it was being ignored," Ruhama grinned. "I think she was expressing the way she feels at home sometimes. She's feeling resentful toward Shoshana."

"What did you tell her? About ignoring K."

"I said it's not being ignored. We know it's there. I told her that sometimes we know something is there even though it's hidden. The way we read the Name of God with our eyes on the page, but we don't say it out loud. Like a special secret we know but keep to ourselves."

"Like having faith," Gershon said. "God is like the K at the beginning."

"Listen. If you want to stop having children, Gershon, you'll have to get a *heter* from the *Rav*."

"Who said anything about stopping to have children?"

"You've been distant lately. I thought there was a problem. Some people have those kinds of problems. I can accept it. Just go see the *Rav*."

Ruhama knew that some families in the community were having fewer children, though she couldn't name a single one that had only two. The families that had fewer than five were the ones who couldn't handle the pace, the stress and money issues they faced in daily life. She also knew that speaking with the rabbi frequently had a soothing effect. He discussed problems with couples in need of advice. He didn't only give them permission to stop having more children, he also offered them perspective and encouragement to continue. She thought that if Gershon went to see the *Rav*, there was a chance he might be convinced to change his mind.

"I never said anything about not having more children. I don't need to see the *Rav*. Why would you think that? What did I say?"

"You said it by not saying anything."

"Like the silent K," Gershon said, smiling at his wife. "You know how I am, Ruhama. I get a bit off track, preoccupied. Your job is to straighten me out. I never thought you had so little faith in me."

"I have faith in you, Gershon," Ruhama said softly.

"Me too. I won't disappoint you. Just have a little faith in me, okay. I need it."

"I know."

There were small faiths a person had to maintain. The trust a person had in other people to deliver on their promises, or to keep their word, or to hold up their end of the bargain, was a separate matter altogether. Trust was a temporary bond between people, it was what a person needed to have when they went into an airplane, or got behind the wheel of a car hoping to arrive safely at their desired destination. All the little trusts didn't add up to anything substantial. As he spoke to Ruhama, Gershon was thinking about a deep underlying faith, a foundation of unspoken meaning that affirmed and supported the love they shared. What he maintained with Ruhama was faith. When people maintained faith, it was big time. It was larger than life, a soaring mountain, a Mount Sinai where God could come down and deliver the purpose and significance of the world. This was what Gershon had in mind when he asked Ruhama to have faith in him. It was also what he meant when he said, "I need it."

Ruhama understood immediately without him having to explain it any further.

"Okay, we're talking in circles. You're hiding something. I can feel it. There's a secret you're itching to reveal," Ruhama prodded.

He looked at his wife seriously and said, "Someone's been stealing electricity from Joey Putkin and I don't know how much to tell him."

Ever since the onset of Sholem's illness one thing became apparent to Gershon: 99 was a nicer place. On his collection rounds, or touring the building to show vacant spaces to prospective customers, tenants no longer ducked behind corners or slipped into their offices to avoid him. Now they opened their doors and made detours to greet him, just the way they used to with Sholem. They asked about his father's health.

Gershon could tell from their voices and facial expressions they were genuinely concerned.

People had been nice before; it was an epidemic in places of business. Smiles, handshakes, jokes and friendly inane conversation were exchanged like a virus that burrowed deep in the cells, hidden from view along with ulterior motives. Sholem had taught Gershon by example when it was advantageous to be nice.

But *this* niceness spreading through 99 carried sympathy and compassion. Rent cheques arrived unattached to resentment. The regular waves of complaints subsided. Even Irving Roth, who at the best of times ignored Gershon, now approached him in the lobby and, with hand extended, asked how his father was doing. Gershon answered shortly "stable" and added "*Boruch Hashem*," knowing that under the unfortunate circumstances, Irving wouldn't retaliate with one of his patented curmudgeonly comments against religion. Gershon enjoyed the unusual treatment, though he felt slightly uneasy. He appeared to be profiting from his father's misfortune.

It was in this atmosphere—when Gershon was feeling, for perhaps the first time, like a real businessman in control of his enterprise, a captain at the helm of his own ship—that he came to a decision on how to handle the problem of Joey Putkin's electricity.

Repairs

GERSHON FOUND two hundred and fifty dollars steep for a simple electrical report. What did Krantz have to do? Spend a couple of minutes writing something up. A sentence or two. And sign the bottom. What did a little fiction cost anyway?

"What's the price of *your* reputation?" Krantz replied rhetorically. "You're asking me to put my name on the line. What if the truth came out. Word might get around and my respected professional name would be damaged forever." Krantz argued that Gershon was lucky he agreed to do it at all. Most electricians wouldn't. It really wasn't worth the risk but he was doing Gershon a big favour.

Gershon spoke boldly. "Let's put our cards on the table. You're not doing me any favours. You're going to do it on the chance that you'll get more work from me in the future. You know it and I know it. Work worth a lot more than two-fifty. And you know dealing with me is not like dealing with my father. I won't cut you down. At least, not after the fact."

Not only did Krantz agree to furnish the report, Gershon also managed to convince him to drop his price. He asked Alfreda to prepare a cheque for Krantz in the amount of one hundred and fifty dollars. As he watched her pen scribble numbers ending in zero, Gershon said under his breath, "the value of a reputation."

Handing the cheque to Krantz he said, "Start by cutting the line on the second floor and work down. The basement tenant must not be aware the work is being done. When you enter his premises to disconnect the line from his meter, if he asks, tell him you're doing a last-minute verification for your report."

Krantz stepped from the office with the cheque folded between his fingers, his *tzizes* bouncing around his waist. Gershon hoped he'd thought things through carefully enough to avoid an outcome he hadn't accounted for. Krantz was certainly the right man for the job. He was both a Lubavitcher and an outgoing, friendly person. Putkin was unlikely to question his integrity or be suspicious. Gershon hated to admit it, but he was thinking of religion as the perfect cover.

When the job was completed that afternoon, Krantz came to deliver his falsified report. Gershon made a copy for his files and handed the original to Alfreda. He asked her to put the paper back in Krantz's envelope and leave it in Putkin's mailbox downstairs. Let Putkin think that the report came directly from Krantz and Gershon hadn't intervened.

Gershon didn't want to be seen by Putkin. Not yet. He wanted the inevitable confrontation to be on his own terms. He needed time. Putkin specialized in ambush and Gershon didn't want to be caught off-guard. Let Putkin examine the report and then, in a day or two, he would go down to ask what the electrician had said.

In the interim, Gershon walked the halls of 99 cautiously, trying to steer clear of Putkin. Even an encounter with Joey's father, normally a pleasant experience, was fraught with hazard. When Gershon arrived at the office the following morning, Alfreda said that Putkin had called. He left a message that he wanted to see Gershon as soon as possible, signalling that the report had been received and studied. Gershon ignored the message. He didn't want to seem anxious. He liked the feeling of being in control.

If Putkin accepted the report at face value, Gershon decided he would demand immediate payment of all rental arrears. But probably he would reject the report. In that case, Gershon would challenge him to get his own electrician to confirm Krantz's findings and demand the money he was withholding in the meantime. Either way he resolved not to leave Putkin's presence without a cheque.

"Everything alright, Gyerry?" Niko was coming down the hallway toward the management office. Hearing Niko, Gershon stepped through the doorway into the corridor.

"Fine. So what brings you up to the sixth floor?" Gershon asked.

Niko held up the paper bag and styrofoam container he was carrying.

"My delivery man is sick today. The third time in two weeks. I have to get rid of him and find a new one. Too many late night binges. He's not interested in working, that guy. And speaking of being interested…" Niko shuffled his feet. He turned his head to see if the coast was clear and leaned closer to Gershon. "I thought it was Michelle Labelle you were interested in."

"What?"

"The girl you asked me about that time. The one in the elevator."

"I know who Michelle Labelle is," Gershon said, "but what are you talking about?"

"Don't worry, Gyerry. I know what it's about. I have experience too."

"Experience? What experience? What are you talking about?"

"Like french fries," Niko said, grinning. "Once you have one, you want more. I know," he said with a nod.

"But *what* do you know?" Gershon was becoming exasperated. He couldn't decipher Niko's meaning. His body language conferred intimacy, but why? What did Michelle Labelle have to do with wanting more french fries?

"It's okay," Niko said. "Just take my advice, be careful where you eat."

"Where I eat?"

"Maybe doing it here in the building is not such a good idea, Gyerry. Me, I never mix business with pleasure. Not a good recipe."

Business and pleasure? "Come to the point Niko," Gershon demanded, his exasperation changing to worry.

"Two rules. I don't do it with a regular customer. And never in the restaurant. It can become troublesome. Word spreads too fast. Anyway, the food is getting cold. I don't want to keep my customer waiting." Niko turned to leave.

"Wait!" Gershon clasped Niko by the forearm, immobilizing him. "Word about what? What have you heard?"

"Estella. StayMore Finishing," Niko confided. "You know, about *you* and *her*." He lengthened the words.

"What about me and Estella?" Gershon demanded in a panicked whisper.

"Don't worry, Gyerry. I understand. We all do it. Just take my advice. If you're not careful it can come back to hurt you." Niko shook his arm free of Gershon's grip and trotted down the hall.

Gershon's chest boomed and drops of sweat began forming on his forehead. He stared at the hand that had held Niko's arm. The curved fingers of his empty fist floated in mid-air. The image of mating insects came to his mind. Some insects copulated in mid-flight. They climbed on top and pounded one another, flapping their wings madly. Somehow, in the frenzy of passion, those bugs did it in the air and avoided crashing to the ground.

Estella had gone on the offensive by spreading rumours. Gershon felt violated. When they met he had treated Estella with respect, given her more time, and this was the gratitude she showed. He was being sucked down by the undertow. How was he going to stem the tide of gossip and innuendo? He was becoming one of them, no different than all the cheaters in the building he'd heard about.

Rumours about tenants cheating on their spouses proliferated in 99. It was an epidemic in the industry. Sometimes the pairings were haphazard and difficult to fathom. For instance, Gershon had heard that the head shipper from one company was sleeping with a secretary from another. The shipper was slovenly and dim-faced. The secretary he was reportedly having sex with was sweet and unassuming. Gershon surmised that, if it was true, the frequency of contact between them had been the critical ingredient of their affair. They were two people who had bumped into each other enough times in the restaurant, shared enough smiles in the elevator, or said enough friendly words passing one another in the hallway, to eventually create sparks. Under the right conditions, two stones that struck together enough times to spark ultimately produced a fire, which is why Gershon was careful not to engage his female tenants in inordinately long or overly personal conversations.

Most of the time, the rumours that spread through 99 involved buyers sleeping with manufacturers. These pairings seemed more probable to Gershon. The manufacturers courted the buyers, who, it was well known, bought merchandise from the manufacturers they liked personally. Kickbacks and payoffs, standard practice for decades, had been eliminated as the retail chains cracked down by rotating their buyers between departments and scrutinizing their accounts. Financial favours may have been in decline but sexual favours were not. The manufacturers used all the means at their disposal to woo buyers. Flirtation and charm were effective means of building relationships. They were also low cost. It was not a huge leap from wooing buyers with charm and flirtation to outright debauchery. Anything to keep the customer satisfied, and adding thousands more garments to their orders.

Now, as far as anyone knew, it seemed Gershon was one of them. No different than the head shipper and the secretary, or the buyers and their sales studs. He had to extricate himself from this den of iniquity. Flee. Gershon would do just about anything to block out the thought of his name being paired with Estella Mora in conversations taking place all around the building.

He decided to leave 99 and visit Sholem in the hospital. "To offer support," he told Alfreda as he rushed out of the management office.

At the front entrance of the Jewish General Hospital, Gershon admitted to himself that he had no idea what supporting his father entailed. Pressing the heavy glass doors open, he fought the certainty that whatever it meant, he was ill-equipped for the task.

He passed doctors and nurses in the hallway and noted that the two classes of workers were distinguished by their costumes. Doctors on their rounds, male and female alike, wore long white lab coats. The colour and garb indicated a neutrality of gender, and the stature associated with science. The nurses were dressed in green or blue cotton pants and shirts. It was clear from their garments that they did the dirty work, while the doctors gave instructions.

The doctors had plasticized security passes pinned to their lab coats, with their names printed in bold letters and written backwards underneath photos. Dr. MASUL, Darius. Dr. COHEN, Heidi. Dr. MERCER, William. Dr. SHUSTER, Arnold. Dr. GUPTA, Ravindran.

Gershon matched the faces on the lapels with the ones perched between their shoulders. He was surprised that often the pairs looked dissimilar, like two different faces from the same family, brothers or sisters, or first cousins. The ID portraits were frequently more youthful than the persons they claimed to identify. One bald doctor with a bushy grey mustache, Dr. THOMAS, Francis, carried on his chest the image of a much younger man sporting a full head of thick black hair. Dr. MADDEN, Victoria, had short, brittle, dyed blond hair and her puffy face was pasty with makeup, although a smooth-faced woman with sharp features framed by long flowing golden hair appeared on the laminated photo pinned over her heart. Every person was two-faced. The image in the photo smiled and appeared hopeful, while the real-life face looked grim, strained and in a terrible rush. This is a place of former selves, thought Gershon. And not just for the patients in their beds who lay there idly recalling previous vigour.

Gershon paused in front of the nursing station on Sholem's floor. A group of nurses and doctors was behind the counter joking and chatting. The nurses held shot-glass-sized plastic cups of pink liquids in their hands. They smiled coquettishly, batting their eyelashes. At least that's how they looked to Gershon. They waved file folders in front of their faces like coloured fans. The nurses looked sexy, he supposed, in their one-piece green work outfits. In contrast, the doctors looked mystical in their lab coats. They uttered long ancient Latin phrases that might have been spells or charms. Stethoscopes were curled around their necks like trained poisonous black adders. Even here, thought Gershon, in a place where there was suffering and pain, the men and women flirted with each other. Then it occurred to Gershon that perhaps they flirted not in spite of all the pain and suffering they confronted daily, but because of it.

Sholem's room was hushed and smelled harshly of ammonia. It immediately reminded Gershon of one his mother's rituals. Every spring she poured capfuls of some corrosive noxious liquid down the kitchen drain even though it wasn't blocked. She said it was necessary to rid the pipes of bad spirits. Gershon associated the stench of ammonia with springtime.

Sholem's eyes were closed but he was not sleeping. He opened them as soon as Gershon entered his room.

On earlier visits, conversation was at a minimum. Not that Sholem was unable, but speech exhausted him. He preferred pointing to a pitcher of water and cup to indicate that his mouth was dry. Gershon obliged, asking Sholem if he was comfortable and if there was anything else he could do, not really expecting an answer. Maybe his father needed his body repositioned, his pillows fluffed and shifted, or maybe he wanted something to read, a book of *Tehillim*, Psalms, brought from home. Sholem didn't want to read.

In fact, Gershon had always been uneasy around his father and now he sensed this more acutely. A vortex of discomfort spun silently around them with Gershon draining down the centre of it. The only way to save himself was to fill the void with his voice. This time there was too much on his mind. Gershon knew he could speak freely now without fear of reprimand. Sholem was a captive audience.

Gershon told Sholem about Joey Putkin's electrical problem. He took pride in telling his father how he dealt with the situation, explaining in detail his plan. Sholem listened blankly. Periodically, he closed his eyes and reopened them without expression.

Finally, Sholem said, "You fix it."

"Pa, I did. The job's been done. Putkin's already read Krantz's fake report."

Sholem raised his good hand slowly to Gershon, pointing. "Tell da trooos," he slurred.

"Tell what?"

"Da trooos," Sholem breathed out.

Blood rushed to Gershon's face. "The truth? What do you mean tell the truth? It'll cost us a fortune. He's claiming we owe him thousands of dollars. You know we'll never get it back."

Sholem didn't answer. He rested his eyes.

"This way, at least we have a chance. Maybe he won't find out."

Sholem opened his eyes. "Not styoopid. You pay," he whispered.

What is he talking about? Gershon asked himself. He paced the room. It must be the medication. He's not thinking straight. Gershon saw how even this brief exchange between them had tired his father out. But Gershon needed to talk more. He approached the bed, leaned close, gripping the cold metallic bars.

"Pa, it's okay. Don't open your eyes. Don't answer. I'll take care of everything. Don't worry. I know about the shares in the building. Your holding company. I know about the Will. It's okay." Gershon paused to catch his breath. Then a thought came to him.

"Pa. I was thinking. When you get out of here, when you come back to work, we'll find a minyan in the building. For *Minhah*. You'll have a place to *daven* in 99. You won't have to go down the street to the minyan at Chabad for the afternoon prayer service."

Chaim entered the room. He looked at Gershon standing by the bed, leaning next to their father's ear.

"Is he alright?" Chaim asked, approaching the bed.

"The same. No change," Gershon said, taking a step back.

Hearing Chaim's voice, Sholem opened his eyes.

"I was thinking," Gershon said to Chaim. "Talking with Pa, I was thinking that we could have a minyan at 99. When he gets better, we can find ten men to *daven Minhah* so he doesn't have to go down the street for the afternoon prayers."

"It's a good idea," Chaim said, looking at their father. He raised his face to Gershon. "That is, if you can find ten men in the building who would pray."

"You'll come, Chaim, won't you?"

"Yah."

"So with me, you and Pa we have three," Gershon said.

"It looks like Pa will be here for a while. You'll need every minute to find the other seven," Chaim said.

Traffic along the Metropolitan Autoroute was heavy on the drive back to 99. The car jolted forward, slowed, stopped and rolled forward again in concert with a long line of vehicles slithering spasmodically across the city. We're all dependent on one another, thought Gershon. The car in front relied on the car in the rear-view mirror to heed the flow, antici- pate subtle movements, read accurately the decisions of other drivers. Complete strangers. An unexpected lane change, a lapse in concentration or judgement by any single person could spell tragedy for many.

Hulking eighteen-wheel trucks loaded with products were paired next to schoolbuses filled with wild, noisy children banging at the windows. Mothers with shopping bags in minivans advanced shoulder to shoulder with carpenters, probably hardworking fathers, in flatbed pickups, ladders sticking out the rear with red scarves hanging off the end. Couriers in inexpensive compact models trailed salesmen in souped- up sportscars, who chased bosses in their gas-guzzling luxury vehicles. Gershon was pleased to participate in this widespread profusion of trust. If complete strangers were trustworthy enough to advance along the highway in an orderly fashion, was it so crazy to trust a few tenants in the building to help him form a quorum for prayer?

At the office, Gershon sat at his desk and made a list on a sheet of white paper. Sholem, Chaim, Gershon, Shimmy Solomon, Sonny Lipsey, Arnie Free, Joey Putkin, Avi Putkin, Charlie Roth, Hyman Roth, Irving

Roth. Eleven. He paused to let his mind roam through the building. He continued. Sid Markovitch (Chairman Mao), Stanley Sarna (Stalin), Larry Superstein (Superman), Lenny Luterman (Lex Luther), Yossi Alfasi. Sixteen. Is that all there were? Probably there were others, but Gershon couldn't think of any. Shimmy Solomon's company was large enough to have several male employees who were Jewish. The Roths too. Rosie K was ineligible, but Gershon thought of him anyway. He knew Rosie would have felt honoured to be asked and was someone who could be depended upon to join in, unlike many of the other genuine Jews-by-birth on his hit list.

All in all the group held little promise. They were a sorry lot. Gershon began crossing off names. Those who were unlikely to consent. As he did this, two thoughts came to his mind. First, he looked over to the other list waiting on his desk, the receivables, tenants who owed money. Like the minyan list, the receivables told Gershon how much work he had ahead of him. But there was a distinct difference. He wanted the minyan list to be as long as possible. A long receivables list told him he was not doing his job properly. Striking names off the receivables was a sign he was succeeding. Rents were being collected. The bank account was filling up. As he drew his pen across names on the minyan list, another account was emptying. A sign he was failing.

The second thought that came to Gershon was not really a thought but an image. He saw Sholem, sitting at his desk, a supplier's invoice on the table in front of him, a red pen poised between his fingers. Gershon thought about how Sholem decided whose price to pay and whose to renegotiate. Would the minyan list require such bargaining? If he went to Shimmy Solomon or Arnie Free or Sonny Lipsey, would they expect favours in return for participating in the daily minyan? If so, what kind of prayer quorum was that?

One by one, names came off the minyan list. Shimmy and his crew were dashed without further consideration. As were Joey Putkin, the Dolphin Brothers, Superman and Lex Luther. Avi Putkin was a maybe. Arnie Free and Sonny Lipsey too. Arnie might do it because he did business with religious Jews. He might consider it bad luck to refuse. Sonny had a soft heart. He might accept the invitation out of sympathy. Either way both Arnie and Sonny, if they agreed to participate, were not likely to make a habit of it.

Gershon was left with Yossi Alfasi alone. As a Sephardi, Yossi could be relied upon to join in. Moroccan Jews were known to be mystical types. They had a reputation for being both unfettered by ethics in their business practices and equally unambiguous when it came to religion. Many of them saw no contradiction in eating *traif* and, with the taste of unkosher food still on their lips, kissing the ubiquitous pictures of a revered sage kept in their wallets like cherished family snapshots.

Yossi, on the other hand, was more consistent. A few years earlier he had gone through a spiritual transformation. He had rediscovered his family roots which could be traced back several centuries to the great Alfasi line of rabbis from the Golden Age of Spain. He abandoned the fast, reckless, freewheeling life of a Garmento and made the decision to become observant. His business was downsized so that it would not overly impinge on his time for learning Torah. He attended *kollel* in the evenings and his home library of *seforim* grew. Several volumes were brought to work each day and Yossi delved into texts between serving customers at his store on the fourth floor. When Gershon passed his premises in the hallway, Yossi invited him in to ask questions concerning Jewish law, or to share a midrash, a homiletic insight into Torah. Yossi attended the daily minyan at Chabad. Gershon knew that providing him a place to pray at 99 would offer Yossi an appreciated convenience.

So that was it. From an initial list of sixteen only a total of four remained, including Gershon, Chaim and Sholem. The challenge ahead of Gershon was monumental. What if the six others could not be found? And in truth, six wasn't enough because backups were needed if one or two could not attend regularly. The prospects were not good. Gershon nonetheless refused to lapse into despair. He was on a mission. A sacred mission. There was no other way of looking at it.

The bathroom door slanted open on its hinges. A waft of shower steam escaped along the ceiling, dissipating to nothingness. Ruhama stepped carefully onto the beige carpet, a yellow towel draped over the slope of her breasts. It hung loosely like a tent, flaps drawn tightly across her belly down to her knees. A second towel, twisted and rolled, sat on top of her head like a melted gold crown. Gershon sat stiffly in his street clothes on the edge of the bed.

Rather than proceed with her nightly routine of smothering her skin in scented powders, perfumed creams and moisturizers, Ruhama stood in front of Gershon. She said nothing. When she moved even closer to him, Gershon pushed her away.

"I want you to undress for me," he whispered, removing the *kippa* from his head and putting it in the pocket of his trousers. Gershon leaned over to click off the room light.

Ruhama hesitated, her eyes adjusting to the darkness. She took three steps across the room along the edge of the bed and paused. The toes of her right foot dipped into a dimple in the carpet left by the wheel of her bed, after it had been shifted back from its former location along the opposite wall. She didn't know what to make of Gershon's attitude, his desire to have her showcase herself. Her impulse was to resist.

In the past, their lovemaking had always been done in silence. Gershon had never told her what to do and when to do it. He had never said what he liked or desired. Ruhama had the curious feeling that she was being tested. Was it some kind of erotic fantasy he was playing out? Gershon had told Ruhama that managing a building in the fashion district was one step above working in the sex trade. Part of the reason she kept Gershon on such a short leash was that she felt he had to be protected. Was his behaviour now a result of influences he'd picked up from years of working at 99? She could not deny that their sex life was mechanical and that she'd been bored by it. What would happen if she went along? What if, instead of a clash of wills, she allowed Gershon his way and their love-making was like play-acting? Maybe it would add something fresh to the experience. A new dimension. If behaving like a different person was going to help Gershon get into the mood, she would oblige by meeting him halfway.

Gershon waited, sitting on the side of the bed. The carpet transformed before his eyes. Watery moonlight streamed in from the high window, bathing the floor in a translucent liquid blue. Ruhama, gone for an instant, floated back into view. She opened the towel around her waist from the centre, extending edges of fabric out like wings.

"Not too fast," he whispered.

Ruhama refolded the towel and tucked the corners inside the envelope of her cleavage. Turning her back to Gershon, she raised her arms up and held the peak of her turban. She kept the position, feeling the towel around her middle loosen slightly.

Gershon's fingers rose up and caressed the underside of her arms. She breathed in, arching her back. His fingers trickled down, in and out of the smooth troughs of her underarms, along the V of her back, bumping into the towel's edge and dropping off the sides. He touched her again and again. Ruhama's skin shuddered. Less and less with each pass of his hands. She closed her eyes. Her face felt warm. I am a candle, she thought. I am soft as wax.

Gershon's hands moved up through the covered dampness of her hair, catching tangles. The heat of his fingers tingled against her scalp. She let him untie the head-wrapping from underneath. The towel unknotted and fell to the floor.

She turned to face him, feeling released. Gershon stroked the sides of her temples, probed the clefts of her ears, skimmed her earlobes, his palms cupping the angle of her chin. Her spine slackened and with eyes sealed shut, Ruhama bowed her head as if in a moment of supplication.

He raised himself off the mattress and kissed her lips. He kissed her cheeks. Her nose. Her eyelids. As his lips travelled up and down the surface of her face, his beard alternately tickled and scratched. Before, these sensations would have been intolerable to Ruhama, prompting her to slide backward and clamp Gershon's head steady between her hands. In a gesture meant to be misconstrued as affection, she would have pressed her lips against his, positioning his beard safely away.

Now she allowed her husband the freedom to explore with his mouth, feeling a wet trail under the ledge of her chin and further down, circling the scroll of her neck, along the protrusions of her collarbones. Gershon's hands came up the back of Ruhama's legs. His fingernails pressed along the horizontal crease where thigh met buttocks, back and forth, squeezing, kissing her lips, and up further, under the towel, to the hardness of her hips and down again. The towel loosened and cascaded to the floor. At that very same moment, Ruhama felt a thin barrier, like an invisible membrane that had existed between them, drop too.

Gershon gathered her fingers, her hands, her legs, all the parts of her body up in his arms. He placed her on the bed and knelt over her. His hands slipped behind her shoulders. Gershon's lips pressed gently against Ruhama's nipples, as if they were made of glass. Apprehension, if there had been any left within Ruhama, was now completely gone. She felt drained, weightless, utterly absorbed. Her flesh coursed with energies. She abandoned herself. She abandoned anything she might have known about herself or Gershon or the world. Lying back, she saw through the slits of her eyes a blur of disembodied limbs as they hovered above her. They moved back and forth, luminous arms and legs, his enmeshed in hers, slicing the darkness. And she sensed that her body was merging with his like a diaphanous layering of light.

The next day, Gershon marched into the reception area of Putkin Leather Designs Inc. He had decided on a surprise attack. He arrived at the basement office unannounced, believing his strategy would give him the edge he needed to walk away with money.

The receptionist was talking on the phone. Before Gershon could demand to see Joey, she smiled and waved an envelope under his nose like a small white flag.

"Joey left this for you," she whispered aside, blocking the mouthpiece.

Gershon took the envelope without reply. It was thin. A cheque.

Normally, when Gershon received such envelopes he would slip them into the inside pocket of his black jacket, say thank you and leave. It was protocol. A way of maintaining confidence between tenant and landlord, abiding mutual expectations. To open the envelope in front of the tenant was an insult. Like screaming "I don't trust you," in his face.

Gershon did not hesitate. He was emboldened by the fact that Putkin was not presently standing in front of him, and he smelled a rat. Why had Putkin left the cheque at the reception? The message was clear. He was avoiding Gershon, cowering behind his secretary. There had to be a reason. He tore into the envelope.

The amount stamped in blue ink across the face of the cheque was several thousand dollars off the mark. Gershon lost his composure.

"I will not accept this!" he screamed to the receptionist, eyes nailing her to the chair. "This is not acceptable. It won't be tolerated!"

She pushed the hold button, and cradled the receiver. "It's what he left with me," she said innocently.

Gershon looked at the signature on the cheque. The low, cavernous loop of Joey Putkin's "J", the empty chamber of his "P", the jagged heartbeats of "ut" and the unfinished flatline letters of "kin."

Since there was no one to talk to, Gershon negotiated with himself, deciding on his next move. Putkin was clever. He must have known it would be difficult for Gershon to relinquish a payment, even one substantially less than expected. At least he had gotten something, and Sholem had always taught his son never to refuse money.

Gershon also came face to face with his resolution to himself not to leave the premises without money. If he shredded the cheque in a display of outrage, the dramatics would be wasted on the receptionist. Putkin had backed Gershon into a corner, pulled the carpet out from under him and stolen his advantage, again. He turned and walked out, leaving the ripped envelope on the front desk.

Upstairs, Gershon stormed into the management office. Slapping Putkin's cheque down on the blotter in front of Alfreda, he said, "Call up the lawyer. It's time to initiate legal proceedings against StayMore Finishing. We're evicting Estella Mora."

Lease

IT WAS PLEASANT TO WATCH Alfreda dialing the telephone, her fingers springy, her voice gleeful. She was singing, composing a ditty, "StayMore stays less. The finishing company's finished." She chanted while waiting for the secretary on the other end of the line to answer. Alfreda appeared victorious, though Estella Mora's departure was a long way from a foregone conclusion. She was delighted to begin the process, and that was all that mattered at the moment. Gershon genuinely enjoyed watching her in this rare condition, and, as premature as it might have been to sing a victory song, he was determined not to say anything that might spoil the atmosphere.

Four. That was the number of tenants evicted from 99 in the time Gershon managed the building. Admittedly, "evicted" was not the right term. All four had left on their own. They had skipped out in the middle of the night. Packed up their machines and merchandise and under cover of darkness abandoned the building.

When a tenant abandoned their premises, it came to Gershon as a welcome relief. Typically, the prelude to skipping out was a painful, herky-jerky dance. The tenant would make earnest pleas for more time to pay, appeal to Gershon's sympathy and compassion. This would last for a few weeks. When it became apparent that payment was not forthcoming, the management would respond. They sent a registered letter. This could only mean one thing, legal action. Another few weeks would pass, followed by a series of bounced cheques from the tenant. Meanwhile, one month had moved quickly into the next and then the next, sucking more money down the drain.

Deadbeat tenants who stayed on were the worst. They were a double loss to the landlord. Not only did they neglect to pay, they added insult to injury by rendering the space unrentable to a new tenant who would. Tenants like Estella held their spaces hostage.

Sholem hated spending money on lawyers. The policy at 99 had always been to work with the tenants, which meant negotiating, getting as much owed rent as possible and then convincing the deadbeat that it was in his own interest to leave peacefully. Sholem had calculated that if a tenant owed five thousand in rent and fifty percent could be obtained by bargaining, the other twenty-five hundred was roughly equal to the cost of hiring a lawyer and pursuing the matter through the courts.

If a tenant refused to negotiate and also wouldn't leave, there was little choice but to go the costly legal route. After making a demand for payment on legal letterhead, giving a forty-eight hour deadline, the lawyer would formally petition the court to have the lease cancelled. In the best circumstance, the legal motion would go uncontested, a judgement would be handed down on the spot and the management could take possession of the premises by forced entry and changing locks.

As for the payment of rental arrears, they would generally be awarded to the landlord upon judgement, including a sum for damages, which might total as much as six months of future rent and court costs. Collecting the money was an altogether different matter. Deadbeat tenants usually didn't have money, or there were other creditors, like banks and the government, standing in line ahead of the landlord, so effecting a seizure of merchandise was a costly and dubious procedure. The most likely result was the tenant declaring bankruptcy, in which case, the landlord had wasted a lot of time and money for nothing.

Sholem had structured the leases at 99 solidly. Dozens of clauses, sprinkled over sixteen pages, protected the landlord against every imaginable eventuality. In addition to the standard indemnification against fires and floods, the management could not be held responsible for broken toilets, blocked pipes, disturbances of any kind, real or imagined, from co-tenants, damages caused by extreme cold, extreme heat, fog, wind, hail, rain, ice-pellets, snow, frost, smoke, power black-outs or Acts of God. The only unforeseen plagues missing from the list were infestations of frogs or locusts. The Pharaoh in Egypt could not have been better protected.

The document was intentionally lengthy and laborious, filled with long, impenetrably convoluted sentences. "The Lessee (tenant) does hereby agree to indemnify and save harmless the Lessor (landlord) from and against any and all liabilities, damages, suits and actions arising out of damage to the property of the Lessee (tenant), any breach of the Lease, any injury to any person or persons including death, and failure by the Lessee (tenant) to fully and faithfully comply with all legitimate requirements of any public or quasi-public body."

At the very end of the lease, below the space for a tenant's name signalling his complete and unreserved acceptance of everything contained herein, there was another place for a second signature under the phrase, "I hereby personally, jointly and severally guarantee the payment of rent under the terms and conditions of the present contract." The more savvy tenants refused to sign here, realizing it meant they were personally warrantying their company's debt. Those who signed, out of ignorance or laziness, were liable to have their personal assets seized by the landlord. The first question asked by the lawyer initiating a procedure was always whether or not the tenant had personally guaranteed the lease.

A personal warranty was leverage, but it hardly ever ensured payment. Quebec law stated that only household property exceeding six thousand dollars in value was seizable. Rented assets like cars and socked-away retirement savings were out of bounds. Also, the assets had to be personally owned (which meant that property under the name of other family members was untouchable). Hence, the businessman's first law: *Thou shalt not own anything personally. Make thy name scarce.* Gershon abided. His house was put under Ruhama's name. Their two cars, his Lexus and her Toyota minivan, were leased by the business.

Despite the fact she had initialed and signed everywhere required, Gershon was sure Estella Mora was a lost cause. He knew the costs of proceeding with legal action were prohibitive. She had no means of paying her rental debt. But rent was not the main reason he was setting lawyers on her. This was a special case. The cost of keeping Estella in the building was too high.

Watching Alfreda's glossy fingernails performing a supple tapdance on the telephone keypad made him lighthearted. Maybe the exorbitant price of lawyers was worth this sight, along with her bad puns and unmelodic rhymes. "Estella go to hella, get yourself another fella. Estella

Mora you're a bore-a, I'll show you the door-a, and then we'll do a hora."
Whore-a is the right word, Gershon said to himself.

Such times accentuated their friendship. Alfreda was one of the few
people Gershon felt was truly on his side. When she griped and criticized
he knew it was for his own good. When he struggled with a tenant, she
struggled along with him, offering frank comment, advice and technical
assistance. She spoke up and said what was on her mind, a personality
trait Gershon appreciated. Of course when Sholem was nearby, she was
silent, taking orders, responding with strict deference. But she would level with
Gershon. He could not imagine treating Alfreda like a regular employee.
He respected her experience too much, just as she respected Sholem's.

Gershon sometimes wondered about Alfreda's private life. He knew
precious little about it in spite of her many years of devotion to the
Stein family. Obviously she was careful not to let her personal life interfere
with her work. But this much he knew. She was married. Her husband
Sheldon sold wholesale men's and ladies' undergarments: socks, stock-
ings, briefs, bras and related items. They lived in Chomedey, a district of
Laval, part of a small Jewish enclave off the island of Montreal. She had
a daughter and a son. Both lived out of town. Her son was an accountant
in Toronto, the daughter was studying marketing at a university in
Vancouver.

"It must be difficult for you, with your children living so far away,"
Gershon had once said.

"I encouraged them to leave," Alfreda replied. "There's nothing for
them here. No future." Like so many Montreal Jews, Alfreda had given
up on Montreal after two provincial votes on Quebec sovereignty in the
past twenty years. "The way I see it, sending them away saved them. It
gave them a new lease, a chance to make a better life for themselves away
from all this craziness. The politics."

There was not the slightest hint of regret in her voice. Gershon was
continually impressed by Alfreda's neutral, even-tempered disposition.
She seemed prepared for anything, emotionally fortified, as if she lived
under the security of one of the building's airtight leases. He also sensed
Alfreda's depth. Gershon realized that somewhere at the bottom was
fine print and a line with a signature guaranteeing personally everything
she said and did. Alfreda cared about the Steins, the business and the
building. She handled her responsibilities, all of them, with diligence.

And how did Gershon show his appreciation to Alfreda? He remembered how one day, when Alfreda was out, a delightful bouquet of flowers arrived at the office. Since Alfreda wasn't available, Gershon accepted the delivery. He turned the clay pot wrapped in cellophane around in his palms, and shoved his nose between petals. Who could they possibly be for? The obvious did not immediately occur to him. He spotted Alfreda's name on a tiny card slotted between the stems. Gershon was surprised. He was not intentionally being cold. He simply couldn't imagine the type of man who might send Alfreda flowers. Gershon didn't even know it was her birthday.

The house was a mess. With Bayly now in school and Shoshana at Kinder-Lach Nursery for part of the day, there was more time for Ruhama to restore an equilibrium, a semblance of order from chaos. But she was feeling extra tired lately and to make matters worse, she was anxious about the fast-approaching High Holy Days. Rosh Hashana brought the preparation of feasts. Usually, the cooking was shared with her mother-in-law. Sholem was in the hospital and Masha, beside herself with worry, was incapable of helping. Ruhama knew that this year the responsibilities would fall completely on her shoulders.

Seven days after Rosh Hashana, Yom Kippur arrived. Five days after that, the harvest festival of Succot, the Feast of Booths. It lasted for eight days and then came the celebration of Simchat Torah. Holy Day after Holy Day after Holy Day, which, for Ruhama, constituted an explosive chain reaction of household chores. Even before it had run its course, the sheer anticipation of the cumulative impact overwhelmed her.

Succot was Gershon's favourite of the Holy Days. He would fold up the plastic lawn chairs and tables and stow them underneath the back balcony where the *succah* would be erected. He brought out from storage a bag of butterfly screws, armfuls of aluminum rods and a long silver tarpaulin. About three hours was required to screw the *succah* frame together and enclose it with fabric. Bayly and Shoshana would get busy making pictures to cover the floppy walls. With Ruhama's help they hung papier-mâché and rubber fruit on string from the bamboo-mat ceiling unrolled on top.

Gershon had bought his *succah* from a local company that manufactured portable ice-fishing shelters, which is what it actually was. He liked to imagine thousands of frozen lakes all over the Quebec country-side dotted with *succahs* with men inside them praying for a bite.

On Succot, Jews were meant to emulate the ancient Israelites when they had lived in makeshift huts in fields for the duration of the harvest. Most religious families were like the Steins, eating all their meals in the *succah*, weather permitting. Montreal in mid-October tended to be rainy, blustery and chilly. The keenest, heartiest Jews also slept in their *succahs*.

Although the *succah* was intended to stay up for eight days, it could get blown over and have to be reconstructed halfway through the festival. This didn't bother Gershon. Dressed in a warm parka, he would stay in his *succah* all afternoon learning Torah. Seated in the center of his ten-foot by twelve-foot booth, his pages of scripture were illuminated by slivers of sunlight seeping through slits in the roof. He listened to the wind slap at the shelter's walls. He watched the structure bend and twist. The precariousness of the structure was part of the meaning. Succot reminded Jews of both the abundance of nature and the fragility of life. Gershon remained stalwart, staying in his *succah* with his books, drawing confidence from the texts that the walls would not cave in and bring the roof crashing down on top of him.

Ruhama spent the days leading up to the High Holy Days taking inventory. Rooms were re-organized. Clothes and footwear were inspected to make sure Gershon and the girls owned appropriate attire that fitted properly. The kitchen cupboards, freezers and refrigerators were stocked, and then overstocked, with provisions.

This was not the manic, obsessive cleaning which preceded Pesach in the spring, when the house was emptied of leavened products, the *chometz* sold off. For Passover, no corner was left unswept, no drawer unwashed, no countertop unscoured. Pesach meant life had to be scaled back. It was stripped down, and the load lightened—only the bare necessitities were brought on the fabled journey ahead. The Holy Day of Pesach memorialized a hurried escape, a flight from oppression to freedom. The night before the first *seder*, the family would gather around a lit candle and holding a spoon and a feather as their tools, seek out the last breadcrumbs, tiny as gold dust, in every nook and cranny like a team of spiritual prospectors. As her mother did when she was a child, Ruhama hid some small morsels of bread wrapped in tinfoil in different corners of the house so Bayly and Shoshana would partake in the *mitzvah* of finding and disposing them.

Unlike Pesach-time, the days leading up to Rosh Hashana were for looking backward, not forward. Ruhama became acutely aware of the repressiveness of her accumulated mistakes and errors. Burdens, before they could be lifted, had to be acknowledged. The Hebrew month of *Elul* before Rosh Hashana was traditionally marked by intense, sober introspection. Personal failures were admitted, responsibility for sins was taken. The full weight of conscience and guilt had to be supported, until the supreme Day of Judgement. An individual's capacity for change and renewal was tested during this month. Intense soul-searching was part of a slow, lumbering approach toward the final, monumental confrontation with God. The verdict was delivered on Rosh Hashana and a person's fate was sealed on Yom Kippur. Success, if it could be called that, was determined by how well one was prepared to accept their fate.

As Gershon put it, the High Holy Days was the time you renewed your lease with the Almighty. The potential for repentance through *teshuvah*, spiritual return, always existed. It was the Jewish way. But Ruhama didn't feel up to the negotiations this year. She felt fragile and out of sorts. It was not only that she would have to do without her mother-in-law's help. Common sights, like a half-built city of Lego blocks lying in ruins at her feet in the dining room, upset her. Orange juice stains on Shoshana's bedroom carpet, ignored for months, nearly brought her to tears. The carnage of Shoshana's dolls strewn across the hardwood floor of the living room shook her: a disjointed arm contorted out of its socket, a leg twisted lamely to the side, decapitated bodies with hollow necks. Nothing could be done for them. It was too late. The conditions were irreversible. She was powerless to make corrections. There had been too much abuse, the fabric was damaged beyond repair.

Compounding the situation, Shoshana hadn't been sleeping well the past four nights. She awoke every two or three hours and cried out for mama. She's just having nightmares, Ruhama told Gershon.

"Nightmares? How can a three-year-old have nightmares? What do they know from nightmares?" he responded.

"You think they don't have fears?"

"Of course, I know they have fears. I'm not talking about fears. I'm talking about nightmares. There's a difference. You're the one who called them nightmares," he accused, as if teaching Shoshana the word was sufficient to make them happen. "Now you've handed her a word that can make her mother appear in the middle of the night like magic. You think she's not going to use it every chance she gets. Meanwhile, look at you. You're a wreck."

Gershon was having enough of it. The next time Shoshana cried out for mama in the middle of the night, Gershon went to her instead. He scooped her tiny body out of bed and carried her to the threshold of her bedroom. The sudden ride in Gershon's arms was enough to silence Shoshana. Gershon kissed her on the cheek and pointed her face toward the doorframe.

"You see that? Do you know what that is?"

Shoshana looked at the *mezuzah* and then back at her father.

"That's your protection against nightmares. That's why we put it there. So you won't have nightmares."

Gershon took Shoshana's right hand and rubbed her tiny index finger along the square edge of the Hebrew letter *shin*, the insignia for *Shadai*, a name of God.

"Do you know what that is? It's a *shin*. It means a tooth."

Shoshana looked at it and touched the edge again. Then she brought her index finger back to her mouth and ran it along the tops of her own lower teeth.

"You see how the letter looks like teeth sticking up. That's because it's God's sharp teeth. The nightmares are scared of God. They know He'll chew them up. They won't come into your room. You have nothing to worry about. Now go to sleep."

Gershon tucked Shoshana back in bed. "Remember, God's *shin* is protecting you," he said to her with a kiss.

"What did you tell her?" Ruhama asked, as Gershon flopped down on the mattress next to her.

"I told her that there was nothing to worry about. God is protecting her. And He feeds on nightmares."

Shoshana was soon sleeping through the night. A better night's sleep also took the edge off Ruhama's fatigue. Still, every morning she faced the tumult of the house.

Ruhama was a tidy person. By the age of six she was performing regular household chores. She had been raised to respect the orderly condition of the house, and she helped her mother by clearing the dinner table, rinsing dishes and sweeping under the chairs. Particularly at Holy Day times, the monumental tasks of cleaning, cooking, tidying and shopping were regarded as the fulfilment of a *mitzvah*. Ruhama contributed to these domestic duties with enthusiasm.

When she first moved to Montreal, Ruhama lived with her in-laws. Gershon had warned his new wife in advance about his mother. He called her a neat-freak. Ruhama found out that "neat-freak" didn't begin to describe her.

She immediately noticed how immaculately Gershon's family home was kept. Masha maintained the house by constantly cleaning up after herself, and not just a normal tidying, putting things back where they belonged. She dusted and wiped incessantly. The sinks were scrubbed several times a day. The bathroom was cleaner after her mother-in-law used it. Ruhama watched Gershon's mother wash her hands and then reach for a rag to dry out the basin and polish the faucet until it shined. It was as if Masha cancelled her history, erased traces of her presence as she journeyed from room to room.

This standard of cleanliness was utterly foreign to Ruhama. It was beyond clean, more like sterilization. She began feeling extremely self-conscious and resentful, devising a discreetly sadistic game to express her discomfort. She created disorder, shifting the angle of family portraits on shelves, displacing ritual objects an inch or two and changing the order of books when no one was looking.

She stood aside and observed her mother-in-law enter the room and unconsciously move things precisely back to their original positions. Her fingers extended and clutched robotically. It spooked Ruhama. The room was quickly back to its previous, perfectly undisturbed state. Ruhama couldn't wait to depart her in-laws' house.

After three months, Ruhama and Gershon moved into their new home. Ruhama had all the walls painted off-white to mark a fresh start. She intended every room to be a separate project. Colour schemes would be decided upon later, one room at a time. She imagined covering the floors with gorgeous oriental area rugs, filling spaces with stately bookshelves and handcrafted cabinetry, plush sofas with handwoven cushions, and an antique Canadiana dining room set with seating for ten.

The dining room was soon painted mauve and furnished as planned. The living room sofas were bought, but that was all. The rest of the house remained virtually untouched. The children's rooms were decked out in cheap, self-assembled furniture. Gershon had said they were too young for better quality product. Let them live with furniture that could be damaged. The basement was large, an empty room with unfinished walls. It gave the kids a place to run around and act wild, he said.

However, instead of seeing projects in motion, a home in various stages of completion, each colourless room symbolized a different form of inadequacy for Ruhama. The kids' bedrooms were one kind of failure, the master bedroom was another, the living room still another. She could not articulate exactly what it meant, but the feeling was there. It was like the discomfort of being partially clothed, or worse, the anxiety of living in layers of blanched, leperous skin.

She sometimes thought about the Chazon Ish, the *gadol hador*, a *tzaddik*, the most righteous of his generation. It was said that every second of the sage's life was accounted for and that he kept only enough food and material possessions necessary for him to live a single day. Revered by thousands for his wisdom and humility, there was a well known story about an American Jew who travelled to *Eretz Yisroel* to pay his respects to the great man. He arrived at the Chazon Ish's house and found a diminutive figure seated on a hard bench behind a simple wooden table in an empty room. The man was learning Torah by the light of a single naked lightbulb hanging from the ceiling on a chain. Feeling disappointed, the American asked, is this the great Chazon Ish whose sage reputation reaches every corner of the world? Is this how a giant of his generation lives? Surely, a man of such stature should not suffer such deprivation. Where is your furniture, your chest of drawers?

The Chazon Ish looked at the man curiously and questioned back. If I may ask, where is your furniture, your chest of drawers?

Well, the American answered, I am only here temporarily, for a brief visit, passing through.

The Chazon Ish replied, as am I.

Ruhama felt like the encumbered American. As a mother and wife, she needed to have a house filled with furniture and knicknacks and chests of drawers. The bare necessitities were not enough. She wanted nice things, beautiful things to enhance her surroundings, everything that a respectable family might need. Yet, as a Jew, she loathed rooms packed with stuff, particularly when it got out of hand and there was a mess behind every door.

But the heaviness she felt in her bones was more than just the untidy contents of her house. It was the contradiction of impulses which she knew could never be reconciled.

When she was a little girl, Ruhama went with her parents to the banks of the East River to rid themselves of sin. She watched her father and mother, their faces grave, sprinkle small pale scraps into the water. This was the performance of *Tashlikh*, the High Holy Day custom of symbolically casting off sins by uttering penitential prayers while emptying pockets of breadcrumbs and tossing them into water.

The bread floated like stars, dots of light suspended in airless black. Ruhama watched and waited for fish to rise from the dark depths to gobble up the scraps. She decided this must be what God did. He swallowed the confessed sins of people scattered in the universe, taking them away, making them disappear forever. The notion comforted her.

But this year, the memory of her chilhood *Tashlikh* seemed quaint. The ritual in general seemed calculated and trite. This year, she felt breadcrumbs wouldn't do the job. Loaves of bread were required, or entire bakeries. And she wondered, could God digest all that? Would He? What was the tipping point? When was there too much accumulated, even for God?

Come Rosh Hashana in two weeks, she would have to wish family and friends the traditional greeting "*Shanah tova tikatevu*, May you be inscribed for a good year." The prospect of saying the greeting annoyed her. The words had started to sound insincere. And she didn't think she had the strength to stand in synagogue for *Unetaneh Tokef*, feeling certain that the instant the mournful notes of that song reached her ears she would break down and collapse on the spot from sadness:

On Rosh Hashana it is recorded, and on Yom Kippur it is sealed.
How many shall pass away, and how many shall be born
who shall live and who shall die,
who in the fullness of their years and who before his time.
Who by fire and who by water,
who by sword and who by wild beast,
who by hunger and who by thirst,
who by earthquake and who by plague,

who by strangling and who by stoning.
Who shall be rested and who shall be restless,
who shall be calm and who shall be distraught,
who shall be serene and who shall be tormented,
who shall be poor and who shall be rich,
who shall be downcast and who uplifted.

This year Ruhama could not bear the litany of tragedy.

The problem wasn't in the prayers themselves. The words hadn't been emptied of meaning. On the contrary, they seemed too real. Heavy, wingless, grounded in the here-and-now. Prayer was supposed to belong to another realm altogether. An ascendent realm. It was supposed to whisk the spirit away to a higher altitude, unfetter and rejuvenate the soul. Ruhama had a strange, dreadful thought. What if words traditionally meant to carry the spirit away had become like overcrowded city buses? What if they were so cluttered with the tedium and sadness and grief of quotidian life, there was no place left for the soul? What happened when words no longer did the job?

Every Jew knew that a time came when words were insufficient. During the High Holy Days, the stakes were highest, the sound of pure prayer, or rather, the prayer of pure sound was relied upon to reach the Almighty. The blowing of the ram's horn.

TEKIAH SHEVARIM-TERUAH TEKIAH

The shofar's wail, its plaintive stutter, echoed the unuttered fear of Isaac as Abraham lashed his hands and feet for sacrifice. The shofar produced a dense, multilayered sound that reached across history, in which the groan of a father's uncertainty could be discerned and joining it, in unison, the pitched silence of his son's confusion. Underlying the shofar's call, the frightful stillness as God descended on Sinai in thunder and lightning was felt. And the unspoken question present on every horror-struck Israelite witness's mind was recalled: Is this how *we* will be consumed? If the Egyptians were drowned down in the depths of the sea, have we been brought to the foot of this desert mountain to be taken up by incineration? Redeemed in smoke?

The shofar commanded faith and perseverance. Ruhama had always maintained an abundance of the former, but the latter was in short supply at the moment.

~

Gershon exited the elevator on the fourth floor and rounded the corner in the direction of Sonny Lipsey's premises without lifting his head. He was deep in thought. Having decided to ask Sonny to join the minyan, he knew full well that even if his response was positive, he was unlikely to be reliable. But there was also a chance that Sonny could suggest others.

Gershon couldn't say whether it was catching a whiff of that certain unmistakable perfumy scent which he'd stored in his memory, or if something had appeared within the boundary of his peripheral vision, but just as his body turned the corner he paused and raised his eyes. Seeing them standing at the far end of the hallway, Gershon took a quick step backward. He placed his fingers on the edge of the wall and peeked out from behind the corner.

Rosie K was talking with Michelle Labelle. Rosie loomed large over her. His body was twice as thick as hers. Had he been a grizzly, reared up on its hind legs, he could have swallowed her whole. But there was no antagonism between them, only conversation. It appeared to be congenial. In his right hand, Rosie carried a block of fabric samples, red and white rectangular swatches that waved in the air as he spoke. Each gesture brought them up and down like small coloured banners, the way two passing ships bouncing on ocean waves raised flags to communicate by semaphore over distances. Gershon imagined that Rosie was sending him coded signals. Two reds meant danger ahead. One red and one white meant caution. Two whites: the coast was clear.

While Rosie spoke, Michelle kept her head down. Her bony shoulders sagged. She looked defeated. Rosie kept talking, then paused. After a moment in which they looked like they might be praying together, or like Rosie was blessing her, the empty mitt of his left hand rose to Michelle's chin and Gershon could swear he saw it gently caress her right cheek.

Then the volume of Rosie's voice rose a notch. Rosie bid Michelle adieu. This was it, they were done. Gershon hopped swiftly out of sight and scooted through the doorway of Yossi Alfasi's store.

A tall, solidly-built man in his fifties, with dark eyes and a greying moustache, Yossi always sat at a narrow table tucked behind two neatly attired headless mannequins. Today, one mannequin wore a red and blue checked pant-suit, the other a brown blazer and wool skirt. Yossi's line of clothing was designed for the working woman. His table was covered in religious texts and next to them was a spiral-bound blue notebook in which Yossi jotted down quotes and his own ideas. From his place in the corner, right by the front door, Yossi could both learn Torah in relative privacy and size people up as they walked in, lifting his eyes from his books to decide whether or not they were important enough to take him away from his studies. In a glance he could distinguish between bonafide buyers, competitors looking to copy his styles, thieves hoping to grab a garment and make a quick getaway, and window shoppers. He ignored the French-speaking Haitian women who frequented his shop, knowing that they liked to browse but rarely bought his pricey styles. Hijab-wearing Arab women, who usually pushed baby-strollers, elicited insults from Yossi under his breath.

Born in Morocco, Yossi had immigrated to Canada from Israel after doing his military service. He had fought in a tank unit during the 1973 Yom Kippur War. His intense dislike of Arabs was forged in the northern Negev, where he faced platoons of Egyptian soldiers across the desert battlefield. He didn't go out of his way to express this hatred, but he also made no bones about it.

Yossi sometimes recounted to Gershon stories of his wild youth in the Israeli military. After the war, in Canada, he opened his business and acted the playboy. Over the years, he had made and spent hundreds of thousands of dollars, he told Gershon, maybe millions. "I don't give a shit about that now," he said. "It means nothing to me."

Occasionally, when Gershon was with Yossi in his store and they were conversing about some aspect of Torah, they would be interrupted by a woman who openly flirted with Yossi. "From my past," Yossi would say to Gershon after she left. He never elaborated. The incident would pique Gershon's interest, but he stopped himself from prying. He didn't want to put Yossi in the uncomfortable position of having to explain himself. Still, he wondered about people who lived with "a past." The concept was alien to him. He knew that everyone held secrets, decisions they had made but wished they hadn't, or actions they preferred to forget about. But living with *a past* was something else entirely. There were people who carried around within them previous identities, former incarnations of themselves. When they changed, as Yossi had, Gershon imagined it was like they threw a party—a going-away party, a birthday party, or a re-birthday party—in which all their former selves were invited guests, and from that moment on they walked around like rooms crowded with old acquaintances, people with whom they wanted to avoid making eye-contact.

Gershon had only ever been one person. He had only himself to bear, which was difficult enough most of the time. If it was tough to manage himself, how much more difficult was it to tolerate the presence of previous selves, Gershon wondered.

For Yossi, becoming Torah observant was a major overhaul. As a successful Garmento, in his earlier life Yossi had probably participated in all the unsavoury practices the manufacturers were known for— wooing buyers with flirtation and gifts, kickbacks and payoffs. If Yossi had been as fervent a businessman back then as he was a Torah-observant Jew now, Gershon could imagine that maybe he'd been a gambler, taken drugs, perhaps hired prostitutes. Gershon was astounded that Yossi could change so radically. He saw that most overweight people, himself included, couldn't even keep to their diets, let alone metamorphose into a totally different person.

Yossi appeared to have succeeded in his metamorphosis. From his previous incarnation as a high-flying wheeler-dealer concerned with making money and satisfying his own personal pleasures, he had become a God-fearing pious Jew who adhered strictly to both the letter and spirit of the Law. It had to be said, however, that Yossi had been given a head-start.

The Alfasi name was well known, among Moroccan Jews in particular. Picture postcards of Yossi's grandfather, the great Rabbi Yehoshua Alfasi, were found in Sephardi homes and places of business all over the city. To this day, there were working rabbis in his family. His first cousin, Rabbi Meir Alfasi, was a revered *Rosh Yeshiva* in France. The religious institute he had founded in Paris taught thousands of students from all over Europe. Yossi had said with pride that his cousin could read a person's *neshama* and predict their future. People travelled across oceans to receive Rabbi Meir's blessing. Rediscovering his Jewish identity was less a matter of outright creation for Yossi, than finding and reattaching himself to the unhooked tether of his family legacy. By becoming Torah-observant, Yossi was no different than any wayward son who had decided to return to the family business. Chuckling with embarrassment, Yossi told Gershon that Moroccans had started coming to him to be blessed. Yossi had no regrets about his wild and crazy days. He said he learned from those experiences. His mistakes, and Gershon surmised that they must have been doozies, had made him a stronger and more deeply committed Jew.

Gershon wondered if, having had himself what can best be described as a tepid youth, he had missed out on something. In the stories Gershon heard, it was often those who had been the most spiritually debased and had, by some miracle, acknowledged the errors of their ways, that reached a higher level of spiritual understanding. Maybe in his earlier life Rabbi Meir Alfasi was a drug-addicted rock star or acted in pornographic movies, and those experiences had earned him his powers of clairvoyance and ability to read auras. Maybe, if Gershon had been more carefree he would have attained greater enlightenment and perhaps even gained some supernatural powers. Of course, Asheknazi Jews didn't usually talk in such mystical terms. They were less concerned with supernatural occurrences than the rigours of following and interpreting the Law. But the mere fact of Yossi's transformation was proof that some miracles were in the realm of possibility. Certain changes were not to be underestimated, least of all, changes of heart.

"Gershon, come in. I'm preparing a *d'var Torah* for *Kol Nidre*," Yossi said, looking up from the Torah commentary he was reading, delighted to have an unexpected visitor in his store who wasn't an Arab or Haitian.

"Hello, Yossi. I'm sorry to disturb you," Gershon said, peering back through the doorway into the corridor. He waited anxiously to see if Rosie and Michelle would pass.

"No, no, no, I'm happy you came. I wonder what you think of what I'm writing."

"I'd love to hear it, just not right now."

Yossi's enthusiasm would not abate. "It's such an honour that they asked me to make a speech in my shul *erev Yom Kippur*."

"Yes," Gershon said. His eyes were glued on the rectangular block of hallway visible through Yossi's door. "It's a great honour."

"Let me read it to you. I'm talking about *Nedarim*. Why we are required to renounce our vows on Yom Kippur."

"Yes, I know."

"Today is not different from the time of the Spanish Inquisition.

We are like Marranos. Jews on the inside but another person on the outside. The world forces us to do and say things which go against our *neshama*. That's what I'm talking about for *Kol Nidre*. The renunciation of vows is the liberation of the soul, Gershon. The world corrupts us. We say and do things every day that we shouldn't. The world covers our souls in thick mud, layers that harden and become heavy. We cannot bear the weight. When we renounce our vows on *Kol Nidre* we free our souls from the burden of our double lives. It brings our souls back in line with our essence. Who we really are."

Gershon was lost in thought. He had no idea Rosie K and Michelle Labelle knew each other. From their exchange, it was obvious they were well acquainted, maybe even friends. He had touched her face. He had done so in a comforting, consoling way. She had let him do this. Was it possible that he saw her light too? There was nothing sexual in the gesture. Gershon decided that as soon as the opportunity presented itself, he would ask Rosie in private about the nature of his relationship to Michelle.

"So what do you think, Gershon?" Yossi asked.

"About what?"

"*Kol Nidre*. That we are Marranos. The renunciation of vows allows us to be who we really are."

Something in what Yossi said instantly irritated Gershon. He wanted to pick at it. Test Yossi. "Then I guess *you* must know," Gershon said.

"Know what?"

"Who you *really* are."

"Of course. I'm a Jew."

"But you haven't always lived as one. Maybe a Jew is just what you *want* to be. Maybe who you *really* are is the way you were. Your past. When you didn't care about living as a Jew. Maybe you're just pretending."

Gershon's mouth stumbled on the word *pretending*. He hadn't wanted to accuse Yossi of pretending. He hadn't really wanted to put Yossi on the defensive. Or maybe, deep down, that was exactly what he wanted to do. Gershon couldn't help feeling that at some level Yossi was acting a part.

"Yes. It can't be denied. What I was. I'm not ashamed. Who I am is where I come from."

Gershon understood what Yossi meant. He was not referring to his life in the dress business. He was going deeper. Far back to the Alfasi rabbis.

"And what if where you came from wasn't so wonderful? We can't all come from great rabbis and scholars. People never come from beggars and whores. You ever notice that? What if you came from a terrible place?"

"You can always find something good if you look hard enough," Yossi answered. "Every family has someone to be proud of. Someone with nobility. Some redeeming accomplishment. It all depends on how deep your memory goes."

"What if there's a blank? What if you can't remember, or don't want to remember?" Gershon asked more forcefully.

"Then you're dead," Yossi replied.

"What if you want to forget?"

"Then you remember."

"What if you have to avert your eyes from what you see when you look back?"

"Then you keep digging until you find what you're looking for," Yossi said, smiling.

"Aha! So it's all about what you're looking for, not what's already there. That means you're pretending," Gershon said, feeling for once that he'd cornered Yossi. "Like a Marrano. You have to pretend to survive."

"It's not pretending, Gershon, if you put your heart and soul into it. Survival isn't enough. You have to *live*. If you're only concerned with survival then you're right. You're just a pretender. A Marrano."

Yossi's words stung Gershon. He instantly realized why he had been aggressive with Yossi. He'd attacked Yossi because *he* was the one pretending. In the building. In his job.

Gershon thanked Yossi and slapped a kiss on his *mezuzah* as he exited the store. He never caught up with Rosie K, losing him in the stairwell between the second and third floors. And he never found out why Rosie had touched Michelle Labelle's face. But he didn't feel bad about not knowing. The gesture between them lived on in his mind as an image of genuine tenderness, perhaps consolation. He was grateful for having witnessed it. They had not been pretending. Gershon knew that not everything that went on in the building was his business. He acknowledged to himself that Yossi wasn't pretending either. Yossi put his heart and soul into being a Jew. That's what mattered most.

Address

ESTELLA MORA'S CONTINUED presence in the building was becoming intolerable to Gershon. The legalities of eviction took time. Notices had to be served and motions presented. The lawyer was working as fast as possible. Getting rid of Estella felt to Gershon like having an abscessed tooth extracted. The process was both excruciatingly painful and essential to stop further misery and damage.

He only heard the rumour once, from Niko. It was possible it hadn't travelled any further. On the other hand, if Estella had told Niko that she and Gershon were having an affair, she was undoubtedly telling others too. Gershon could not come out publicly with denials. That would be as good as spreading the rumour himself. He decided the only thing to do was to keep quiet, act like nothing was happening and focus on other problems, like collecting the balance of Joey Putkin's rent. He knew he would inevitably have to confront Putkin again.

The main thing that interested Gershon was the minyan. Putkin and Estella were distractions. Better to be a collector of souls than a collector of rents.

Of all the difficult questions Bayly regularly asked her father—questions about God and the six days of Creation, about miracles and plagues, signs and wonders, about Moshe and Miriam, the Hebrew slaves in Egypt and their wanderings in the desert—the most difficult one Gershon ever had to answer was possibly also the most universal, frequently asked question. The inevitable query every child, Jewish, Christian, Hindu, Muslim, or Buddhist, poses to their parent: What do you do at work?

Without a second thought Gershon answered, I'm a rent collector, to which Bayly, then a mere four years old, predictably returned a puzzled stare. Considering how to explain what a rent collector did, Gershon squirmed. It wasn't like being a policeman which could be described to a four-year-old with the simple phrase, I catch bad people and put them in jail. Or a fireman: I put fires out and save people. Or a doctor: I make sick people healthy again. Or an architect, an artist, a truck driver, or a garment manufacturer, for that matter. Rent collection was not as easy to describe as what a banker did: I keep people's money safe. Or a computer programmer. Nowadays, most four-year-olds understood something about computers. Gershon could not even say that like Bayly's *zaida*, Sholem, he was a builder. He hadn't built anything.

These were occupations that could be explained by referring to a tangible accomplishment, something physically produced, or a service virtuously rendered. Most of them accorded a person the integrity and status of a title. Doctor So and So, Professor X, Captain Y, Rabbi Z, or just plain Sir. But a rent collector? The only job Gershon could think of which might present equal difficulty was insurance agent. And for a moment Gershon felt a certain peculiar empathy for people who sold insurance.

Like all questions leading to more questions, an explanation of rent collection presented many problems. People gave him money to occupy space. Was there a cost to occupying space? It sounded silly. After saying to his daughter he was a rent collector, Gershon felt embarrassment, a pang of shame wash over him, as if he were engaged in an illicit activity. He realized the question was not really about what he did to earn a living, *what* he was, but rather *who* he was.

Who was Gershon? An overseer of space. It sounded synonymous with being a spectator. A sideliner. A non-participant. A nothing. He was not even Mr. Stein. Mr. Stein was his father. Gershon did not possess the dignity of proprietorship. The floor under his feet was not his, neither were the walls surrounding him. He might well have been a speck of dust blown from one corner of his father's building to the next. A rent collector was a dust collector.

Bayly judged as scrupulously as any learned adjudicator sitting on the Bench, and as he stood trial before her, Gershon feared he was incriminating himself. What if he said he was a property manager? She would never understand what a manager was. And how could he possibly explain everything he did in the building on a daily basis? It was not simple to sum up the complications of tenant-landlord relations, the subtle legalities of lease negotiations, the complexities of maintaining plumbing, heating, electrical, elevator and security systems, the market-economics of keeping the business running profitably. What about all the mind-games landlords and tenants played with each other? Maybe, he could just say to his daughter, Honey, I play mind-games. That is what I do. Who I am.

Calling himself a rent collector, Gershon decided, was demeaning. It was a term he had himself become accustomed to using as a way of divesting himself from the relationships he cultivated on the job. If he was more than a rent collector, it meant he cared more. Or to put it accurately, if he cared more, it meant he was more than a rent collector. But all along he had been busy avoiding caring too much.

When he first came to 99, the property showed obvious signs of neglect. Garage door panels hung loosely off broken hinges. Large leaves of paint flaked from hallway walls. Plaster chips cracked and dropped to the floor, leaving gaping holes. The central stairwell of the building was covered in graffiti. Thick, black explicit calligraphy. Cartoons of squirting penises and large breasts. There were anti-Semitic epithets scrawled in the elevator cabins, the spiralling hooks of swastikas. Gershon smelled the acrid stench of urine in the loading dock area where truckers regularly relieved themselves. He occasionally came across small, brown, putrid piles of feces under the steps. Sholem was the proverbial slumlord, concluded Gershon. He was horrified.

He asked Sholem why the building was kept in such a state of misery and disrepair. Why hadn't the stairs been washed with bleach, the halls re-plastered and painted, the graffiti erased? His father answered that in a week or two it would come back. There was no sense in wasting money. The tenants were *chazzers*, pigs, he said. After so many years his father had tuned out. Milked the cow and left her for dead.

A greenhorn, Gershon refused to abide. He ordered 99 to be cleaned top to bottom. The hallways were fixed. The expressions of lust and hate were eradicated. The tenants, he argued to his father, treated the building like a garbage dump and a toilet because the owner treated it that way. Gershon invested.

In time, there was more graffiti, more feces, more hate. Sholem was right. People were *chazzers*. Gershon persisted, scrubbing, wiping, disinfecting. But he was getting tired, losing hope. He became numb. He began not seeing. And like Sholem who had survived the death camps many years ago by denying the smells that wafted to his nostrils, ignoring the views that appeared before his eyes and blocking the sounds that came to his ears, Gershon stopped noticing.

Now when Gershon exited through the front doors of the building, the huge 99 under which he passed appeared to be hanging there like two enormous, tired, droopy eyes. They stared out blankly at the indifferent city, the cars speeding by, the buses screeching to a halt, passengers disembarking and scattering in the street. Back in the lobby he would rub his palm along the cool grey reflective granite and pause in front of the building directory to scan down the list of companies and their suite numbers. He took in the names silently, like he was reading from a war memorial.

They came here to die, Gershon admitted. This was the last stop. When they couldn't afford the expensive rates of the newer buildings down the street, they came to 99 where the rent was cheaper. The successful brand-name companies had all moved on, and left the dregs behind. Rent collecting at 99 was bottom-feeding.

Gershon peered up at the ceiling, through grills covering eight-foot fluorescent fixtures. Several burnt tubes had been left dimly in place. What was a light that no longer lighted? An empty piece of glass? A useless ornament? A non-light? He waited under the shadow of the non-light for an elevator.

Of the four elevators, one wasn't working. He could see this from the floor indicators that ran along the top of the lobby doors. Elevator number two was blocked on the second floor. The light didn't flicker on and off to demonstrate movement. Number three arrived suddenly, doors thwacking open. He entered alone and pressed his floor. The number lit but nothing happened. The car didn't move. He waited twenty seconds then pressed the door-close button. Nothing. He pressed again and again. Nothing. An Arab man hurried into the cabin. He pressed two floor buttons, fourth and seventh, then slammed his hand against the door-close button. They came together slowly. Gershon gazed at the man quizzically.

"How can you get off at two floors at the same time?" he asked.

"This elevator does not stop at seven unless you press four too," the Arab replied. "Funny machine. I come here enough times to know how it works."

Doors opened at four. Gershon and the man turned to each other and smiled without budging. Doors closed. He knows more about the building than I do, Gershon said to himself. Where have I been? The building is alive. Why haven't I seen it? The building is sick. Maybe dying. Who will care, if not I?

There were times, pacing the hallways of 99, when Gershon felt overwhelmed. The building was a complex microcosm, a compact world of swirling energies both hidden and apparent. The concrete walls coursed with metal veins, plumbing pipes and electrical wires enmeshed with steel and concrete. Gershon knew that the building's very existence expressed a narrative. As a religious Jew who studied scripture, he was predisposed to noticing and speculating on the meanings hidden inside everything. Everywhere he looked he saw clues of origin, beginnings. On the outside was a structure of painted walls, polished floors, wooden doors and grimy windows. Yet locked within its materials and assembled parts was a story, about how and when and why it came into being. Before there was a building there was a plot of vacant land that begged to be filled. There was the need for a building—which begat the idea of a building, which begat the hope of a building, which begat the blueprint of a building, which begat the building of the building. Gershon walked down the hallway toward the management office. He could almost visualize the layers of 99's existence, tucked inside the housing that surrounded him, its past folded neatly into its present like seeds inside a fruit.

Which of Gershon's tenants ever thought about what went into the creation of 99? Who ever paused to think about the creation of anything? Taking the building for granted was one thing. It was to be expected from his tenants who went blindly about their businesses. But Gershon was sure that on a deeper level, even the most hardened, jaded business types, who occupied themselves with the task of producing quantities of apparel, reducing costs, optimizing efficiencies and making profits, were attracted to something more real.

Even in these days of autumn, 99 emptied out early every Friday afternoon. The Jewish businessmen flocked north to their Laurentian cottages. They got into their Mercedes and Cadillacs and raced to beat the rush-hour traffic out of the city. Gershon also left early on Fridays, heading home to help Ruhama prepare for the Sabbath. The parking garage was already half empty by the time he was leaving the building.

Beginning two generations earlier, the Jews had bought tracts of land in the Laurentians. They built country houses in the villages of St. Sauveur, Ste. Adele and Ste. Agathe. In some instances their country houses were more palatial than their city homes. There was even a synagogue up north, boasting more than a thousand members. Although few actually attended religious services, the Jewish cottagers dutifully paid their annual membership fees as a matter of pride. They remembered how only decades earlier several communities in the Laurentians had restrictions against Jews owning homes.

Owning a house in the Laurentians indicated status and prestige. But Gershon was sure there was more to it than that. More than having a place for relaxation, a refuge from worldly hassles. Disengaging from the workaday world was what the bosses did at home every weekday after five or six o'clock, when they unwound in the comfort of living room armchairs by the static light of television screens, glasses of scotch or rye in hand. For the Jewish businessmen, leaving behind the ordered malaise of Montreal—the paved roads, traffic signals, street names, directional arrows and addresses—was their way to recapture the world they lost slaving away in buildings. After the deadening tick-tock pace of industry and routine, the weekend trips they made to their lakeside cottages were all the bosses could do to feel fully alive once again.

This desire to feel fully alive, Gershon believed, was what the mass migration north at the end of each week was really all about. The businessmen sought to unhinge themselves from the concerns of market competition. They abandoned, if only for a brief time, the impulse of personal gain. They wanted to love the world again, sensing that hidden deep inside each of them there was also an untouched, undeveloped plot of land. Although the Jewish businessmen may not have abided the Law explicitly, or thought about it in those terms, to love the world, to find a connection with it, was precisely why God had decreed the Sabbath in the first place.

~

"How is your father?" Shimmy Solomon called out to Gershon, who was standing at the threshold of Shimmy's large office.

"Thank God," Gershon answered, waiting to be invited in to take a seat. "The doctors say he has a good chance of recovery." It was gracious of Shimmy to begin the conversation. He waved Gershon to advance into the room. "Thank you for asking," he added, addressing Shimmy respectfully.

Gershon would never have gone to see Shimmy under normal circumstances. In the first place, he didn't ever speak with him. Shimmy was hardly someone who engaged in casual conversation. When there was a problem with building services, Shimmy didn't bother with Gershon. He contacted Sholem directly. As the oldest tenant who occupied the most square footage in the building, he always got satisfaction. Gershon was compelled to pay Shimmy a visit now in the hope that a few more names for the minyan list could be garnered from the bloated employee ranks of Simple Dress. Anyway, with Sholem out of the picture for the moment, Gershon thought it might be a good idea for the two of them to get better acquainted, even at the risk of it being an exchange between unequals.

Shimmy was a designer by training, and uncompromising by nature. His offices on the third floor had been modelled according to his personal specifications and taste. The walls and doors were covered with imported Indonesian teak. The floors were tiled in Turkish marble. Shimmy had his eccentricities too. Light switches were unsightly to him. So when his offices were built, he demanded they be installed out of view, inside closets and cabinetry. Shimmy also disliked the appearance of door hinges. As an alternative, he commissioned the design and manufacture of specialized hardware, invisible joints that could be implanted inside doorframes. With the office doors shut, the long rectangular hallway leading from the reception area to the warehouse had the enclosed, spare elegance of a wooden casket.

The Great White Father presided from the back of his spacious office, behind a Spanish antique bureau, circa 15th century. It was exquisitely carved in a floral pattern. Shimmy was known for his impeccable dress. A red silk tie hung down from his chin like a moist tongue. His shirt was freshly pressed and his collar was starched. Gershon noticed the SS monogram embroidered into his cuffs.

"He's a strong man, your father. I have a tremendous amount of respect for him," Shimmy said, looking placid. "You know, he and I go back a long way. To the very beginning."

"Yes, I know," Gershon said. "I'm sorry for disturbing you. I just wanted to ask if —"

"He worked hard, a real pioneer," Shimmy interrupted. "When the business was downtown, they thought I was crazy to move out here."

"Yes."

"But, your father … he saw the future. He had confidence. It took guts to do what he did," Shimmy said.

"He has no shortage of that … guts," Gershon agreed. "Hopefully, enough to carry him through his current difficulties."

"Illness," Shimmy continued, "what can you say about getting sick? He's a fighter. Your father's a real survivor."

Shimmy's silver hair reflected light from the window behind him. The dome of his head appeared to emit an aura. He gestured deliberately as he spoke. His hands hovered above the dark bureau, moving back and forth like an ancient priest performing rites over an ornamented sarcophagus.

"I don't want to take too much of your time. I was hoping you might help me." Gershon wanted to verbalize his request and exit quickly. Shimmy interrupted again.

"Illness," Shimmy muttered pensively as he slid a drawer open, extracted a cigarette, lit the end and inhaled. "Your father's sick, the industry is sick." Plumes of smoke rose from his nostrils.

"Your father and I… we've known much better times." He paused. "All this was built on a lousy dress," Shimmy said, opening his palms and circling his body with his arms to show off his surroundings.

"Actually it wasn't a dress. First, it was a lousy blouse. In the early forties when I started out, the wholesale price of a blouse was a dollar ninety-nine and it retailed for between three and four dollars. Back then, each operator sewed a complete garment. I knew there had to be a better way. I saw how manufacturing could be streamlined like an assembly-line. I was hungry as hell. After apprenticing with my uncle for a few years, learning the nuts and bolts of the business, I went out on my own.

They'd eat me alive, my uncle told me. He said I didn't stand a chance. I'd come to him on my hands and knees begging for my old job back." Shimmy hauled on his cigarette.

"One day, a couple of months after I left him, he showed up at my door. He wanted to see how I was suffering. He walked through my factory shaking his head, mumbling that I didn't have a clue what I was doing. He took one of my blouses off the rack and inspected it. Decent quality, he said. I suppose he thought he was making me feel good. How much are you selling it for? Eleven ninety-nine, I told him. You'll go bust, he laughed. Per dozen, I said. I put that *putz* out of business in six months."

Gershon listened stiffly in his chair. Hearing Shimmy swear startled him, like a student in a classroom hearing his teacher curse.

"I think about what we had and how we gave it all up."

"What do you mean? Who gave it up?" Gershon asked.

"We did. The label. We have no one to blame but ourselves. When we gave up the label, we gave up the business. At one time we owned it all. The stores came to us for *our* product. Now we beg them to produce *their* garments. They own the customer. It's all about the name."

"I don't understand."

"We Jews have always re-invented ourselves." Shimmy began philosophically, leaning forward and stabbing his cigarette out in an ashtray. Gershon noticed a mound of small brown butts, like hungry maggots crawling over themselves.

"Re-invention has always been the Jewish speciality. The immigrant manufacturers who came from the old country chose names. Fancy-sounding, hyphenated, *goyish* ones. In those days I used 'Jessica-Lynne' and 'Carla-Ann' on my labels. I tacked on the word 'original' and called one of my lines 'Jessica-Lynne Originals'. What a sham. There was nothing original about it. The styles were knocked-off from European product. Canadian women always wore 'original' designs that were really nothing more than hand-me-downs.

"I was one of the first to give up my label. What choice did I have? I had built the largest dress manufacturing operation in the country. Profits depended on producing in volume. I had to grow my markets continuously. After a while it became a problem. I came up against a wall. My customers, the boutiques and chain-stores, were reluctant to carry the same labels as their competitors. They wanted to differentiate themselves. I needed to devise a way of hiding my identity to sell them more dresses. I replaced my label with names chosen and owned exclusively by the stores. We handed them on a silver platter the ability to build consumer loyalty. The name. We sold millions and million of privately-labelled units to hundreds of retailers across the country. We made minor alterations, added a pocket or changed an elastic for a zipper, but the styles were basically all the same."

Shimmy paused to light another cigarette. The stench of smoke, which Gershon had tolerated successfully at first, was beginning to make him feel light-headed and ill. A few smoky hauls and Shimmy was ready to continue, his train of thought undisturbed.

"For a long time it was a boon to the industry. We became rich. We didn't care that by copying designs and giving up our labels, we were becoming invisible to the consumer. The purchaser only cares about the brand. The retailers realized the power they had in their hands by owning the name. The end-purchaser was loyal to them, not to the manu-facturers. We became obsolete. The chains could have anyone, anywhere, produce their product for them. They began demanding cheaper and cheaper product. We dropped our pants and gave them what they wanted, like a bunch of whores. Anything to keep their business. They ate into our profit margins until there was nothing left. Then, when that wasn't good enough for them, the chains turned to imported product from God-forsaken places like China and Bangladesh. All because they owned the labels. When we gave up our names we ransomed our future."

"So that's why the industry is in decline today."

"Everything is imported now. The Montreal *shmatte* business is finished, kaput. The Jewish manufacturers are dying a nameless death."

With talk of death, the moment seemed opportune. "I'm looking for a minyan in the building. I'm hoping you can help," Gershon spat out.

Shimmy glared at him, amused.

"Help? With a minyan in the building? I'm afraid praying won't work." He grinned.

Gershon was quiet. Then he said, "With my father ... those days when everything was healthy ... good ... sometimes, I think ... it's better not to look back."

It's better not to look back. Gershon turned the phrase over in his mind. He didn't know why he had said that. He didn't believe it. Or maybe, in a way, he did. He believed something like it. Looking back could be a good thing to do, or it could be bad, depending on how far back and how deeply you looked. And that depended on what you were prepared to see in the first place.

Gershon *looked back*, which meant looking inside himself. He thought about his father. A series of what-ifs assaulted him. What if Sholem had made one wrong decision along the way? What if a German soldier, doing his job, had thoughtlessly put a bullet in his head? What if Sholem hadn't had luck and faith on his side? What if he had died in the camps? What if Sholem's parents had not survived their pogroms, innumerable atrocities and misfortunes? And their parents had not survived their hardships?

The what-ifs stacked up like dominoes in a line, each falling into the next and the next and the next, hundreds and thousands of lives, experiences and decisions, each dependent on the one before it. At the end of the line was Gershon, sitting right here, right now, today. One mistake, one gap in the chain and it would have all ended. Come to nought, forever.

There was no such thing as looking backward or forward. There was only the present, the constancy of being that encompassed past and future. Gershon realized that his own presence was an unlikelihood. He was here against all odds. It was nothing short of a miracle. Suddenly, he was filled with profound feelings of gratitude, a sense of his own wealth and depth.

"You may be right, Gershon. About not looking back. We were on top of the world in those days. You have no idea what it felt like. And now to see how far we've fallen, to witness it all happening. That's what makes it so difficult."

Gershon had learned something listening to Shimmy. His stature in the industry may have been big, but Shimmy's life was small. He sounded bitter and regretful because when he *looked back* he saw only what he had taken. The little he gleaned from the past represented all he was capable of holding in the shallow cup of his own heart. Inside, Shimmy saw his own reflection peering back up from a reservoir so empty he could see the bottom. Now that the end was near, what he saw was his own shallowness.

"We were kings. Now look at us. After the war the money flowed like a river. All we had to do was dip in and drink. The only thing stopping us was how much we were capable of holding in our hands. In '64 this building was the future. It was full-steam ahead. Now look at it. The elevators don't work. The walls are cracking. The hallways are filled with garbage."

Gershon had a strange thought. When a person died their soul lived on. It went forward into the next world, the *olam habah*, where it merged with the Eternal. But what happened to an industry when it died? Where did it go, the way of life, the culture, the language, because wasn't an industry all of those things too? If they were lost forever, wasn't it possible that the demise of an industry was a greater tragedy than the death of a person, or at least as tragic?

"I feel bad for you, Gershon. Look at what we've left for you, the shit your generation is inheriting."

"I don't feel like I'm inheriting ..." Gershon did not want to say it.

"It won't be too long now," Shimmy said, not listening to Gershon.

"Too long?"

Shimmy raised his eyes. "Before we pack it in. It's finished."

"Finished?"

"I've had enough. I'm getting too old for this crap. The government is back. Bastards. They won't let us survive. Scratch out our living. I'm getting too old for it. First it was the Separatists and their goddamn laws to make everything French. Now they harass us for the sales tax. I'm tired of it."

"What do you mean, finished?"

"Thinking of putting a key to the door, Gershon. Closing up. We'll see how they like it when I put a few hundred people out of work, those bastards."

Gershon's stomach dropped. If Simple Dress closed, twenty percent of the building would instantly become vacant. The restaurant would lose a substantial number of customers. The stores on the fourth floor did a lot of business with Simple's employees. They would suffer. Gershon imagined more closures, more vacancies. He felt the pit in his belly grow.

How would Sholem have responded to Shimmy? His father always had a way of saying the right thing when the situation looked most grim.

Sholem used words that instilled confidence. It was a talent honed in the death camps. At the moment, Gershon felt speechless.

"I hope your father gets well," Shimmy said, staring down at the dark surface of his desk.

Gershon sensed that he was being dismissed. There was no reason to ask Shimmy again about the minyan. The conversation had ground to a halt. He rose from his chair and turned to leave. "I pray he does too," he said, without looking back.

As Gershon stepped from the office into the hallway, the red fire bell on the wall above the emergency exit started clanging, BING BING BING BING. He looked at it calmly, walked to the elevator, pressed the arrow pointing up and waited. He was willing to wager a month's gross rental this was another false alarm, the third in less than a week. Nothing to get excited about.

If there was one reason Sholem was still alive after more than eighteen months in the camps it was because he worked hard. In the fall of 1944 he was still labouring, breaking stones with a hammer, filling wheelbarrows, lugging heavy loads down a dirt path and dumping them on a pile. He gasped for air, his nostrils thick with dust. When somebody working nearby dropped to the ground, Sholem rushed to their side and tore the shirt from their body without bothering to check if they were still breathing. He wrapped his cracked, bloody hands and feet in protective fabric.

Three hundred metres down the path from the mound of stones another pile was growing faster than the pile of stones. This was a heap of corpses. Sholem had almost ceased seeing any difference between the two inert, misshapen piles. As time went on, though, the matter crystallized in his mind. One pile meant a great deal. The pile of stones meant life. He tended it. He made it grow with all the energy he could muster, as if it were a bed of flowers.

With the end of the war in sight, his captors had decided to increase the rate of prisoner exterminations. The supply of corpses had begun to outstrip the capacity to incincrate them. Workers were ordered to take the stones they quarried and begin building more ovens.

When the war was going well for Germany and reports of victory reached the camp—news of conquered lands, territories being made

Judenrein—the soldiers marched about serenely. They held the barrels of their weapons delicately in the crooks of their elbows like infants. They even joked with prisoners on occasion. The beatings came less often, and less viciously; their hearts were not in it.

Now Sholem heard the German soldiers repeating "vier" to one another. Vier. Vier. They wanted *four* more ovens built as quickly as possible. They were agitated and short-tempered, beating the workers to the ground frequently, kicking them and then commanding them to get up and work. Lazy Jewish dogs, they barked. For the first time since his arrival, Sholem heard the fear in their voices. He surmised that the tide of the war had shifted against Germany. I will work hard. Harder than ever before, he told himself. I will be like a machine, unstoppable. But his brain and body argued. Months and months of cracking stones had sapped his extremities of their strength. His legs were wobbly. The tool began slipping from his grasp, his arms shook and his spine ached more with each lift of the hammer. Gravity tugged at him, pulled him down. He could perceive the ground opening beneath his feet. He was slowly being swallowed.

He hadn't seen it coming. The soldier's heel against his chest. It hadn't even occurred to him that he was on the ground until the bottom of a boot told him so. Up was down and down was up. The rocks were grey clouds and the clouds, grey rocks.

I can still work, he told himself, looking up through the haze of dirt and dizziness at the soldier's face partially eclipsed by the dim hole of his gun. Sholem pushed out the words *Ich arbeit*, I work.

The soldier lifted his boot off Sholem's chest doubtfully. Sholem rolled on his side, arched his back and pushed with all his might to balance himself up over his bent knees. Arms extended to the ground, he took another breath and repeated *Ich arbeit*, this time trying to convince himself. He brought his knees up underneath his chest and steadied the weight of his body over the balls of his feet. He rested. If he'd been preparing to walk a tightrope fifty feet off the ground, without a net below to catch him, he wouldn't have felt such trepidation. Falling meant certain and immediate death.

He strained to raise his body. Fully erect, he tottered like a child learning to walk, his arms outstretched for balance, hands grabbing the air for support. The spinning world slowed and came to a stop.

The soldier waited impatiently behind him. Now that he was standing, Sholem looked down to the sledgehammer lying at his feet. He could not do it. He knew if he attempted to pick it up the gravity of the earth would not let him go. The spot where he stood would be his grave, the camp his final address. What was he going to do now? How would he get the hammer into his hands? Incredibly, the internal debate became moot when the soldier reached around Sholem's body, scooped the hammer off the ground and handed it to him. Go ahead, work, he challenged with his gesture. Or let's get this over with, and you can die already.

The solid weight of the hammer passed straight through Sholem's palms as it was given to him. His hands were as useless as the appendages of a ghost. The hammer's head thudded to the ground, its wooden handle catching against his knees and pivoting upward within reach. He leaned his body against the tool, using it as a balancing prop while he spit into his palms, indicating to the soldier his readiness to get back to work. He rubbed his hands together and wrapped his fingers around the cool, slender shaft of wood. He tested the weight at the end, trying to raise the metal head off the ground a fraction of an inch. It didn't budge. His palms burned with opened sores. He tried again, wincing with effort and pain. Nothing. And again. Nothing.

Watching Sholem, the soldier was quickly coming to his decision. Three more ovens had to be finished. Time was being wasted. He slipped his pistol out of its black leather holster and pointed the barrel toward Sholem's neck, at the base of the skull where it connected to his spine. Sholem didn't have to see the gun. He felt no fear, not even resignation. He was empty. If his hands were already those of a ghost, in all likelihood, the rest of him was not far behind. He stood immobile, his fingers still resting against the handle of the hammer. He began a final prayer. *Shema Yisroel Adonai El…*

Then Sholem thought he'd heard the crack of gunfire. He believed a bullet had been released from its chamber and passed through him. But he felt nothing. It was uncanny. He *had* become a ghost. He was weightless. Energy and light encircled him. Stones glowed like lanterns. His body was dissolving. The air sifted through his presence like a filter. Am I entering the *olam habah*? Shall I be joining the realm of pure spirit? No. The moment he asked himself these questions, he knew he could not be entering the afterlife. In heaven there are no questions.

Familiar sensations returned—the ground pushing up under the weight of his body, the slight shifts of his feet, a chill along his arms. The wooden handle of the hammer slipped off his knees and kicked up dust as it hit the ground, sending a dry, chalky mist to his nostrils. He was standing in a quarry, alive, somewhat. He sensed an absence. He was alone. Out of the corner of his eye he confirmed that the soldier behind him was gone. He twisted his head further around and witnessed movement, uniformed men running in the distance, like tiny grey rodents scampering to their burrow. The soldiers were surrounding the most recently completed oven. The one put into service just a few days ago. It now lay in a smoky heap of rubble.

Poor workmanship, thought Sholem. What else did they expect from buildings constructed by the walking dead? With this last rhetorical question still lingering in his mind, Sholem collapsed too.

Basement

GERSHON CIRCULATED among the tenants for a week, using his best salesmanship to make it as difficult as possible for them to refuse to join the minyan. He appealed to their compassion, asking them to do it for the sake of his sick father. He told them that they didn't have to pray in the formal sense. If they didn't know how to read Hebrew they could follow along in English. The Talmud says a person shouldn't pray in a language he does not understand. If they didn't know the *trop*, the melodies, they could just hum. Prayer was not just words. Or they could just stand in place doing nothing, reflecting quietly. But they said no. Not to disappoint Gershon, others said maybe, but they meant no.

"When do you know you've hit rock bottom?"

Why did Gershon ask her? Did he expect Alfreda was some kind of expert?

"What's the matter, Gershon. Rent collection getting you down?"

Gershon hadn't mentioned to Alfreda anything about his quest for a minyan. Arnie Free had said he would come to the daily minyan, but Gershon knew he couldn't be depended upon to attend regularly. Arnie might forget the appointed hour, lose track of time while perusing a sexy catalogue. Or hung-over from one of his infamous late-night 'business trips', he might not make it into work the next day.

Sonny Lipsey had bargained with Gershon. "Increase your donation to *I VAIT* by twenty-five percent and I'll come," Sonny had said.

Yossi Alfasi, as expected, was enthusiastic about participating in the minyan. He even took it a step further, suggesting after prayers someone could prepare a brief *d'var Torah*, share a few words of insight on the weekly Torah portion.

"It's not just rent collection," Gershon said to Alfreda, though in truth, rent was definitely part of it. The time he had spent working on the minyan came at the expense of his routine rent collection rounds.

"I've noticed you're behind this month," Alfreda said to urge him onward.

"Every day it gets harder and harder," Gershon said.

"Rock bottom, eh? Well, if you were a drug addict, I'd say you'd hit rock bottom when you couldn't think of anything else except getting your next fix."

That's it, thought Gershon. I'm an addict. When I do my job, the rent is like a fix. I'm a rent addict, living from cheque to cheque. The thought disturbed him. He cancelled that notion with another one.

"I'm a God addict," he proclaimed thinking about the minyan, the collection of souls.

"A God addict? In that case—no difference," Alfreda said without missing a beat. "Maybe that's what's taking you down. Forget about God for a while. Focus your energies on collecting money."

It would be simpler. Still, Gershon couldn't get the minyan out of his mind. Why was it so difficult to convince people to give twenty minutes of their time? It was easier for them to give cash. Wasn't their time more valuable? What was it about prayer that made them so reluctant? It frightened the tenants.

Standing quietly was intolerable to the them. It was so excruciatingly difficult they preferred to pay. When Gershon went to see Superman and Lex Luther about the minyan they gave him rent cheques to hurry him out of their offices. Anything but prayer, was the message they communicated by handing over money. The minyan could be an effective form of coercion, thought Gershon, an incentive to remit rent. Instead of asking for the monthly rent he'd threaten: pay or pray.

Somewhat in jest, Irving Roth had said, "For Sholem, I might come. How much of a rent reduction will we get if we show up?" Then he asked, "How many more do you need for the minyan? I might even be able to scrape up a few bodies. I'm sure some of our Jewish employees can be persuaded."

Gershon did not want Irving Roth to twist employee arms. He did not want *bodies scraped up*. He decided relying on Irving Roth to twist arms and scrape up bodies was likely a sign he was near rock bottom, if he hadn't already landed there.

Had Gershon really been that naïve to suppose he could gather a minyan from the tenants of 99? Even the most impious Jews prayed when they were in trouble. If they could not muster the humility and gratitude that underlied the observant Jew's daily prayer, surely, at the very least, they were capable of desperate prayer. One that cried to the Almighty "get me out of this mess." Surely they saw that the industry was in a shambles. Maybe Gershon had overestimated this too. It seemed that his tenants had come so far down they didn't even recognize that they were in trouble. Or worse, they acknowledged privately that they were in trouble but their souls were in such a degraded state that the last resort option of prayer had not occurred to them. Instead, as in every business situation, they stubbornly hung on to the belief that they could bargain their way out, which is what they did with Gershon.

Ruhama told Gershon he was wasting his time. "I know how much you want your father to get well, but a minyan at 99 won't make it happen," she had said. Her words clawed at his insides. Ruhama had a way of saying things that sometimes made him feel immature. She liked to see him as a child. Regardless of Ruhama's opinion, Gershon felt the burning sense that there was something much greater at stake than his own wishes and impulses. Was hoping a waste of time? Was it something to be ashamed of?

Whatever the reason behind it, at least he had tried to collect the ten righteous men to form a minyan. *The ten righteous men.* He repeated the phrase in his mind. *The ten righteous men.* He hadn't really thought of it that way, but that was exactly what the minyan was. The number needed to form a quorum for prayer was the minimum of righteous men God required to save the cities of Sodom and Gomorrah.

When the Almighty announced that He would destroy those dens of perversion and iniquity, Abraham had the chutzpah to bargain with Him. Surely a merciful God would not let the innocent die for the sake of the guilty, Abraham had pleaded. Would the cities be spared if fifty righteous men could be found among the inhabitants? Yes, the Almighty had answered. Forty-five? Yes. Forty? Yes. What about thirty-five or thirty? Yes, God had responded. When they arrived at ten, the discussion came to a close, like a tenant and landlord settling on a final price for rent.

Gershon thought about Abraham's courage and temerity. Bargaining with God was his way of testing the limits of Divine Mercy and Justice. Abraham was experiencing his own crisis of faith. Does a God who slaughtered the innocent together with the guilty deserve his faith? Abraham must have asked himself this question. What kind of justice was that? What kind of God would do such a thing? Or maybe it was the other way around. God wasn't the one on trial. It was Abraham who was being tested. The destruction of Sodom and Gomorrah was God's way of determining if Abraham was worthy of founding His People. The Almighty wanted to see if Abraham would defend his fellow human beings. And Abraham had proven his merit by caring enough to bargain with Him in the face of impending calamity, trying to save as many souls as he could.

Perhaps that's what the minyan meant to Gershon. His search was not motivated by a childish desire to bring his father back as Ruhama had claimed. Gathering the ten righteous of 99 was a test of his own faith. But did his faith depend on finding ten righteous souls among the businessmen of 99? How absurd was that? And if he succeeded, did Gershon think the city would be saved? The industry? Gershon would be the saviour of Chabanel. The notion sounded ridiculous.

Gershon spent so much of his life in this place, on this street, and it was still such a mystery to him. Even the name. He was ashamed of himself. He had not even cared enough to at least find out what, or who Chabanel was. People had spent decades working on this street and he was willing to bet that few if any knew what "Chabanel" meant. He reckoned that Chabanel must have been a person. So many of Montreal's streets were named after famous politicians and historical figures, heroes to some, villains to others. The city teemed with significance, the famous and the infamous, people who had left their mark.

For example, Camillien Houde Drive bisected Mount Royal. It was named for the bulbous-nosed, charming, populist politician who ran the city as mayor, on and off, from the late 1920s through the early 1950s. Those were the years when Montreal was a wide open city, known for its brothels, fancy night-clubs and illegal gambling establishments. Beloved by corrupt city-councillors, crime-bosses, cops on the take and constituents alike, Houde was a master of exploiting the patronage and largesse afforded him by his office. A supporter of Mussolini and the policies of the Vichy government in France, he called for Quebeckers to defy conscription in 1940 and was interned by the RCMP for four years in Ontario as a result. After his release, Montrealers welcomed their cigar-smoking "favourite uncle" back by promptly returning Houde to power in the elections of 1947 and 1950.

René Lévesque Boulevard, a main artery through the centre of downtown, was named for the former Premier of the province. Lévesque was the founder of the Parti Québécois. In 1980 he had very nearly succeeded in turning Quebec into a separate country. René Lévesque Boulevard had been called Dorchester Boulevard for decades until it was changed by government officials who saw merit in replacing the 18th-century Loyalist British military commander and former Governor with the 20th-century Quebec separatist. The downtown municipality of Westmount, an Anglo bastion for generations, kept the name Dorchester. Walking east along Dorchester, perhaps enjoying the sights of buildings or idly daydreaming, a person crossed Atwater Avenue and found that, without veering left or right, a frontier had been invisibly traversed. A shift had taken place from one era, one history, one mindset, one language, one political stripe into a completely opposite one. It was like magically moving from one dimension into the next, like walking through the boundary of an *eruv*, indicated by a change in street names.

True to its staunchly Roman Catholic past, a great many Montreal roads and avenues were named for religious personages. The city was criss-crossed by a patchwork of sainted routes and martyred thoroughfares. Ste. Catherine Street was the main shopping strip downtown. Large office buildings and fancy retail complexes lined Ste. Catherine along with small boutiques, seedy bars, cinemas, fast-food restaurants and neon-illumined triple-x strip-clubs. The Santa Claus, St. Patrick's Day and Saint-Jean-Baptiste parades all took place along Ste. Catherine. The route was adorned in red, green or blue at different times of the year depending on the festivity being celebrated.

The Jews did not believe in saints. They had *tzaddikim*, righteous people, but not saints. The *tzaddikim* were individuals of unusual piety and wisdom, but otherwise not much different than regular folks. They possessed the same faults and grappled with the same temptations and personal dilemmas. Even the greatest Jewish prophets had made errors in judgement for which they were held accountable. The price they paid for their mistakes was usually severe, which was also part of Jewish tradition. Moses the Deliverer, who had led the Jews out of slavery, guided them through forty years of hardship in the desert and brought down the Tables of Law at Sinai, had himself not been permitted entry into the Promised Land because he had made mistakes.

Some *tzaddikim* were decidedly unsaintly. King David, the greatest Jewish political leader, the poet of the Psalms, the man from whose lineage the Messiah was expected to come, had sent an innocent man to his death because he desired the man's wife Bathsheba. Gershon was sure that the Jews loved and admired their heroes as much as the Christians, probably more. But they did so, not in spite of, but in large part because of their flaws, their inner conflicts, their transparent humanness.

The sheer numbers of Christian saints Gershon saw memorialized on street signs populating the metropolis always surprised him. Most of the time he had no idea who they were. He recognized St. Marc and St. Mathieu, two downtown streets, as names from the Christian Bible. But who was Ste. Catherine? What had she done to warrant the honour of being Montreal's most prominent shopping route? And what about St. Antoine? Who was Saint Antoine? Who was Saint Viateur for whom a street close to Gershon's house was named? Who was Saint Urbain?

The west-end municipality of Côte St. Luc was ninety percent Jewish. Gershon knew that Luke, like Mark and Matthew, was one of Jesus's disciples. 99 Chabanel was located just west of St. Laurent boulevard which was called "The Main" by the immigrant Jews who settled there. But who was St. Laurent? Lawrence the saint? Was he the patron saint of something? For a time, St. Laurent was the patron saint of struggling Jewish immigrants, until they got rich and left that district for Côte St. Luc. Lawrence the saint was traded in for Luke who became the patron saint of Jewish prosperity.

What about Chabanel? Was there a Saint Chabanel? Gershon had no idea where he might find information about Chabanel. He asked his brother to help him with research. Chaim searched the internet and arrived one day with several pages of biography.

"What do you want with this stuff?" Chaim asked, handing Gershon the document.

"Just curious," Gershon answered. "You know how I am."

Noël Chabanel was thirty-six years old when he died in 1649. Gershon was also thirty-six, an important number in Judaism because it was *tvei mol chai*, two times eighteen. When spelled out in Hebrew letters the number eighteen meant life, *chai*. It was why, when the Steins made donations, they gave a hundred and eighteen dollars instead of just one hundred. Eighteen, or permutations of that number was considered good luck.

Chabanel was one of the so-called eight North American Martyrs. There were four North American Martyrs of the first order and four of the second. Chabanel had been a second-class martyr. He'd arrived in Quebec, then called New France, as a Jesuit missionary. During his brief mission he distinguished himself by being uniquely unsuitable for converting the natives to Christianity. According to accounts from the *Jesuit Relations*, despite years of study and effort, Chabanel was unable to master the Indian language. His inability to communicate with the Indians made it impossible for him to contribute to the expansion of the Huron Mission. As a result, Chabanel remained in the village of Ste. Marie. Lamenting his failure to participate in more ambitious missionary adventures in the outlying regions, Chabanel called himself, "a bloodless martyr in the shadow of martyrdom."

Acknowledging that his role was fated to be a secondary one, he suffered constant self-doubt, loneliness and discouragement. Even as he dreamed of the day he might die a painfully glorious death for the sake of Christ, he accepted his station and humbly served his mission in whatever way he could. His personal failures, he believed, were a cross he was given to bear.

Gershon read two accounts of Chabanel's death, both by the Jesuit mission's chief chronicler Paul Ragueneau. The first account said simply that he was caught in the wilderness while fleeing the murderous Iroquois. Christians who had escaped the rampaging hordes had reported witnessing Chabanel as he dropped to his knees in the snow and declared, "What difference does it make if I die or not? This life does not count for much. The Iroquois cannot snatch the happiness of heaven from me."

The second account of Chabanel's martyrdom was considerably more precise and apparently more reliable. Ragueneau wrote that Chabanel was betrayed by a Huron apostate. A member of his flock,

Louis Honareenhax, bragged publicly that he had murdered Chabanel with a hatchet and then tossed the mutilated body into the half-frozen Nottawasaga River. He blamed the priest for the misfortunes that had befallen the Huron Nation ever since they had embraced the Christian faith. Honareenhax claimed that the sacrifice of Chabanel was necessary to expiate the scourge and terror his tribesmen now faced from the advancing Iroquois.

No doubt this second account was promoted by the Church because it linked Chabanel neatly to Jesus, the model of martyrdom. Like Christ, Chabanel had been betrayed by one of his own flock, a person who had resisted reform and could not be converted to the ways of the new faith. For Gershon it echoed the repugnant lie the Christians taught for two thousand years about how the Jews had committed deicide. How they had resisted change and turned on one of their own, making him into the ultimate scapegoat. Gershon was repulsed by the effort to glorify death. The rabbis had always taught that there was nothing noble in dying. It was a tragedy. He hated the Christian myth that attempted to make death otherwise.

His death-wish and gory ending notwithstanding, it was how Chabanel lived that Gershon found most intriguing and sad. He read one final biographical note. In the official image of Noël Chabanel, the martyr was pictured solemn-faced, holding a closed book in his hand, the symbol of both his devotion to God and a closed life. It was apparent to Gershon that if Chabanel was a saint, he was the patron of misfits and failures, those who were perpetually disappointed and suffered in repressed silence.

Repeating the words *Noël Chabanel* in his head Gershon realized something. *El* in Hebrew meant God. All Hebrew names that ended in the suffix "el" referred to the Almighty. Ariel was "Lion of God". Daniel meant "God is my Judge". Gabriel was "Defender of God". Joel meant "The Name is God," Israel was "One who wrestled with God" and Michael stood for "Who is like God". The name Noël could not be coincidental. Did it mean No God? And what about Chabanel? It was French, pronounced softly, like the name of the famous fashion designer, Chanel, *shun El*.

Just as the rabbis loved to search for hidden scriptural meanings in words and the arrangements of letters, Gershon played with the name.

Hardening the word "Chanel" hebraically, it sounded like *kan El*, "God is here." Reversing the syllables, he arrived at *El kana*, "God is jealous." If there were secret meanings in the words it could be that God was absent, *Noel*, or God was shunned, *Chanel*, or God was here, *Kan El* and He was jealous, as in *El Kana*. Maybe like the inhabitants of Sodom and Gomorrah, the businessmen of Chabanel had incurred the Almighty's wrath because they ceased to worship God, or they worshipped other gods, the god of sin, the god of flesh, the god of money.

Another name insisted itself upon Gershon. An *El* name. An important one. He said it slowly, at first only in his head. *Mi-chelle La-belle*. Michelle was the French feminine form of Michael, "Who is like God." He broke the full name Michelle Labelle into Hebrew words, uttering the syllables aloud and translating as he went along: *Mi* – Who, *shel* – Of, *leib* – Heart, *El* – God. It was not a name at all. It was a Hebrew sentence. A precise phrase, crystal clear. A message: *Mi shel leib El*— "Who is of God's heart."

Gershon took a pen and a sheet of lined white paper. He wrote the name Michelle Labelle. He immediately saw that the words did not end in the suffix "el" but rather "elle," the French word for "she." "Elle" could also be understood as the name of God in a palindrome, readable either forward or backward. Did it represent both an inward turning, and simultaneously, an outpouring of the Divine spirit? Every syllable and every letter had to be significant. Did it mean that godliness moved in two directions? Did it mean that the God of our innermost hearts and the God of the outside world were one and the same? If that was the case then the task of every person was to seek the connection between the two, to conjoin the world within with the world without, to fuse the earthly with the heavenly we felt in our hearts. For a moment Gershon couldn't catch his breath. He was stunned by what he'd divined from delving into the names. The questions in him multiplied. Meanings begot questions and more meanings which in turn begot more questions and meanings.

Maybe he was blowing all of this out of proportion. The search for a minyan hadn't been about the salvation of Chabanel or the industry or anyone else. Gershon was not Abraham. Far from it. More like the biblical Lot. He was an occupant of Chabanel and made his living from the fashion business as much as any of his tenants did. He was a participant, as guilty as any inhabitant of Sodom and Gomorrah. He may have been pious, but he was hardly righteous. Maybe it was a mistake to think that he wasn't one of them.

Gershon hadn't wanted to save the street, the industry or the city. All this time spent looking for the minyan wasn't about saving his father, either. Gershon knew that already. He was really only after saving one person, himself. As foolish or naïve or crazy as his endeavour had been, he hoped that having had enough faith in his fellow Jew to attempt finding a minyan at 99 demonstrated something worthwhile. Just because the outcome had been unfavourable it didn't mean he had wasted his time. He hoped that God took pity on the ones who tried and failed.

His quest had yielded one pleasant surprise. Avi Putkin had said he'd come for the minyan, no strings attached. Gershon believed him. Avi's credibility derived from the fact that his wife had passed away not too long ago. Jews often acquired a taste for prayer when they experienced a personal loss of such proximity and magnitude.

Gershon had unexpectedly bumped into Avi in the parking garage. Confident that his request would be treated respectfully, Gershon did not hesitate to speak about the minyan. He spoke frankly, dispensing with the foreplay and verbal niceties he had used with the other tenants. Avi responded positively. With the discussion proceeding smoothly, Gershon decided to ask Avi about something else. The next subject was handled with more delicacy.

"The other day, when I came to see Joey, I was looking at the pictures in your office."

"Really. I'm shocked." Avi grinned.

"I had to wait for him. What else was I supposed to do? There was no choice. They're all over the walls." Gershon spoke nervously.

"I'm kidding. Take it easy. They're meant to be looked at, Gershon. That's why we put them there. Did you see anything you liked? You can say. They're just pictures."

"Well, there was one … behind the receptionist's desk."

"That one? You liked that one?" Avi knew precisely the photo Gershon was talking about.

"No. Not exactly."

"I didn't know you had such good taste. But isn't that one a bit sexy for you?" Avi's tone dropped a notch, to a level of intimacy.

The image came to Gershon's mind. The model standing with legs akimbo over a bare-chested man, his thick rhinoceros horn sticking up at her crotch. "Yes. I mean no. It wasn't the picture."

"We were going after an African theme. You can almost hear the rhythm of drums beating. Yes, I like that one." Avi nodded, looking self-satisfied.

"When you say, *we were going after a theme,* do you mean *you* took the picture?" Gershon asked, stunned.

"No. I didn't take the picture. I helped to set it up. It's one of the things I do for Joey. I get the models together, hire the photographer and the studio. I really enjoy working out themes and scenarios for shoots. You didn't know I was so creative? I'm an arrrrteest, Gershon." Avi rolled his 'r's, exaggerating his Israeli accent and he flicked his index finger in the air like he was stroking a paintbrush.

"*You* chose the models?"

"It's the best part. The shoot itself is quite bor-ing actually. You can't imagine how long it takes to get the perfect image. I have an eye for beautiful women. It's one of my specialties. A God-given talent. For models you need a special eye. Just because she is beautiful in person does not mean she will look good in pictures. The camera has a unique way of capturing beauty. Sometimes you find a model appealing in the flesh, but when you get them in front of a camera, there's ugliness. At other times they seem quite unappealing in real life, but the camera does them justice."

"Their faces are covered in that picture," Gershon said.

"In that shot, yes. With those two models it was something about their forms. The energies they gave off. There had to be something more, a kind of inner beauty that the camera understood and could bring out and capture. I can't explain it, Gershon. It's a matter of light and dark. The camera only understands light and dark."

The moment Avi mentioned light and dark, Gershon knew the truth. The woman in the picture was Michelle Labelle. It was confirmed. He didn't have to inquire further and risk exposing himself.

Gershon had made a wrong assumption. Joey Putkin hadn't been the one to see Michelle Labelle's inner light, his father had. Avi was the connection, not Joey. And when he had seen her light, what had he done about it? He had exploited her, covered her face and dressed her up like an animal for the camera. Gershon suddenly became flushed and irritated. Joey was crass and vulgar because, at base, his father was that way. The son took after the father. He instantly disliked Avi, almost as much as he disliked Joey. To continue being friendly now felt to Gershon like a kind of heresy. He wanted to cut the conversation short, or take it in a different direction. Since they were talking about the technicalities of photography, although it could hardly have been of less interest to Gershon, he decided to follow Avi's lead along that track.

"Interesting," Gershon said, stroking his beard and feeling the space between him and Avi grow. "I didn't know it was so complicated to take a simple picture."

"Oh yes, Gershon. More complicated than it seems. The trick is to make it look simple. She was very good, that model. I handed her a role and she played it like a real pro. You would never know it was her first time."

Avi's reference to Michelle Labelle stung Gershon. "You must be a very good director," he said, still trying to steer conversation away from her.

Avi persisted. "I'd like to use her again for another shoot. But I haven't been able to find her. After that photo session she vanished."

"I'm sorry for you," Gershon said through clenched teeth, his jaw beginning to throb.

The slap of Avi's heels reverberated off the garage's cavernous walls as he walked away. Gershon watched him move into the distance, getting smaller. He looked down and saw that his hands had curled themselves into fists. He was raging inside. Glancing over to the far corner of the garage near the boiler room, he half-expected to hear the hum of flaming furnaces and the screech of pumps that sent heated water circulating up through the building during the wintertime. In a couple of months they would be running again. Now, of course, the boilers were ominously silent.

Cars were lined up between huge rectangular pillars. Many were like Shimmy Solomon's Mercedes Benz and Irving Roth's Jaguar, freshly washed and gleaming. Other cars were less fancy. They belonged to tenants like Arnie Free whose nine-year-old Maxima had scratches and small rusty dents.

Gershon walked deeper into the garage, bending slightly to peer inside the back windows of vacant cars as he passed them. He looked into a succession of dim interiors. He saw a series of small rear-view mirrors hanging from front windshields. Stopping for a second behind each vehicle, he tried to spot his own reflection looking in from the back, but the mirrors were angled for someone seated in the driver's seat.

He stopped behind Joey Putkin's silver BMW parked in the farthest corner of the garage under a dip in the ceiling. When the garage door opened, a draught entered the building and pushed dirt from the outside into this corner, where it was trapped and accumulated. Gershon looked down and saw that the toes of his leather shoes were scuffed and covered in a thin layer of dust.

Behind the pillar to the right of the BMW, Gershon noticed bags of garbage piled up. Tenants who didn't bother bringing their trash to the compactors on the loading dock stuffed them in this distant corner of the garage out of public view. Under the heap of plastic bags filled with coffee cups, crushed aluminum cans and cut fabrics, Gershon saw construction materials, broken pieces of Gyproc, twisted metal studs, planks of wood and discarded steel piping used for hanging garments. He bent down, clutched one of the steel rods in his hand and gripping tightly, pried it out from under the mound of trash. He inspected the rod, shaking it in the air and swinging it like a baseball bat. The weight and action of cutting the air was exhilarating.

He looked around and listened. Silence. Then he stepped back over behind Joey Putkin's BMW.

No one would see me, he said to himself. No one would suspect me either. Not in a million years. He thought about how much pleasure he'd get from bashing a hole in Putkin's rear windshield. Gershon imagined the cracks that would appear on impact, traveling across the glass in a spray of directions like a spider's web. My little trap for him. If only I could see the look on his face when he arrived. I could wait for him to come, hide somewhere. Maybe I can move some bags and make a space for myself behind the garbage to peek out, watch his horrified reaction.

He swung the metal rod through the air again. It felt powerful and controlled in his fist. His eyes moved back and forth between the two red brake-lights on the BMW. What sound did a windshield make when it broke? Did it shatter? The crash would be heard. People might come running, he said to himself. I'm in a corner here. If someone came how would I escape? I'd be caught red-handed.

He raised the steel rod above his head like a hammer.

"Gershon! I meant to ask you…"

Startled, the slim piece of metal slipped from Gershon's grasp. It rang like an alarm bell as it hit the concrete floor, a loud BING echoing through the garage.

"About the minyan. I wanted to know the hours." Avi Putkin strode toward Gershon quickly.

I'm caught, thought Gershon. It was inevitable. He saw the metal bar in my hand. He watched me swinging it, knowing what I was going to do.

"Is everything alright?" Avi asked, seeing Gershon standing alone in the darkness.

Gershon panicked. His mind raced. Avi knows. But what does he know? I didn't do anything, Gershon rationalized. Avi can't know what I was thinking, can he? A person can't be held responsible for having criminal thoughts. People have those kinds of thoughts all the time. If he accuses me I'll deny everything. I'll say that I don't know what he's talking about. I'll play innocent. I'll tell him that he was mistaken. I'll plant the seed of doubt. I'll say that whatever he thought he was witnessing was nothing more than a trick of light. In the basement we sometimes see things that aren't really there. Illusions. Under such conditions it's best not to draw conclusions. But he'll know that it was precisely here, in the half-light of the basement, that acts of vandalism happened regularly, windshields were smashed, car stereos and mobile phones were stolen and hood ornaments were yanked off fancier vehicles. I need to make him doubt what he saw. I'll fake it with every fibre of my being. I'll act stupid, like nothing's the matter. Yes, it's good to know that sometimes, if you play your cards right, you can bluff your way out of any situation. I'll draw his attention elsewhere. Misdirection, I think the magicians called it. So now I'll be a magician, an actor. I'll pretend.

"Look! Look at this garbage," Gershon stammered. He kicked the metal rod at his feet back toward the mound of trash. "Look at what the tenants do—the way they treat the building." Thinking quickly, he added, "It doesn't bother your son that he has to park his nice, clean, expensive car next to a pile of trash?"

Avi nodded in answer to Gershon's question. They stood together staring at the BMW and the pile of trash. Not wanting to seem like he was running away, Gershon didn't budge from Avi's side. He resisted the urge to glance askew at Avi. Better to act like everything was normal. Make him think that Gershon was doing nothing more than touring the garage to inspect its cleanliness.

"It's shameful," Gershon said. "It's gotten to the point where people have no sense of shame anymore. And *that's* shameful." Avi nodded in agreement. Gershon hardly knew what he was saying. His pulse slowed after a few quiet moments. He began to calm down. He felt confident that his ruse was working. It was increasingly clear from his reaction that Avi Putkin didn't realize he was being duped.

Bayly asked Ruhama, "If you had to be blind or deaf, which would you rather be?"

"Blind or deaf? Why would you ask such a thing?"

"In school, we talked about handicaps. The teachers made us play a game. We put our fingers in our ears and tried reading lips. We closed our eyes and walked around the room holding a partner's hand."

"Well, that's good."

"I didn't like it very much. It felt bad."

"What did you learn?" Ruhama asked.

"I don't want to be blind or deaf."

Ruhama smiled at the way Bayly cleverly stated the obvious.

"God willing you won't be. But some people are. Now you know how it feels."

"I didn't like it," Bayly said. "I didn't understand what my friends were saying. I bumped into chairs and desks. My legs hurt."

People were courageous, some more so than others, some hungering for the world around them, caring so much they reached out and held on to it with whatever abilities they possessed. "Imagine how hard it is for people with handicaps," Ruhama said. "They have to be so strong."

"Blind people use special animals to help them. That's neat," Bayly said. "It would be nice to have a trained pet like that. What would you rather be, blind or deaf?" She asked her mother again.

"Well, if I was blind I wouldn't know what colour was. I wouldn't be able to drive because I couldn't see the red of the stoplights. I wouldn't know what the sky looked like, or the colour of a sunset." Ruhama thought a bit. "I think the worst would be not seeing your beautiful face."

"So you'd rather be deaf?"

"Well, no. Not necessarily. If I was deaf I couldn't hear music, or the sound of your beautiful voice asking these interesting questions."

"They showed us how blind people read special books with their fingers and deaf people talk to each other with their hands."

"They need to have special skills. Not many people understand the hand language."

"Is that why they are called 'handicaps'? Cause they speak with their hands?"

"Not really." Ruhama chuckled.

"It must be lonely for them. Like they live in a different country with a different language no one understands but them."

"You're right, sweetheart," Ruhama said, pleased with Bayly's expression of empathy.

"Does *Hashem* understand? Does He understand the language deaf people pray in?"

Ruhama had never thought about the prayers of deaf people.

"Of course, He does. He understands all languages."

"But *Hashem* speaks Hebrew. The Holy language."

"Actually, the Holy language is ours. *Hashem* doesn't speak language. Or maybe He speaks in all languages so everyone understands Him in their own way."

"But the Torah is in Hebrew. In the Torah, *Hashem* said, 'Let there be light.' Didn't He say it in Hebrew?"

"Oy Bayly, so many questions you have. You tire me out."

"Doesn't Hashem speak Hebrew?" Bayly asked, insisting on a satisfactory answer.

"Hashem understands all languages. Hebrew belongs to the Jewish people. It's our language. When He gave the Torah, He gave it in a language we would understand."

"So, when He created the world, when He said the words that made everything, what language did He speak?"

Ruhama thought longer. She wanted to be careful. Visions came to mind. The molten fire of Creation. The golden glow of the burning bush. The jagged finger of flame that carved the Law into hunks of stone on Mount Sinai.

She realized the answer that came to her would probably confuse her daughter more, but she said, "He spoke in the language of light."

"Uh oh." Alfreda was looking from her desk through the glass front door of the management office. She pressed the security buzzer to permit two gentlemen entry.

Bailiffs generally carried severe expressions on their faces. They were large, well-built men. Gershon had never seen a woman bailiff, though he surmised that since the days of women's liberation some must certainly exist. His image of a bailiff was a man wearing a suit and tie like a lawyer. In winter, bailiffs tended to wear trenchcoats like secret agents or private detectives. Their hair was neatly combed, and like the ones with whom Gershon had contact in the past, they sported thick, carefully trimmed mustaches. This was the uniform of people who made their profession delivering bad news.

Gershon also imagined that in spite of their formal, tailored appearances and reserved attitudes, they were skilled in self-defence techniques, martial-arts or some other form of hand-to-hand combat. Undoubtedly, bailiffs were fierce street fighters who could handle themselves equally well in boardrooms, bars and back alleys.

Either someone was suing, or someone was going bankrupt. Both possibilities were unsavoury. But who was it?

If the management was being taken to court, Gershon knew about it well in advance. Face-to-face arguments, terse, threatening letters sent "Without Prejudice" and a final demand on legal letterhead were preludes; the arrival of a bailiff represented the *coup de grâce* of a conflict that was ongoing and unresolved. Gershon quickly discounted the possibility of a lawsuit since he had not been engaged in any heated disputes which had gotten to that point. He assumed that the reason for this visit was bankruptcy. He began with worst-case scenarios. A list of nominees ran through his head, those tenants who owed management the most.

He greeted the bailiffs respectfully. It was unusual to receive two of them. Bailiffs typically worked alone. One was older than the other.

Gershon concluded that the younger man was a trainee. He placed the tense men at ease by inquiring how their day was going. The bailiffs were offered hospitality. Perhaps they might like a drink, a glass of water or a coffee. As someone who appeared at tenants' doors to demand rent, Gershon knew how it felt to be an unwelcomed guest. He empathized with the bailiffs, offering them a seat and implying with this gesture, that he knew how difficult it must be to perform their job.

He signed for the scrolled documents and handed the tube to Alfreda. The bailiffs smiled, rose and departed. Gershon was glad to have made the experience a pleasant one for them.

"Wait. Wait. Don't peek yet," he said to Alfreda, playfully. "Who do you think it is? Go ahead, guess." Alfreda held the papers sternly.

"No, no, wait a second. Don't say anything. You're much better at this than I am. Let me guess first," Gershon insisted.

He thought for a moment, scratching his beard.

"Estella Mora," he announced. "Definitely, Estella." Alfreda peered at him.

"Nope," she replied, shaking her head. "I don't think so. Definitely *not* Estella."

If not Estella then who?

Gershon thought about Shimmy Solomon. He had mentioned to Gershon at their meeting that he wanted to close, but so soon? It was unlikely. It was not Shimmy's style to declare bankruptcy. When he decided the time was right, Shimmy would probably pay off his creditors and leave discreetly, his reputation intact. Anyway, there was nothing to worry about. His account with the building was clear.

What about the Roths? They hadn't given any hint of trouble. No. Like Shimmy, they were old school. They wouldn't hurt people on the way out. They'd drop out without a fuss.

"O Great One, do tell. Seer of Futures. Diviner of Truth, Destiny and Misfortune. Master, reveal your secrets."

Alfreda grinned, feeling complimented.

"Well," she said, "bankruptcy is like making a quick escape. You only declare bankruptcy if you have something to protect. Estella has nothing."

"So, you think it's someone who has money."

"It's someone shrewd enough to move assets strategically out of their dying company, leave their suppliers crying, and start their business up again under a new name."

"No. No, don't say it." Gershon suddenly knew who Alfreda was thinking about. It struck him like a bolt of lightning.

"You don't think…"

"Yup."

"He wouldn't."

"Yup."

"Give me that thing," Gershon said, grabbing the scroll back.

"Don't tell me he's done it again." Gershon's eyes raced down the page.

CANADA
PROVINCE OF QUÉBEC
DISTRICT OF MONTRÉAL

SUPERIOR COURT
(In The Matter of Bankruptcy and Insolvency)

NOTICE OF INTENTION TO MAKE A PROPOSAL TO
CREDITORS
(Subsection 50.4 [1])

Take notice that:

1.   I, PUTKIN LEATHER DESIGNS INC., an insolvent person, pursuant to subsection 50.4(1) of the Bankruptcy and Insolvency Act, intend to make a proposal to my creditors.

2.   THE MALACHI GROUP TRUSTEES INC., a licensed trustee, has consented to act under proposal and a copy of the consent is attached hereto.

3.   A list of the names of the known creditors with claims amounting to $250 or more and the amounts of their claims is attached.

4.   Pursuant to section 69 of the Bancruptcy and Insolvency Act, all proceedings against me are stayed as of the date of filing the present notice with the Official receiver in my locality.

Gershon flipped the page. Creditor number seven leapt out at him, 99 CHABANEL INC. Next to the name an amount, $21,643.33. Gershon felt nauseous. His eyes sunk down to the bottom of the page. The total owing to creditors was more than two million dollars.

Gershon handed the document to Alfreda. He dropped down into his chair feeling weak. He lifted his index finger over his ear, tucking his *payas* behind. Why had he hesitated? He should have smashed the windshield of Putkin's BMW when he had the chance. It was clear now why Avi Putkin had agreed to participate in the minyan. He wanted to pray, not only for his own sins, but for his son's too.

Gershon inhaled and exhaled deeply. He thought about what would happen next and began to feel even worse. Putkin would approach him with a request to sign a new lease under a different company name. As an incentive, Putkin would offer Gershon some money to pay at least part of his debt. And because Gershon was taught that getting something was better than nothing, he would oblige.

Roof

GERSHON OFTEN FOUND HIMSELF on the rooftop of 99. A lot happened there. He went to check the source of rain leaks, and to verify the operation of the massive cooling-tower which chilled the water circulating through tenant air-conditioners. He also traversed the roof to enter the elevator machine rooms, where motors hummed, turning the huge grooved wheels and steel cables that sent cabins dropping and rising between floors.

The expanse of the roof was so great it had to be built in four flat quarters. The top of 99 had an inverse construction, which meant it was upside down, like a lined winter hat worn inside-out. The insulation was above, covering a rubber membrane over a concrete base, all held down by a layer of tons of chipped stones.

The inverse roof design had both positive and negative aspects. On the positive side, it was known to be extremely durable and long-lasting. Great care had been taken in the construction of the building to give it a strong, protective roof. On the negative side, the design's special nature was such that only a handful of companies were willing to fix it and repairs were usually expensive.

When it rained heavily, water became trapped under the top layer of insulation and gravel. Sections that had shifted and didn't drain properly became spongy. When he went on the roof to find the source of leaks during torrential rainfalls, Gershon bounced, as if he was stepping on the mattress of a waterbed. Feeling weightless, he sometimes imagined himself walking across the gravity-deficient surface of the moon.

He enjoyed his sojourns up to the roof. For one thing, the view was breathtaking. Gershon could not traverse the roof without pausing and planting himself. He felt exhilarated by the harsh wind that pressed against his body, threatening to carry him off the edge of the building. Staring straight out at the sky he felt at one with the world. He didn't think he would feel such awe had he been standing on the moon itself and looking back through space at the glowing light blue marble of planet Earth. What he saw from his place on the roof was Montreal. Specifically, the round dormant volcano heart of Montreal. Mount Royal, which was not really a mountain, but everyone still called it *the mountain*. Montreal which was not really a city, more like a collection of communities, an encampment of tribes and yet everyone still called it a city. His city, his mountain.

Montreal was not particularly beautiful. At least not looking outward from the centre. Standing at the tourist look-out on the eastern side of the mountain, the square grey duplex and triplex rooftops were spread out like ceramic bathroom floor tiles. These were laid down in neat rows, all the way out to the porcelain-white Olympic Stadium, which appeared to sit on top of everything. From the chalet on the western side of the mountain, you looked directly out on a clump of downtown office towers, and then further away the distant arcs of bridges spanning the St. Lawrence, like tiny bent metal struts binding the island-city to the river's opposite bank.

Montreal was one of those cities which was most glorious when perceived from the outside looking inward. The view from atop 99's roof was proof. Gershon saw the mountain of his childhood. He remembered family promenades around Beaver Lake, which was not a lake at all, but really a manmade pond. There, people fed stale chunks of bread to seagulls and ducks in the summertime, and in the wintertime, when the lake was frozen, they went skating. He remembered climbing with his brother Chaim on the large, geometric, formed-concrete shapes in the mountain's sculpture garden. They competed with each other, testing their mettle to see who could be fastest to the top of the awkward eight and ten foot structures. And he recalled the sight of expatriate Israelis, *Yordim*, holding hands and circle-dancing on Sunday afternoons to Hebrew folksongs blaring from loudspeakers near the recreation centre.

Despite the acres and acres of tombstones scattered over the mountain's northern slopes, suggesting the Mount of Olives, Gershon didn't relate Mount Royal to the Judean hills surrounding Jerusalem's Old City. Instead, the flat-topped fortress of Masada near the Dead Sea came to mind. Masada, where two thousand years ago a small band of pious Jews fought off vastly superior Roman battalions, eventually choosing martyrdom over surrender.

But in reality the mountain was neither a fortress nor a tomb, it was a kind of haven, a place to seek refuge. You could get lost in the twine of forest paths that twisted around the mountain's crown.

The heart of Montreal was many things. A secluded clearing where families gathered for picnics and celebrated the seasons together. A park where children played imaginary games all year round. And a final resting place for the dead.

These were the thoughts that came to Gershon as he stood in the central stairwell in front of the metal security gate that barred access to the stairs that led to the roof. There was supposed to be a fat chain wrapped around the gate. The lock was missing and the chain hung limply to the side.

In most circumstances, this would not have been cause for concern. The elevator repairmen had a key and went up on the roof to do monthly maintenance. But Gershon was not aware of the presence of repairmen in the building. The superintendent also had a key. Maybe he was working on the cooling tower. But Gershon normally gave the superintendent a list of his daily tasks and as far as he knew, his employee was working in the basement boiler room today, cleaning the furnaces, getting them ready for winter.

Gershon was hesitant to climb the stairs, frightened by what he might find. There was good reason for the added security of gates and padlocks. It protected the rooftop machinery against vandalism. It also deterred any mentally unstable person who might contemplate using 99 as a launching pad.

Gershon wondered if the missing lock might have something to do with the spate of false fire alarms in recent weeks. The frequent ringing of the bells, intially a minor annoyance, had become a cause for concern.

There were yearly tests of the fire alarm system; the tenants were warned a day or two in advance by posted notifications on every floor. Once in a while, a malfunction would trigger the bells. False alarms were not an unusual occurence at 99 and the tenants grew to expect them.

When the alarm was tripped, they rarely fled their premises automatically as they should. Alfreda would be inundated with phone calls. "No, this is not an unscheduled test," she would answer. "I don't know if it's a real alarm. Yes, I think you should exit the building." Tenants were reluctant to evacuate their premises because it cost them to interrupt production. The tenants of 99 were a notoriously unpanicked bunch.

Officials from the city's fire department visited 99 routinely. Once a year they came to perform an annual examination of the building's evacuation procedures. The fire alarm was set off and the inspectors stood at the base of the stairwell by the front entrance with stopwatches. Tenants strolled leisurely down the stairs. Some passed the inspectors smoking cigarettes while others arrived in the lobby on the elevators. Ten minutes later the building would be mostly empty, though combing the corridors Alfreda always found a few dozen more occupants still in their offices, on the phone or working in their factories. The inspectors visibly disapproved. A building the size of 99 was legally required to be completely evacuated in ninety seconds or less.

Having failed the test so miserably, the management would receive a fine from the city, accompanied by a stern letter warning that if procedures were not improved increased penalties would be levied. In the years Gershon worked in the building, no improvements had been made and the city had never backed up its threats of steeper fines. Gershon and the municipal fire department inspectors agreed on at least one thing, that 99 was a hopeless case.

However, this latest epidemic of false alarms was extremely unusual. The system had been tripped ten times in the last two weeks, sometimes twice in one day. Now, when the bells rang through the hallways tenants did not even bother to call Alfreda for verification. They immediately discounted the possibility of a fire, assuming it was either a prank or another technical glitch. The tenants didn't appear to hear it anymore. The loud clanging elicited no response. Workers pushed carts filled with merchandise through the hallways unfazed. Salespeople stood blankfaced with sample bags strapped over their shoulders waiting passively for the elevators. Everywhere it was business as usual.

The situation had deteriorated to such an extent that Alfreda suggested scrapping the fire system altogether. It had become obsolete, she said. "The only thing that will get their attention now is if I go running naked through the building with my hair on fire, waving my arms like a madwoman, screaming Fire! at the top of my lungs. And even then, they'd probably stop me to ask if it was a *real* fire."

A pattern was noticed. The false alarms would happen at around eight o'clock in the morning or four o'clock in the afternoon. Business hours. The main control panel in the lobby indicated that emergency switches had been pulled in two specific locations, on the fourth floor near Sonny Lipsey's premises and at the bottom of the stairway next to the fire exit on the east side of the building. Gershon had quickly surmised that it was an inside job. The saboteur worked in 99.

He had begun looking at tenants suspiciously, inspecting the faces he passed in the corridors for signs of guilt. He suspected the newer occupants first, the least familiar faces. Then he realized that the culprit could be anyone. An older occupant who, for whatever reason, had suddenly gone batty. Chief among his suspects was Sonny Lipsey who was still complaining about Crooners putting garbage near his door. Maybe he set off the fire alarm as a means of garnering added attention to his problem.

After a while, Gershon had judged certain occupants to be beyond reproach. He recruited them, asking that they be extra vigilant and report anything unusual to the management. Even with informants scattered throughout the building, the saboteur evaded detection and the false alarms continued.

The longer they went on, the more paranoid Gershon became. He took the matter personally, thinking about who might want revenge against him. Estella Mora or one of her henchmen. Joey Putkin. No, as low as Putkin would sink, it was beneath him to go around setting off the alarm bells.

Without an obvious suspect, Gershon concentrated on preventive measures. He had been researching tamper-resistant trip-switches. The emergency hall stations at 99 were old models from the 1960s. Nothing about them detered a thrill-seeker. He thought about replacing them with newer models sealed in glass encasements. He called for quotations from surveillance companies to install hidden cameras and monitors.

Now, two weeks into the fire alarm fiasco, this breach in security, he was standing at the base of the last flight of stairs leading to the roof, looking at an open gate and not finding a lock which was supposed to be there. He felt anxiety building inside him. Maybe he should call the superintendent to find out why the gate was open and have him accompany Gershon up the stairs. No, he was being silly. There was little sense in traipsing down to the boiler room and interrupting the man's work.

The gate creaked on its unoiled hinges as he pushed it wide, rattling the loose chain. He bounded up the steps to the landing, paused to catch his breath and felt a sudden, cool breeze. Looking up the next flight of stairs to the black door which led directly onto the roof, he saw that the lock there was missing too. Blown by the wind, the door was swinging back and forth. Sunbeams strobed through the gap in steady rhythm with the swinging door.

The fluorescent tubes above Gershon's head seemed ineffectual. In comparison to the intrusion of sunlight, the fixtures emitted an electric shadow. Gershon squinted his eyes and realized it was true, the whole building was cloaked in electric shadow. People worked all day long in this shabby light and grew accustomed to it.

The open door at the top of the stairs beckoned. Come, it seemed to say, waving him up. Okay, he thought of the reward that awaited him on the roof, the view of his city. He took several more steps, counting backwards, starting at six, five, four, three, two, one. Blast off. An image came to Gershon: perfect prayer. Blasting off and shooting up into the stratosphere. A person who prayed was like a rocket. He stood still on his launch pad, grounded and solitary, waiting for the reduction of a countdown. Arriving at the utter self-effacement of zero, the fuel ignited, combusted, propelling him ever higher, breaking gravity. As the spirit went up and up, soaring through the clouds, the praying person shed stages of himself, becoming smaller and smaller, lighter and lighter. When he reached the smallest, most compact, shining kernel of his being, at the apogee of his trajectory, he was gripped by another, more mysterious cosmic force. One that buoyed him in the pitch blackness of space, carrying him along without weight or friction, into the distance, as a dream.

Gershon was at the top of the stairs. The air was cold. The door slapped open and shut in front of him.

Now there was a certain process of reassurance that seeped into Gershon's mind. There were some journeys, he said calmly to himself, that had to be taken solo. In every experience there was something to be learned and tackling it alone meant you couldn't hide, couldn't find excuses, couldn't blame anyone else. The superintendent might be reprimanded for leaving the gate unlocked, Alfreda for not informing him work was being done on the elevators, if that was the case. But for now Gershon knew he had to step out onto the roof by himself. He had to walk through that door.

The September sun warmed him immediately as he broke through the threshold of the door. He faced the hazy, grey humpback mountain. It did not look lovely today as he had expected. Not even remotely. It was a giant deformity. An ugly tumour rising out of a heated, tortured city at midday. The sleeping mountain, that dormant volcano, seemed as if it was on the verge of erupting. Gershon was gripped by anguish. It hit him hard. This was a disappointment that should not have been. Not today. Today was a day for overcoming anxiety and moving forward and going higher. The missing padlocks were only part of it.

Ruhama had awakened Gershon that morning at six a.m. He was deep in sleep when her icy fingertips touched an exposed shoulder and burrowed against his neck under his beard like a small creature. He rolled over, but the creature persisted, caressing the nape of his neck, becoming entangled in his hair, getting free and tickling his forehead.

He heard his name. "Gershon, Gershon." It was Ruhama's voice, soft and musical, like when she said, "I love you." He rolled back over and twitched his nose, his right hand emerging from the covers.

Before he could open his eyes to look at her, Ruhama's gentle voice floated to him again as if from the back of his drowsy mind. "Gershon. Gershon. I'm pregnant."

He opened his eyes. Ruhama's face hung over him, glowing like a full moon. "I'm pregnant," she repeated. "I did the urine test this morning. I'm pregnant."

Still half asleep, Gershon reached out to his wife. He enclosed her in his arms, bringing her down on top of him and hugging tightly. "*Boruch Hashem*," he said. Ruhama rested her head on his chest. After a few minutes he spoke while Ruhama listened to the thumping of his heart.

This moment made Gershon realize that whatever happened he and his wife were a team. No problem was just his problem, all problems were theirs to deal with. He disclosed the facts about Sholem's Will. He told Ruhama how Chaim had been left the shares in 99 and he, or rather *they,* had been left with nothing. He pledged to Ruhama that he would do everything within his power to get their due. "My father better not die before straightening this out. As soon as he recovers, I'll make sure he changes his Will."

Only after waiting a few minutes, with her head still resting on Gershon's chest, did Ruhama choose to respond. "Try not to be so mad at your father. I don't feel bad about what he did. Actually, he had a very good reason for putting Chaim in charge."

"What? What are you saying?" Gershon asked, surprised by Ruhama's comment and feeling put on the defensive.

Ruhama lifted her head, looked him straight in the eyes and said, "Chaim's the *bechor.*"

Gershon's head sunk back into the pillow as if an invisible hand had slapped him on the forehead. Of course. How could he have been so stupid not to think of it. Ruhama had provided an explanation that was so straightforward he couldn't see it. Chaim was the eldest. Being the first-born son meant privileges and added obligations. According to Jewish law eldest sons were entitled to *pi-shnayim,* double the inheritance of any other child. The law was rarely invoked nowadays, having lost its practicality long ago. But Gershon knew he couldn't fault his father for adhering strictly to code. The answer was tradition, as old and deep as Torah. As the *bechor,* Chaim was responsible for looking after the family when Sholem was gone. Still, Gershon felt shortchanged and remained committed to lobbying for a more equitable distribution of Sholem's legacy. At least now he understood why his father had arranged his affairs in that way. The mere fact that his father hadn't picked favourites between him and Chaim gave Gershon a sense of relief.

Having learned that morning that he would be a father again, and feeling relieved by Ruhama's astute explanation of Sholem's actions, Gershon wanted more than anything to be refreshed by his rooftop view of Montreal. He wanted the mountain to look round and perfect, like a woman's pregnant belly. He wanted the wind to smell fresh and pure as a newborn. He wanted the city to emit the shimmery vapour of prayer, not the thick haze of smog. He turned away, repulsed.

As he turned, the figure of a person appeared, standing several hundred metres away by the north-west corner of the building. She was facing away, looking seventy feet down to the ground. He could see that it was a woman, but didn't recognize the clothing, the shape or posture. He wanted to run and call out, but resisted for fear she would be startled. He walked toward her cautiously.

The woman shifted around to look at him. Gershon stopped. He was not yet close enough to make a positive identification, but he could discern long black hair over a thin frame. He could see the whiteness of her head and neck, like a pillar of salt.

He moved forward. His suspicion was confirmed. Michelle Labelle. She stared at Gershon and shook her head. He took it as a sign to stop. He was now close enough to visually measure the distance between her feet and the edge of the building. Eighteen inches. Two feet at most. He didn't continue forward.

"Why are you here?" he yelled to her. "It's dangerous!"

She didn't respond. Could she hear him? The wind was blowing hard. He thought about yelling louder, anything to keep her faced in his direction, away from the edge.

He took ten more steps. Her hands were holding two shiny gold objects. The missing padlocks.

She didn't move.

He could now make out the expression on her face. Okay, she was sad. She was demolished. Gershon was sure she intended to kill herself. How could he stop her? He thought about backing away, running for help. But if he left, she might take the opportunity to jump. The presence of another person was good, wasn't it? It proved that someone cared. Isn't that what people who killed themselves really wanted? Especially those who made a spectacle of suicide. People who earnestly intended damage did it alone, in parked cars pumped with exhaust fumes when no one was home, or in hotel rooms with bottles of pills on bedside tables. They did not want to make a show of it, unless they wanted help. Roof-jumpers wanted attention. Was he supposed to wait with her until someone came? That might take hours.

Trying to get close enough to have his voice heard, he took a few more steps, then stopped short. Gershon could now see the complexion of her face. It appeared to be melting. Long waxy lines dripped down the sides of taut cheeks. Beneath the trail of wetness he saw pocked, raw skin. Her hair was matted, unkempt and slightly off-centre. A wig. Her features looked drawn, cartoonish. Gershon was shocked. She's a drug addict, he said to himself. The thought popped into his head, even though he wasn't sure what a drug addict typically looked like. They were underfed, weren't they? And had bad skin. Maybe they lost their hair too. If she was a drug addict, that would explain the Hells Angel connection. He was her supplier.

"Please, come with me! Please! Back inside!" he begged.

The wind ripped at her clothes. She shook her head and without saying a word, turned away.

Gershon wished he was Sholem. Sholem would know what to do. He would use his magic, his charm. Sholem would have said exactly the right words to convince her to accompany him back inside the building. He tried to imagine what Sholem would say in this situation, but nothing came to him. Gershon was not Sholem. His mind was a complete blank. He decided then to go for help. He saw no other alternative. If he took another step toward Michelle it might push her over the edge. Maybe he could get Sonny Lipsey to talk to her. If anyone could bring her down safely, besides Sholem, it was Sonny. Gershon backed away.

"I'm coming right back," he yelled. "Please don't move, everything will be alright."

Gershon retreated, his eyes glued to her, walking backwards hoping it would be enough to keep her in place.

He tore down the inside stairwell and burst into the management office.

"What's the—"

Before Alfreda could finish, Gershon said huffing and puffing, "Call Sonny Lipsey. Quick. It's an emergency, his girl. She's on the roof."

"On the roof? What d'you mean?"

"Alfreda, please. Just get Sonny on the phone. Tell him to meet me on the roof. Please, as fast as possible. The gate's open."

Gershon sped out of the office while Alfreda dialed.

OGodOGodOGodOGodOGod, chanted Gershon as he skipped back up the stairs two at a time. The door was wide open. He dashed out onto the roof and came skidding to a halt.

She was gone.

No!

He ran to within ten feet of the spot where Michelle had stood. He did not want to see over the edge and didn't step any closer.

Worse than an ugly scene of unimagineable gore, worse than witnessing horrible gruesomeness and having to grapple with the senselessness of suicide, Gershon could not bring himself to face his fears about himself. It wasn't good enough that he'd wanted to help her, or that he'd thought about helping her and planned to. Michelle Labelle's death—if it was true, if it was over—would be proof of his shortcomings. His incapacity to act rendered him irredeemable.

Alfreda appeared at the door. "Gershon! What happened? Gershon!" She ran toward him. "Are you alright? I tried to get hold of Sonny but he wasn't there. Are you alright? What happened?"

Gershon was momentarily unresponsive. Maybe she was gone, and that's it. Maybe she had simply walked back inside the building.

"She was here," he said as Alfreda approached. "Sonny's girl. The one who does his bookkeeping. She was here, at the edge of the building." Gershon bent down to pick up the two gold locks at his feet. "She had these in her hands," he said, showing them to Alfreda, proof he hadn't imagined the whole thing. "She was a mess. Her makeup—She had been crying. Underneath, her skin was crusty ..." Gershon searched for a word, "... disfigured." He paused. "She acted like a roof-jumper. But I didn't really think she would do it. I can't look. You go. Tell me what you see," Gershon said pointing over the ledge, his voice barely audible.

Alfreda approached the edge of the building. Wind grabbed at her blouse and pants. He was amazed at how bravely she advanced, not seeming to give any thought to the danger involved. She planted her toes less than a foot from where the parapet's metal flashing sloped down and touched the roof's gravel.

"My God," she said, staring down seven floors, her hands coming up to her lips.

Gershon gazed past Alfreda straight off the back of the building out into the endless sky. Beyond the blocks of industrial buildings, grey puffy clouds congealed in the distance. They floated slowly toward 99. In a few hours it will rain, he thought. Gershon may have wanted to avoid seeing what was happening down below, but he could not shut his ears. He heard voices rising and falling, sonic shards of commotion breaking the air, floating and fading. Off the walls of neighbouring buildings he heard the echoing pat-pat-pat of shoes slapping the pavement, the sound pigeons made when they flapped their wings as they landed to peck at scattered breadcrumbs on the ground.

Her head bowed, Alfreda stared, speechless.

"Tell me what you see. I have to know. What do you see?"

"There's no time for that," she said. "I have to get help."

Alfreda spun on her heels and ran past Gershon without acknowledging him. Gershon wanted to stop her from leaving. He wanted to say, "Wait, please don't go. Don't leave me here alone." But he stopped himself. The expression on Alfreda's face as she passed him was not horror at what she had seen, or steely determination for what had to be done. It was a look of disgust.

Gershon felt sick.

The wind slapped at his *tzizes*, the strings getting tangled in his holstered cellphone. He could not stand there doing nothing, freezing and frozen. Gershon lowered himself onto his knees and crawled closer to the edge. Sharp stones jabbed against his shins through his trousers. Closing his eyes, his mind filled with images of gore, pools of blood, shattered bone and splattered flesh. He had to look. He leaned over and stared seventy feet down to the ground.

Gershon was astonished by what he observed. It was a solemn huddle of men. More men were running up to join the group assembled around the girl like air rushing in to fill a vacuum. There were truckers and contractors and deliverymen who had dropped whatever they were doing, the wooden skids of fabric they were unloading and the racks of garments they were loading on the docks. There were Armenians, French-Canadians, Sikhs, Arabs and Chinese contractors. Gershon counted nine of them, a minyan of ten, eleven, twelve, thirteen. Some of the men crouched down on their knees, their backs hunched, their heads bent low and facing inward. Behind them other men stood, gazing over their shoulders into the centre. They were tightly packed in a thickening circle, hardly any space between them. From above, their heads appeared stacked one on top of the other, like a growing mound of smooth round stones.

The girl's corpse could not be seen. The crush of assembled men blocked it from view. There was no evidence at all of her ugly demise. No pools of blood seeped along the pavement. No bits of flesh sprayed out in star-shaped splatters on black asphalt. The only hint of tragedy was the impromptu formation of men. To one side of the group, a trucker held a fat roll of fabric horizontal between his outstretched arms while another man pulled the end, unravelled a length, and cut it with a glinting pair of oversized shears. Had the aftermath been a gory mess as Gershon had expected, the fabric might have been useful to clean it up, soak up the blood. Instead the men were preparing a shroud for the body. Gershon caught his breath. It is true that what he witnessed was not a coming together of Jews, an in-gathering of his tribesmen. Nonetheless, from his vantage point on the roof, the rectangular swath of clean white fabric spread out and spanning the quorum of men looked like a giant *tallit*, an improvised prayershawl, covering them. The scene was elegant, beautiful even.

Gershon was sure, though he could not confirm it with his own eyes, that Michelle Labelle lay dead in their midst. He was not thinking about her *neshama*, her extinguished light. He thought about the way tragedy brought people together, how it focussed them on the task at hand, the urgency of what was necessary. Was there any purpose more exalted than the preservation of life? Was there any *mitzvah* more sacred than *pikuach nefesh*, the Divine Commandment to preserve the soul? The rabbis had said that saving a soul was equal to saving an entire world. The questions welling up inside Gershon had never seemed more obvious and the answers more incontrovertible. Why did people always wait so long to act?

The body of a woman had inexplicably fallen from the sky. Two or perhaps three of the men had witnessed the entire event from beginning to end. The attention of a handful more might have been drawn to the split-second splat of her flesh hitting the ground. The majority of them came running mindlessly, wanting to follow the crowd to see what the excitement was all about. And then Gershon was amazed to see a woman running in among the men. It was Estella Mora. She too had come to join the circle, to witness the girl lying dead in a misshapen heap. The formation continued to grow wider and wider as more people felt called upon to help. And when it was determined that nothing more could be done to save her, they stood in silence, grieving in their hearts. But Gershon knew they were not mourning the departed soul of a fallen stranger. They mourned their own living souls. Standing in the presence of death, each acknowledged privately to himself that *he*, or in Estella's case *she*, was the one who could not be saved.

Gershon crawled back from the edge and stood up. He unfurled his fists and stared at the opened gold padlocks, one in each hand. Their curved metal arms unclasped from the locking mechanisms looked like two 9s. He held them up chest-high and weighed them like a scale. In the end there were only two possibilities, two choices: life or death. He thought about his father. Sholem had walked through the Valley of the Shadow of Death and somehow, by the grace of God, had made it all the way from one end to the other. Gershon's mother, on the other hand, had travelled the same treacherous route but had never quite left it behind. She was still there, in that place, surrounded by mountains of uncertainty, encircled and besieged by memories that reverberated endlessly inside her. And what residue of his mother's hesitation, still echoed inside Gershon?

Had he been more resolute he could have saved her. Gershon realized that from the start his problem wasn't that he had seen the soul of a stranger. It wasn't that, for a brief time, he had become preoccupied by a religious apparition, a *neshama*. Rather, his problem had always been that he had doubted what he had seen, or wasn't completely convinced by it. Her soul was never at issue. It was all about the existence and vitality of his own soul. If only he had possessed the conviction of his soul then the urgency of the matter would have been blatant. He would have run up and grabbed her, hugged her as tightly as was humanly possible and with all his might forced her to safety back inside the building. Now it was too late.

It was clear to Gershon what he should have done. A word suddenly popped into his head, *maintenant*. The French term for *now* was a conjunction of two words *main*, meaning hand, and *tenant*, from the verb *tenir*, to hold. In French, "now" meant holding the moment in hand, seizing it and not letting go. The rabbis had said that each day the world was created anew. They had warned against taking any moment for granted. Why had Gershon not acted *maintenant*? What had stopped him from reaching out to the girl when it counted most and holding her back from the edge?

He had always thought of himself as a maintainer. It was his job to collect the rents from month to month and to maintain the building, keep it running. At some point he had forgotten that maintenance also came from *maintenant* and he had neglected the lesson taught by the rabbis that every living moment, indeed, the very essence of being alive, depended on maintaining faith. If human beings were created in the image of God, then without faith in himself, Gershon realized, there was no faith in God, and without faith in God there was no faith in himself. There were two sides to the equation. The one thing he could never maintain was faith in himself. Doubting himself, as he did all the time, was like standing in front of a mirror and seeing only a cardboard cut-out. A flat, two-dimensional image of himself, and mistaking it for the real thing.

The consequence of his neglect was painfully obvious. Now that the moment had slipped from Gershon's grasp and with it Michelle Labelle, or whatever her real name was, there was no possibility of taking them back. Gershon was gripped by a forlorn sense of loss and regret. He felt shredded. He also felt a certain peculiar desire to know Michelle Labelle's real name, the one given to her at birth, the name that would be inscribed forevermore on her headstone.

Alfreda reappeared at the roof door and trotted toward Gershon. "I've called for an ambulance. We've done all that we can do. There's no sense in staying up here. Come, let's go back inside," she said.

Gershon followed Alfreda and as they walked together over the bumpy gravel surface, stones clicked at their shoes. They entered the dim light of the building, and Gershon handed the two padlocks in his hands to Alfreda. She snapped the first one on the door. From there they descended a flight of stairs and at the bottom Gershon wrapped the heavy chain around the gate. Alfreda handed him the second lock which he threaded through the holes and squeezed shut.

"I think she was the one," Gershon said, "who's been tripping the fire alarm."

Gershon thought about the elevator incident, when Michelle had pressed the stop button, hanging herself on a metal cable between floors. Had he been more vigilant and aware he might have guessed that her actions foreshadowed a more dire eventuality.

He wondered if Gentiles considered it a sin to commit suicide. In Jewish law suicide was an outright abomination, an act tantamount to heresy, which was the reason that Jews who had chosen to kill themselves were buried in a separate section of the cemetery, apart from the rest of the community. Here lay the bodies of failures, the configuration of tombstones said. These were the names of those ungrateful, faithless few who spat in the Almighty's face by willingly taking their own lives. If they weren't disgraced in life, Jewish law ensured that they would be in death.

But what if the life they'd been given, the pain and suffering they'd endured, was simply too much for them to bear? In the death camps, wasn't it true that many Jews had chosen to terminate their own lives rather than continue enduring dehumanization and suffering. Could they be blamed for their choice? In the afterlife, did God allow for exceptions to the rule, or did He expect people to suffer right to the very end?

"People kill themselves all the time, Gershon. It's a sad fact of life."

No. God wants us to fight, Gershon told himself. He wants us to struggle even to the last breath. For Justice and Compassion and Mercy. For all the things that make life worthwhile. *Boruch Dayan Emet*, he said under his breath, *Blessed is the True Judge*.

"One thing I don't understand," Alfreda said. "Why did you leave her alone on the roof? I mean, people in such anguish can't be left alone. You're supposed to keep them talking."

"I tried but she wouldn't talk." Gershon thought about the elevator incident again. He had kept her talking. She had spoken with him through the door. And she emerged alive.

"I had no choice. What more was I supposed to do? I couldn't wait for someone to magically show up on the roof."

"Well, Gershon. You showed up, didn't you?" Alfreda said. Then pointing at Gershon's knotted-up *tzizes* she continued, "Anyway, you could have stayed put and used that stupid thing to call for back-up."

EPILOGUE

THE MIND PLAYS TRICKS. Memory and medicine. Medicine, memory and a stricken mind. A bad mix. And the dreams. The nightmares. And brief moments of lucidity. I don't know which is worse.

Wasting away. Losing my mind. Strapped to a hospital bed. Trapped in the jumbled purgatory of memory and medicine. The beep and tweet of machines. The drip, drip, drip. The visions. Here I am. Or am not. Suspended between past and future. A man without a present. A dangled soul. Neither here nor there. This is purgatory. A soul left to dangle. Between past and future. Merciful God. Let my *neshama* rise up. Or let it fall. But please. Don't keep it hanging. Like a broken elevator. Between floors.

Chaim will be okay. He's a strong, determined boy. His business is doing well. He'll get re-married. Settle down and make children. God willing.

Masha has enough money. I've been a good husband. A faithful husband. Devoted. And a good provider. Masha has enough money. For the rest of her life. Another life too if she wants. But who wants another one anyway? Not me.

Gershon. It's Gershon I worry about. What will become of him? Too sensitive. Thin-skinned. The world comes down hard on him. Cracks him like an egg. I've tried my best. To teach him the business. To toughen his skin. *Ribbono shel olam*. Master of the universe. Gershon seeks You out. How will he learn? What I learned. There are places You don't frequent. Places we won't let you in. I learned it the hard way. Chaim will be his brother's keeper. He'll make sure his brother is okay. Alfreda will take care of him. The building will stand. Chabanel will stay put. Longer than me.

There is no suffering like constant remembering. No pain more true. More deep. My heart is clogged with grit. Why must those faces revisit me? Faces of anguish and hostility. Fake smiles. Corrupt souls. Stop those days of stone from rising up inside me. Like hard cubes of regurgitated vomit. The medicines keep the memories alive. Not me. And the worry. Faces haunt me like ghosts. Poor Shmulik. The tenants. The helmeted hooligans. Angels of Hell. With their jackboots and guns. A purgatorial stew.

Memory and medicine. Medicine and memory. A bad mix. Hallucinations. Those days of stone. I should not re-live them any longer. The hammer slips from my hands. Over and over again. The taste of mandelbrot remains on my lips. Bittersweet. The pebbles drop from my pocket. I am marching through the gates. Always marching through the gates. Even as I lie here. Dead legs. Dead hands. Still, I am marching. Feet crunching gravel. I hear sounds. Always arriving. Never leaving.

Closing my eyes. I am walking the halls of 99. Gershon is there. Alfreda. The tenants coming out from their doors. In the office with Shimmy Solomon. Putkin. Irving Roth. Doing business. Making money. Complaining. Smiling fake smiles. Businessman smiles. Doctor smiles. Bailiff smiles. I smiled those smiles too. Played the game. Played it well. Should I be ashamed? Why do they gather in my mind? Why do I see bankruptcy? Images of Gershon? My hapless Gershon. In the basement. On the roof. Running from tenant to tenant. Trying to find a minyan. To mourn my death. To say Kaddish. To extol Your Greatness.

A *heshbon*. An accounting. Is that what You want? Why You keep me here? In a cage of chrome bars. Attached to machines. Dangling between life and death. What do I need to admit? To gain my release. My deeds speak for themselves. My prayers. My *mitzvos*. My sins. It's all or nothing. But You know how it works. You made the rules. A *yetzer hatov*. And to go with it. A *yetzer hara*. Either I retract everything I did. All of it. Or none of it. If I take back the sins, the *mitzvos* must come with them. A package deal. How else can the scales balance? Are there enough *mitzvos*? Too many sins? Or was it enough for a Jew just to survive?

Ribbono shel olam. You handed me a small corner of Your world. You said, Here. Take it. It's yours for a while. Take good care of it. I played my role. Did the best I could. Under the circumstances. Built buildings. Maintained them. Collected the rent. And from what I collected paid You Your Landlord's share. Now what? My lease has expired. You want more? A rental increase? Wasn't what I offered enough for You? Is it ever enough? If I cheated You. I'm sorry. Forgive me.

Ich arbeit. Ich arbeit. The words keep coming back. I'm finished working. The work must eventually be done. And when the work is done the *teshuvah* starts. How shall I be released? How shall I repent? With all this medicine and memory. Memory and medicine.

What is the right way to die? I am unpracticed at it. Just me and You. Okay. You're my final confidante. You know everything. If You want my sins go ahead. Take them. You want my *mitzvos*? Take them too. You can have all of them. In exchange for peace. Release me. I beg You. You accepted even the souls of Sodom and Gomorrah. Why not mine?

Aching back. Worse all the time. And the pain in my chest. My palpitating, anguished heart. When does she come? The skinny, lovely girl. The one who enters the room silently. At night. Not the fat daytime nurses. Clopping like horses. Neighing and grunting as they shift me on the mattress. A pile of skin and bones. Bones and skin. All that's left. Where is the gentle one who comes at night? The girl who doesn't speak. The one who brings comfort not words. With the long black hair and sad eyes. The oval half-smiling doll's face. Skin smooth as porcelain. Shining. She knows how to turn me. Such a soft touch. Fingers of an angel. I float between her hands. When she shakes out the fresh bedsheet. Sometimes I see a *tallis*. My burial *tallis*. Sometimes wings catching air. Angel's wings. Such visions. Why does she not come back to me?

I scared her away. When she hovered over me. I called out to my wife. Howled Masha! Mashelle! Flailing my arms. Mashelle Libelle! My Masha, my love! How it must have sounded. A sick old man. Slack-tongued. Stiff-lipped. Slurring, Mashelle Libelle! Garbled. Mashelle Libelle! Masha my love! All I could say. From a mouth stuffed with rags. Even those words, you took from me. There is nothing else to say. Nothing left. She must have been frightened half to death. The girl. Scared away. Where is she? The one with thin angel fingers. I need her. When is the right time to die? When does she return? I need her. More than ever. Now.

Photo: Terence Byrnes

B. Glen Rotchin

ESPLANADE
Books

THE FICTION SERIES AT VÉHICULE PRESS

[Series Editor: Andrew Steinmetz]

A House by the Sea
A novel by Sikeena Karmali

A Short Journey by Car
Stories by Liam Durcan

Seventeen Tomatoes: Tales from Kashmir
Stories by Jaspreet Singh

Garbage Head
A novel by Christopher Willard

The Rent Collector
A novel by B. Glen Rotchin

Optique
Stories by Clayton Bailey

Véhicule Press
www.vehiculepress.com